Jenny opened her eyes again and saw black scuffed shoes planted squarely on the carpet near her nose, gray official trousers sloping away into the distance, a gun holstered in a leather belt; the rest of him too far away to bother with. Police. She'd been noticed, all right.

She licked her lips. "We weren't...it was a perfectly ordinary supper party after the opera."

"It doesn't look ordinary to me," said the policeman skeptically. "Perhaps it's different where you come from."

There was food and champagne everywhere. Several glasses were broken on the floor—Jenny remembered toasts. A full plate lay upturned on Pierre Sorbaz's stomach, two bottles had fallen over on the carpet. No wonder the police were hostile, it was the most degrading scene Jenny had ever seen.

More and louder moans were coming from elsewhere in the room, people moving, staring, unable to believe what they saw.

"My pearls," said Jenny clearly, her hands to her neck. "They've gone."

THE BUDAPEST RISK

Mary Napier

IVY BOOKS • NEW YORK

1

IN NEW YORK IT WAS A BRILLIANT, LATE FALL DAY, THE kind of day on which nothing ought to go wrong for anyone on earth. A day born with luck fired into its core. The man waiting on the corner of East Fifty-fourth Street was humming under his breath while he waited, as he had waited for the past week, for a particular woman to appear. Usually he was impatient, glancing at his watch and tapping his toe on the sidewalk if she was even five minutes late; today he was content to lift his half-closed eyes to the dazzling sun, as if he knew that on this lucky morning Jenny Marshall was bound to be punctual.

In fact, she was early. It was only a few minutes after eight when she reached the corner opposite. A few male heads turned as she passed, attention caught more by her vitality than any conventional beauty, although her eyes were fine and dark and large, her cheekbones delicately tilted. Jenny moved briskly and sat erect, her voice was crisp, her mind very quick; even old clothes regained their smartness if she wore them. Usually she looked around as if enjoying everything, but on this lovely November morning she was frowning, apparently so preoccupied by uncomfortable thought that instinct alone enabled her to avoid colliding with the slower crowds around her. Certainly she did not notice the man crossing from the other side of the street, nor sense his watchfulness beside her while they waited together for the lights to change. Jenny was also remarkably free from conceit: if heads turned to watch or try to offer an invitation, then she seldom noticed.

But this man wasn't admiring his quarry, he was assessing her worth. He'd been planning the coup he had in mind for years, knowing exactly what he wanted once circumstance could be made to suit his purpose. Then, quite suddenly, his patience had been rewarded; a time and place that might have been made to order, and now a suitable tool for him to use. A more than suitable tool. When Jenny turned into a block of offices, he strolled past and then stood waiting again. After a week of watching and burrowing into her background, he intended to put her usefulness to the test today. He rolled his lip against his teeth: she had to be useful; there wasn't time to find anyone else.

Jenny was still frowning as she left the elevator for her office. She rented two rooms on a dowdy fifth floor, where a new steel plaque glittered in the sun as she paused to insert her key in the door.

JENNIFER MARSHALL
LITERARY AGENT

Jenny had set up on her own only the year before and was finding the going extremely tough, but that, in her view, was the best of all reasons for replacing an ugly frosted-glass door with pine, as well as splurging by engraving her name on steel. After six years spent in learning the publishing trade in New York and London, she had risked a great deal by starting up so quickly on her own, but a zest for independence won. Ever since childhood Jenny had loved good writing and, at twenty-eight, was still young enough to imagine that the satisfaction of encouraging it was infinitely more important than a safe salary check. Not that she didn't expect to profit; far from it. For the first few years, of course, she would be precariously dependent on selling the work of unknown authors, but Jenny trusted her own judgment and also believed she had discovered a specialty market no one else had touched.

The trouble was, building a good new list took a larger bank loan and more time than she had imagined. Then a stock market crash had neatly bisected her first year and made publishers doubly cautious about backing unproven writers.

She heard a step behind her and turned.

A man, between thirty and forty years old, stood watching her. Smallish and triangular-cheeked, he looked Slavic, although his clothes owed more to Brooks Brothers than Iron Curtain tailors. "Miss Marshall?"

She nodded and glanced at her watch. Eight-fifteen. "I don't often receive such early callers."

"I have to be at work myself soon. May I come in?"

"Yes, of course. Coffee?" She led the way across a tiny outer typing office and into her own room, where there was a panic button behind her desk. So far she had never needed it but preferred being near it all the same, alone with a caller she did not know.

"No, thank you. I have not time." He closed the door and sat down, more at ease than she was. He spoke good English, strongly accented, and looked as if he gave more orders during his day's work than he received.

Jenny sat, too. "What can I do for you?"

"You specialize in selling literature from the Soviet Union and Eastern Europe?"

"I handle any books I'm offered which might make money."

"But you do take work from Eastern Europe?"

"Only if it's exceptional." Because Jenny Marshall was known as one of the few New York agents who even considered acting for writers from Communist states, refugees occasionally found their way to her, offering melancholy and unpublishable manuscripts. Yet this authoritative man didn't seem like a refugee, and because of that difference in him, she added: "My mother came to America from Hungary and I like languages, so I'm interested, I suppose. I had thought I could develop a market for contemporary East European writing when so many Americans nowadays are interested in their roots, but it hasn't worked out as I'd hoped. So now it's more often a personal interest than hard business. Most publishers refuse to touch it: quite rightly, I suppose, when only Solzhenitsyn and Pasternak ever made big money."

"And you are interested in big money?"

Jenny smiled ruefully. "I'd like to be. Now, Mr.—"

"Pushkin."

"I don't believe it."

"No," he replied seriously. "You would be foolish if you did. Perhaps you prefer me to call myself Tolstoy instead?"

She shrugged and did not answer. He was certainly different and just possibly might produce a manuscript worth reading. Some unusual work was coming out of Communist Europe in these less dogmatic days; the trouble was, her gamble that she would be able to develop a market for it had so far failed.

"Then if you have no preference, I would rather stay as Pushkin, who is my favorite writer. Miss Marshall, I come to you because I learn how you try to sell work from socialist countries."

"Listen, Mr.—Mr. Pushkin. I'm not a Marxist pamphleteer, and I'd go bankrupt if I was. It's just that I think some East European writing is good enough to deserve translation. It's different from anything you find in the West, and I'd hoped I could use my languages to help establish Marshall's Literary Agency as a specialist house, then expand from there. But nothing would please me more than a few bourgeois scripts which would pay the bills."

"My idea will pay many bills."

Jenny's interrogatively lifted eyebrows silently expressed her skepticism. A book from the East that sold more than a couple of thousand hardback copies was a rarity.

"How much does anyone know about the private lives behind the Kremlin's walls? Nothing! Why, no one was even sure President Andropov was married until his widow came to his funeral. Gorbachev is better since his fancy wife likes to swagger in Western capitals and waste money in your shops, but I think it would make big news if a book was published which told how our leaders really live, fighting and killing each other like in your stupid 'Dallas.' Gorbachev comes on television as—as soft . . ."

"Bland?"

"Thank you. Gorbachev comes on television as bland as you like to announce a new arms reduction proposal, but I tell you that he, the army, and the KGB have fought each other like Mafia gangsters before each speech. And in gang warfare there are always casualties, are there not? Now some of our southern republics are becoming restless, but most rackets in the Soviet Union can be traced to those same southern party bosses making money. If Gorbachev fires them, they could accuse half his government of complicity in crimes against the state. If he doesn't, who are then revealed as the true rulers of that state? I think you have never read how two southern ministers were never seen again after their last visit to Moscow, nor how our president's daughter made love with a lion tamer?" He paused and added thoughtfully, "I believe she wanted to use his circus to smuggle diamonds, but he became greedy and blackmailed her. So our socialist president, her father, had the poor lion tamer shot and tried to keep his daughter out of further mischief by marrying her to a KGB general. He committed suicide later. Now, suppose a Soviet official kept a diary like that for fifty years while he worked his way up from a low position to a very high one, and suppose he is still keeping it now, at a time when the Kremlin likes to pretend it has changed so much; it would be valuable, would it not?"

"Perhaps." Jenny forced caution into her voice although she felt her heart beat faster. "It would depend on how far it could be verified and whether it was well written. If your diarist possessed an eye for intimate detail and a novelist's flair for making his characters live, then yes. It could be very valuable, providing he was able to convince his readers that what he wrote was even three-quarters true."

Pushkin sat back. "I compliment you. 'She deserves better things to sell than dissident translations and the work of authors still wet behind the ears,' I heard someone say of you recently."

Jenny flushed. She might disregard compliments on her appearance but was childishly delighted by praise of her professional judgment. "It doesn't need much knowledge of the market to realize what a stir the kind of revelations you describe could make. Just look at the fuss over Peter Wright's *Spycatcher*, when everyone is used to scandals in Washington or London nearly every week. But Moscow—" She leaned forward. "Does such a diary exist, Mr. Pushkin?"

He stood. "Yes, Miss Marshall, it does, and though I am not an expert, I believe it is written in the way you described a moment ago. The author is my father. He occupies a position . . . Well, he is close to many decisions which are taken in both the party and the Soviet government. You are interested?"

"I'm very interested." Characteristically Jenny spoke as she always did: precisely, and meaning every word.

"Two hundred thousand dollars interested?"

"If you are speaking of future royalties, it could be even more, but books are always unpredictable. If *Spycatcher* is anything to go by, the more the Soviet government tried to stop publication, the more valuable these diaries would become." She laughed. "Now, if we could only publish in Russia, your father would make a million, I'm sure! In the West, not too many people are interested in Soviet politics, so the way this diary is written would be vital, and at this moment I haven't seen a single page."

"To do that, you have to travel to Budapest."

There was a long silence while Jenny stared at Pushkin's closed, unemotional face. "You came to me because you discovered I was going soon to Hungary," she said at last.

"That, too, of course, but when I made inquiries about which literary agents in New York spoke Russian, everyday Russian scribbled down in great haste, I learned that you not only spoke it well, but also Hungarian, which I dared not hope for. My colleagues tell me it is the most impossible of all languages to learn." He switched into Russian as he spoke, watching her keenly.

"Plenty of other agents would be willing to travel anywhere with a translator if they were promised a look at such a diary." She answered in the same language, but abstractedly, her mind scurrying after supposition.

"Ah, but the person who reads those diaries must also be capable of judging what they are worth. A translator is out of the question when the slightest indiscretion would destroy everything. Really, I did not expect to discover anyone as suitable as you, Miss Marshall! You see, I was able to bring my father's diary as far as Budapest on my way to America three weeks ago, but once you are satisfied it is genuine, then you yourself must bring it the last part of its journey to the West."

"You mean, smuggle it out."

"Of course. The Soviet government does not encourage its ministers to write candid memoirs; why, even Mrs. Thatcher does not like it."

Jenny's brain zigzagged. A minister; before, Pushkin had said the diarist was an official. He must be lying after all, and she had very nearly fallen into his trap. "I'm sorry, but I don't believe you, Mr. Pushkin. I think you had better go."

"Why do you not believe me?"

She smiled and stood, hearing welcome sounds in the outer office. Monica Finsberg came in to type twice a week; it was lucky this was one of her days. "I'm not sure why you've wasted your time and mine, but now I have other things to do. No Soviet high official—much less a minister—who sold his memoirs to the West would survive to enjoy the proceeds. In those circumstances, I don't think he'd consider such an idea worthwhile, and nor do I."

"Sit down, Miss Marshall, and listen." When she stayed standing, he muttered something rude and went over to lean against the windowsill, blocking out most of the light. "I told you before, this diarist is my father. Do you think I would risk his life for this?"

"You might. For something like a quarter of a million dollars." She answered frankly, but the moment the words were out, she would have given anything to snatch them back. Pushkin remained completely still, and she couldn't see his expression against the light, nor did she need to: she knew—*knew*—that just for an instant he wanted nothing so much as to squeeze that hard, cold knot of fright in her throat, until she died.

Why? As he stayed as unmoving as rock, her instinctive panic faded, leaving questions jostling in its wake. Could such intense anger have been provoked because her words unwittingly touched a raw edge of truth, or because they were criminally, hurtfully wrong? Jenny was unable to guess, yet the sheer strength of Pushkin's reaction made it easier to accept the rest of his story.

Meanwhile, the silence between them wound tight and tighter until she felt compelled to jerk out an apology, as if without it, he might stay leaning with folded arms against her windowsill all day. Then he went on with what he was saying as if nothing unusual had happened. "These diaries are in Budapest, as I told you. You can look at them there and see if I have spoken truly. Fifty years inside the Soviet leadership live in those pages, Miss Marshall, seen by the kind of eye you described so excellently to me earlier. A man who could participate in such events and also record them truthfully must be exceptional, don't you think? Well, before his chance is gone forever, my father would like to live in the West, with the opportunity of seeing and doing the kind of things a Soviet citizen can never do. For that he needs money, and he hopes these diaries will give it to him. My father is not unpatriotic, but he is curious. An artist greedy for life before he dies, after so long as a bureaucrat. As for me, I should enjoy the West, but only if I was rich."

Against her will, Jenny was beginning to believe in this diarist, artistic curiosity more convincing than a highly placed Soviet mole. "He intends to defect?"

Pushkin flicked his fingers, looking at her out of calculating eyes. "It isn't too difficult for a man in his position, who sometimes travels. But ministers are watched, and a secretary carries his briefcases. Although he must come soon to Budapest, he did not dare to bring his diaries even that far himself, although for me it was easy. The frontiers between socialist countries are not so carefully guarded as those between East and West. As it should not be too difficult for you to bring them from Hungary to the West, whereas I should find it almost impossible. For Westerners, Hungary is almost an open country nowadays, but not for us."

Minister. He had said it again.

"How could I possibly know?" said Jenny slowly. "Diaries supposed to have been written by Hitler fooled a German magazine long enough nearly to ruin it."

"You can only read and judge and think and wonder. Then, afterward, take a risk. Because if they are genuine, once a story breaks in your press about how you brought such Soviet diaries out of Hungary, you will have all the publicity you need to make your agency well known. As well as for the profitable publication of my father's book. So his reward is money, and yours, fame. Some money, too, of course, but above all, that quick way to future success you told me interested you."

"You must have done a great deal of prowling about in my life, Mr. Pushkin." He was still speaking Russian, but she answered now in English, alarmed because she had never once sensed anyone watching her.

"Not so much as I would wish, since I must keep this hidden and cannot ask the KGB for help."

"If you are speaking the truth."

"If I am speaking the truth," he agreed, and then added, "If you are interested, you must sign an agreement with me now."

"No. That isn't how an agent works. If the diaries are saleable, I negotiate for you with a publisher."

"Ah, but this is not like any deal you made before. I shall not come here again, nor contact you directly."

"What if I can't negotiate a contract you'd be willing to take, even supposing I get the diaries out?"

"Then the book will not be sold. But I am not too greedy. Also I believe publishers in Europe and America will pay what such revelations are worth. I have studied them, you see, and know I speak the truth."

Risk. Huge, unimaginable risk. Under the deal Pushkin proposed, she was left with the entire responsibility for bringing these unknown diaries out of Communist Hungary, after she alone had judged in a few short hours whether they were forged or might, just possibly, be genuine. And even if they were, she could still be chancing years of her life in a Marxist jail for the trivial scribblings of a minor functionary. And yet . . . and yet . . . such an opportunity would never come again. Another year like this one and her first few months of running her own agency would be her last; her painstakingly gathered new authors would have to be abandoned to excite someone else, if they could. As for herself, she would find it even more difficult than they would to start over, with debts to pay and the close world of publishing remembering her past failure.

"I'm not sure," she heard herself say, and despised her weasel words. "There are too many things I still don't understand. I need to think about it."

Pushkin glanced at his watch. "Sign the agreement and think afterward. It doesn't tie you to anything." He slapped a piece of paper on her desk as if he could hardly wait to leave.

The contract was simple enough: the as-yet-untitled diaries of a Soviet official . . . all monies, less commission, to be paid to a firm of Swiss lawyers for the benefit of the Pushkin Fund . . . when and if published . . . Marshall's Literary Agency of New York to handle all negotiations, further and subsidiary rights. Jenny looked up. "What if I lose courage in Budapest and never even go to see the diaries after I've signed this?"

"Why should you? Hungary is Socialist, but not strict any longer in the ways which matter to a visitor. But if you become too afraid, you can walk away. Your obligation begins only when you negotiate for me with a publisher."

Jenny stood very straight, staring out of the window, a slight smile on her lips. The lights on the corner of Fifty-fourth and Second Avenue winked at her slantwise from below: yes; no; wait.

Who wanted always to be safe?

She signed, neatly as always, despising meaningless flourishes.

"Good," said Pushkin softly. "I think you will certainly have arranged to call at the State Publishing House while you are in Budapest?"

She nodded. "Next Wednesday."

"What time?"

"Two-thirty."

"Make sure you keep that exact appointment, then, and carry three hundred dollars in your handbag when you go."

He went out, slamming the door. From her window Jenny watched him stand by the lights, whistle a taxi like any New Yorker, and vanish into the traffic.

"Was he interesting?" Monica put her head round the door. She never just typed letters but spent her two working mornings with her nose firmly poked into Jenny's affairs.

Whatever Pushkin might or might not be, he certainly was interesting, reflected Jenny. "He came to tell me about a manuscript I might be able to buy in Budapest. Have

Morvin, the State Publishing people, confirmed my appointment?"

"They wrote, 'Come earlier and have lunch.'"

"Tell them no, will you?" Keep the exact appointment, Pushkin said. If he planned a contact there, then she couldn't change the time.

Monica sniffed. "I thought you'd be pleased. Not many publishers ask you to lunch. That Mr. Havasi rang."

"Sandy Havasi? Why didn't you say so before?" Jenny went back in her office and shut the door before calling Sandy's number. "Sandy? It's Jenny."

"Jenny, my dear. Come over at once and help me."

"For God's sake, I've only just started work."

"You must have finished a whole day of work already. That Monica woman told me some foreigner who ought to know better had reached you before she could find out anything about him."

Jenny laughed. "She hates anyone to get past her without being cross-examined. But, Sandy, I'm coming to see you tonight, remember? We need to fix a date to meet in Budapest, you said."

There was a brief pause while Sandy's smile somehow squeezed down the line and leapt on her desk. "Last time we spoke, you refused to tell me whether you might scrape up time to go or not. If you have, then we'll celebrate by ourselves tonight, with everyone else cleared out of the house."

"I'll believe that when I find it empty." Sandy lived in half a shabby brownstone, which was permanently filled with a shifting population of his friends, family, and friends of friends.

"I shall personally throw them out on the sidewalk, I promise. But, Jenny, don't think I've forgiven you. I'd hoped you might have begun making up your mind about a few other things by now, and flying off to Europe with only a promise of a single dinner fixed between us doesn't sound like you've spared too many thoughts from your books for me. You know I always go back to Hungary at this same time every year."

"I'm only there five days, and staying with my mother's family in between appointments. They'd be dreadfully hurt if I spent all my spare time with someone I could see any day in New York," she said defensively. Sandy Havasi's parents, and also Jenny's mother, had fled from Hungary as Russian tanks rolled in to crush the 1956 uprising against Soviet power. "Sandy?"

"I'm still here, love."

"Tell you about everything tonight, okay?"

"If you say so, but sure as hell you'd better make it good."

Jenny replaced the receiver, smiling. During all the time she was growing up and then at college or in publishing, she had scarcely given her Hungarian ancestry a thought, although historically it was illustrious. She was American: New York born and molded by this great country she regarded as her own. Molded, too, by her love of American and English literature, so eager to make her own way that she had failed to weigh the risks of setting up her own agency as carefully as she ought. Her mother's forebears had been Hungarian nobles owing allegiance to a Habsburg emperor, but surely few ties remained from that past, fewer still with communist Eastern Europe?

Yet, whether she admitted it or not, there was a tie.

It existed in the faded photographs that filled her mother's apartment, in her own coloring and affinity with languages, the quick rage she felt if she happened to hear Hungary being ignorantly disparaged.

Jenny's mother, Klari Keszthely, had been only one among thousands fleeing westward in 1956, but within a year of her arrival in an Austrian refugee camp, she had married Peter Marshall, an American relief worker. They had lived in New York City for a while, and when eventually their child was born, Klari settled happily into Peter's hometown, Bridgeport, Connecticut. There wasn't much more to say about Klari Keszthely; she lived contentedly in

Connecticut and never wanted to leave America again, clinging to safety as a nonswimmer might to a piece of driftwood in a roughening sea. When her husband went abroad on relief missions, she was delighted that Jenny's needs for stability or schooling made the best of excuses for her to remain behind. Surprisingly, the marriage was successful, since Peter Marshall was the kind of man who enjoyed occasional periods of domesticity rather than living in it all the time. Jenny had seen him only briefly since she left home to enter Barnard College. She visited her mother dutifully every other week, but the paralyzing boredom of Klari's crowded apartment had contributed to Jenny's indifference toward her Hungarian heritage.

Until she met Sandor Havasi, Sandy to all his many friends.

No. Her mind shied painfully. If she was honest, and Jenny valued honesty, then she had to admit that she first became aware of being half-Hungarian rather than wholly American because of the way her affair with Martin Rothbury broke up. But for heaven's sake, she wasn't going to start thinking about Martin again, when nowadays she had more than enough on her hands with Sandy. And Pushkin. She grimaced sourly to herself as she settled down to work. At the moment Pushkin looked likely to become the most troublesome male of the lot.

The rest of the day passed in its usual hectic rush, made worse because she was trying to tie up loose ends before flying next week to Europe. Jenny had already discovered that time was the commodity she had underestimated most disastrously when reckoning up the resources needed to establish her own agency. Working alone except for Monica twice a week, she seemed to need far more hours in each day than she had ever imagined, hours in which to encourage inexperienced but promising new authors brushed aside by the larger agencies, time in which to get herself established without worrying where next month's rent was coming from, time to burrow away at that market for Eastern European writing, which she still believed

could provide a steady contribution to future profit. Time
also to think about her own affairs, as Sandy had edgily
suggested; amusing but volatile, he was becoming increasingly impatient for some answers.

Time that Pushkin might possibly win for her, if his
father's diary fulfilled even half his promises; just selling
the story of how she smuggled it out of Hungary ought to
earn her six months reprieve.

Toward the middle of that same busy afternoon, Jenny
reached for a fresh script from the pile waiting to be read.
She flicked through a few untidy pages half spilling out of
their folder while holding on the phone for an elusive publisher who probably didn't want to speak to her anyway.
After a few minutes she put the phone down to search
among the loose sheets for five pages apparently missing
from the beginning of the manuscript. Once they were
found, she settled to read with precisely honed attention,
the telephone and publishers forgotten. As dusk fell on
Manhattan, Jenny knew that she had found a script—no
need for adjectives like good or interesting. This was a
script that would launch a new writer whose name readers
everywhere one day would recognize.

This lucky day, she thought.

Surely such unexpected twenty-two-carat luck must be
an omen for a secret Russian diary, too. She went over to
the window and looked out, as she had this morning to
watch Pushkin disappear. Green for walk, said the lights.
She laughed aloud. Green for luck, green for get up and
go, green for the kind of once-in-a-lifetime exultation an
astronaut felt when he landed on the moon.

The covering letter sent with the script was grimy and
self-deprecating; the author had been given her name by an
acquaintance and would be grateful for advice after two
years' work on a manuscript with which he now felt thoroughly dissatisfied. Yes, this script needed help, was far
from ready yet. But if the author meant what he said about
advice and was willing to work and work on his script, one
day it would make this young man's fortune. Never since

she joined the publishing trade had Jenny known such certainty. Her eyes sped on down the page, jarred to a stop. Yours sincerely, Simon Druce. He wrote from an address in London, England, and the acquaintance who had advised him to contact her was Martin Rothbury.

2

O N HER WAY HOME FOR A QUICK SHOWER AND CHANGE before going on to Sandy's place, Jenny called in at the travel agent and rescheduled her air ticket so she could fly to Budapest via London. She had already phoned Simon Druce, author of *Let the World Die*, to say she just happened to be in England this weekend and could he meet her to talk about his manuscript? He had been incoherent with thanks and delight, definitely not a genius with the spoken word.

You, not me, are doing the favor, Mr. Druce, she thought as she hung up. Even if that marvelous script does sit up and beg for a goddamn ruthless editor like me.

It also might take as much as a year of painstaking work before *Let the World Die* would be ready to hit the market, a consideration that stifled at birth Jenny's remaining doubts about Pushkin's proposition. Pray God those diaries were genuine, looked worth real money when she reached them, and could somehow be successfully smuggled out.

About all of which Jenny felt cheerfully optimistic. Her

decision taken, she was no longer able to consider even the possibility of failure, and as she walked from the subway toward Sandy Havasi's brownstone, Jenny was thinking far more about how she should work with Simon Druce to edit his book as a potential modern classic deserved than about distant perils in Budapest.

All the lights were on in Sandy's house, and as she had expected, it was far from swept clear of people. Which, she was guiltily aware, suited her pretty well. Jenny guessed that no other woman Sandy had ever wanted to sleep with had kept him waiting even a week, let alone for several months, lack of time only one of her excuses. In fact, the break with Martin had left so many raw emotions that for a time hazarding herself again simply hadn't seemed worthwhile. But Sandy was fun. Jenny liked him a lot and could still be surprised by how relaxed she felt in his company. All the same, a great many doubts remained over letting a man of such an amorous and possessive temperament into her life. Already he was jealous of the emotional energy she put into Marshall's Literary Agency, and perhaps with reason. Tonight, for instance, the momentous events of her day meant she had scarcely given Sandy a thought until she walked through his door, that guilty sense of relief as she saw his house still full of people a measure of the part of herself she remained unwilling to commit to anyone again.

Sandy greeted her at the door, every line of his sinewy, flat-planed face expressing delight at her arrival. He swept her around his sitting room in a flurry of introductions and then out again to the kitchen. "You monster," he said, and kissed her. "Why are you so late? I bribed everyone to leave the moment they'd eaten my *Halaszlé*, but now they've settled down to talk again, God knows how I'll ever get them out."

"What did you say it was?" Jenny peered at lumps in a pan.

"Do you mean your mother never taught you to make *Halaszlé*?"

"If she did, it didn't look like that." She wrinkled her nose. "I shouldn't think it's right, would you?"

"Well, I hope so. Most of the people here tonight can afford to eat in the best restaurants whenever they choose."

"I thought I didn't recognize any of them."

Sandy grinned, a blaze of a grin which knifed right through her and came out the other side. "Don't be rude, darling, although I admit this bunch aren't quite my usual style. But I surely did not bring you into a kitchen to waste time on anyone but ourselves." He kissed her again, reaching her lips by way of the inside of her wrists, her throat, and her ear. Sandy often used small and tender gestures in his kissing, which at first seemed strange in a man whose life was one long extravagance, and later became one of several contradictions in him Jenny valued. Tonight, perhaps because her day had been so filled by excitement and dangerous decision, for the first time her own desire also reached out to twist tight as a rope with his.

Sandy felt this new, instinctive response at once, cherished and teased it before drawing back. His eyes, which sometimes marbled disconcertingly black or gray according to the light, glinted with laughter. "You watch how fast I get everyone eating now, and then out of the house." He released her gently and went over to the door. "*Halaszlé*, folks, then the party's over until Budapest."

Guests in Sandy's house were often of Hungarian extraction, but this was the first occasion when, as Jenny soon realized with surprise, everyone around the table proved to be at least half-Hungarian as well as remarkably rich. Although she had heard only of George Roman, who had become a millionaire out of establishing a chain of Hungarian-style fast-food outlets all over New England, the authentic air of money-satisfaction exuded by the rest was unmistakable.

"Why ask them just because they're rich?" she asked Sandy, low-voiced beneath argumentative chatter. Jenny had long ago decided that Hungarians disguised their affections by arguing incessantly. "I never thought you cared in the least about money, only how to spend it. Why, you told me yourself you chose to work for the government because it gives good vacations and never fired anyone clever enough to look moderately busy." Sandy was reticent about money, but from several hints Jenny had guessed that he gambled heavily on Wall Street, and skillfully, too, since he seemed able to spend as extravagantly after Black Monday as before it. Sandy Havasi's hobby was amateur sports car racing, where he was known on the circuit as either a recklessly successful or fiendishly dangerous driver, although so far he had walked away from all but a few of his accidents. His job had always seemed to Jenny something he flopped into for a rest.

"I don't, *szivecskem*. You're the one who eats work for breakfast, lunch, and dinner."

She shook her head, her body still tingling from their kiss in the kitchen. There were other things in life than her literary agency, after all. "Maybe I enjoy trying to race books on a circuit instead of sports cars."

"But at least you have definitely decided it isn't just so much wasted time to visit Budapest?"

"I didn't need much persuading," she answered, smiling. Actually, her air ticket was an extravagant birthday present from her mother, who adored Sandy and knew he went to Budapest every fall. Probably she hoped that throwing them together where their ancestors had lived and loved for fifty generations might settle her too-exacting daughter's mind. Since Jenny was annoyed by such insidious, old-style family blackmail, this had been one very personal reason why she'd refused until tonight to tell him whether she meant to go or not.

"Everyone here is visiting there as well. It's a kind of bet we had, a gesture if you like, to kick the past up the ass."

"Hungary has changed, Sandy. It isn't the same place you left in 1956."

"Jesus, I know that; I go there every year. It's as free as you can get in the East, and freer than some places in the

West. All the same, if any of the people in this room had stayed there, they'd be lucky to earn three hundred dollars a month. Take Zoltan Zakonyi there; he reached the U.S. carrying a single valise in 1956, and now he's worth ten million dollars. Pierre Sorbaz, his folks settled in France, and now he's one of their top physicists. The French don't count francs when it comes to paying good men well. One night, when we happened to be together—and I guess we'd drunk too much Hungarian brandy—we decided it might show up something which needed showing if we held a celebration party in Budapest."

Show what? wondered Jenny. Modern Hungary did not possess the kind of popular press that reported gestures against the state. Men were childish sometimes, even the best of them. "I'm afraid I shan't qualify for your party, then. Marshall's Literary Agency can't boast its millionaire yet."

"I don't qualify, either, but—"

"No one here would agree!" interrupted Zoltan Zakonyi, who canned fish in Florida to earn the ten million dollars Sandy said he was worth. "Without Sandor Havasi, we would all be going to Budapest different years to look for our roots and never show a goddamn thing to the commies. Wouldn't we, folks? Why, only at Christmas, my wife said, What about Budapest this year so I can see where you were born? And you know what I said? Not this year, hon. Who wants to spend good dollars subsidizing a pack of commissars? I fancied big-game fishing on the Pacific coast. Then Sandor wrote how he was planning to put the commies' nose out of joint by rubbing it in our success, and we changed our minds goddamn quick."

Jenny regarded the speaker with fascination. She loved listening to how people spoke and thought and hid their thoughts; she also felt sympathy for a man who would probably never seem anything other than a caricature in this, his adopted country.

Everyone seemed extremely grateful to Sandy, though. For all their riches, there was something pathetic about these people, which might be why he had succeeded in interesting them in anything as bizarre as a party in Budapest to celebrate capitalist wealth. It was as if they all still felt sufficiently exiled to need to convince themselves by flaunting their wealth that they had been right to leave the land of their birth.

Over the *Halaszlé*, which turned out to be lethally spiced fish chowder, they began to discuss their party in Budapest.

"The others will join us when we reach there," Sandy observed. "You remember Imre Schiller, the central banker from Frankfurt? He's advising the West Germans at the financial conference which is meeting in Budapest next week, and wrote to say he'd enjoy to come along. Gyula Sebestyen is flying in to cover the conference for the *Wall Street Journal*. Her family used to own a town house on the Danube promenade almost next to your grandfather's, Jenny."

"Your folks owned a mansion on the promenade?" asked Zakonyi reverently. "Sandy said your ma is a Keszthely."

Jenny flushed, feeling ridiculous. "It's all a long time ago."

"Have you ever been back?"

"Once, for a few days five years ago."

"And didn't it put you in one hell of a rage to see Budapest strutting with commissars?"

"It isn't. If you're going to Hungary to see commissars, Mr. Zakonyi, you're going to be disappointed. You'll love Budapest, though; it's a beautiful city."

"I bet I'll be able to spot the stooge following me even before I reach the hotel from the airport."

"You won't be followed, unless you punch the first policeman you see on the nose," said Jenny shortly.

"That's what you think," answered Zakonyi. "I know better. Everyone is watched in Commieland; it's just a question of spotting the bastard on your tail."

"Jenny, my dear, you mustn't spoil my guests' enjoyment of the *Halaszlé*," interrupted Sandy. "Where would we all be without enemies to hate? Besides, police have their uses, eh, George?"

The restaurateur, Roman, nodded. "I'd prefer to open new premises in Budapest rather than New York. Sixty thousand dollars vandalism cost me last year. I wish to God we sent the swine to drain the marshes, like I'm told they do in Hungary."

"Then why not open up in Budapest, monsieur? I went there for a scientific congress two years ago, and although the food is quite good when you find it, anyone who does not speak Hungarian must find it nearly impossible to discover which are the restaurants, they are so few and poorly marked." Sorbaz, the physicist, spread his hands with a true Frenchman's horror for such a state of affairs.

Roman grinned. "Because my Hungarian-style fast food isn't even first cousin to the real thing. I'd profit from tourists two months in the year, and the rest of the time the natives wouldn't touch my Danubeburgers."

"Yeah?" Zakonyi stabbed his fork in the air. "You're glue-footed, George. Provided the commies'd let you set up at all, I bet I could make any goddamn Budapester sit up and beg for Danubeburgers, just because they were billed as Western. I read in the papers the poor bastards are just drooling to feel they're part of civilization again."

"Then you could have a grand opening of your restaurant and we would all go." Madame Sorbaz leaned forward eagerly. She was wearing such enormous diamonds that at first Jenny hadn't been able to believe they were real.

". . . wearing all your jewels," murmured Sandy.

"Food accursed by the name of fast is never an occasion for wearing jewels," stated Sorbaz firmly.

Jenny fixed her eyes on her plate, trying not to laugh. Really, they were so absurd, it was hard to believe that each in his own way was an enviable success. Still, successful people often did not think of much except their own affairs. If Schiller, the German banker, and Gyula Sebestyen, the financial journalist, were anything like the rest, then their dinner party in Budapest would be like a bad farce.

Jenny's mind again slipped back to that morning. If all went well, Pushkin and his diarist father would become exiles, too.

"Have you any Keszthely jewelry still, Miss Marshall?" Mrs. Roman leaned across the table.

Jenny snatched at her thoughts, wondering what on earth they could be discussing now. "My mother brought out a lovely pearl necklace set in gold filigree, which, after two hundred years, is nearly back in fashion again. That's all, I'm afraid."

"Oh, you must wear the Keszthely pearls!" She turned to the others. "I always thought George's family stuff quite dreadfully ugly, but I shall just love to take it to Budapest. Imagine, the last time anyone wore it there could have been to an imperial ball!"

"I've only brought my diamonds up from Florida, and they're modern," said Mrs. Zakonyi disconsolately.

"I couldn't imagine you or Madame Sorbaz wearing anything else," answered Sandy gravely. "Jenny, my dear, I would leave your pearls at home if I were you. If they're Keszthely, the Hungarians just might decide they belong to the state."

"How could they? I'm American born, and they're my legal property. Besides, I can't imagine anyone would know where they came from even if I wore them to a state reception."

"Wouldn't that show the commies! A Keszthely wearing ancestral jewels right in front of their whole goddamn politburo," interjected Zakonyi.

"I said, *if* I went to a state reception, which I shan't, because for one thing, there isn't one—"

"Sure there will be, for the financial conference."

"I am not going to Budapest as part of the financial conference."

Sandy cocked an eyebrow at her. "No? I thought maybe you'd picked next week because that prig Martin Rothbury would surely have his legs under any conference table where they're talking about money. He'll be into the vodka at official receptions."

"We haven't met in months, and I don't suppose for a moment he'll be in Budapest, financial conference or not," Jenny answered sharply. Sandy and Martin had met accidentally once and instantly disliked each other. It was a shock all the same, to hear that Martin might be in Budapest at the same time as she and Sandy. But Budapest is a big city, she decided almost instantly. Quite large enough for inconspicuous Jenny Marshall to check the authenticity of some diaries without crossing the path of delegates wrangling over Hungarian debts to the Western banking system.

"If this Rothbury's family came from Hungary, too, maybe he would like to join our party," suggested Roman.

"It didn't," said Sandy shortly. "He's a goddamn British government stiff, and the parties he'd like best would be held in a morgue."

"Of course you must wear the Keszthely pearls," declared Zakonyi. "Jesus, so long as there's the slightest chance our bankers might bail them out, the Reds wouldn't dare touch us if we boated on the Danube wearing the Habsburg crown jewels. I hope this pal of yours isn't soft on Reds, Miss Marshall."

"He will no doubt carry out British government policy," said Jenny coldly. She owed Martin something, after all, for sending her Simon Druce.

Zakonyi immediately launched into a monologue about how allies only fouled things up as soon as they failed to toe the Washington line, but since he had even less idea than they did about what the Washington line was on the banking debts of Eastern Europe, no one took any notice. He had a curiously preoccupied mannerlessness, as if the unquestionable rightness of his views excused any discourtesy, while remaining so innocently enthusiastic that it was impossible to dislike him for long.

So innocent was he that he just might come in useful.

Jenny closed her ears to the rasp of his voice while privately deciding that Hungarian officials must inevitably become so infuriated by Zakonyi that the airport customs would flay his luggage right down to the seams. If she stuck as close to him as she could on the way out, quite likely she'd walk past unsearched.

"God, what snobs they all are," said Sandy, gulping brandy when his guests had gone at last.

"You chose them because they were snobs. You can't start blaming them for being exactly what you wanted."

He shot her a startled glance, then laughed. "Perhaps you're right."

"Why, Sandy? Why invite people who bore you just because you want them to come to dinner in Budapest?"

"A Habsburg dinner," he said dreamily. "Did I ever tell you that for nearly two hundred years my family provided hereditary chamberlains to the court whenever it came to Budapest? You've seen the Imperial Palace there?"

Jenny nodded, remembering the huge building beside the Danube.

"The land it stands on originally belonged to the Havasi. When the emperor wanted to buy a site for his palace, we gave it to him. So he appointed the head of our family as hereditary chamberlain, and we took precedence even over you Keszthely inside the palace walls."

"I don't mind," said Jenny, smiling.

"*Kedvesem*, neither do I. We've wallowed in more than enough nostalgia for tonight. But you can't fool me any longer. Even Jennifer Marshall occasionally feels romantic, too."

Her lips curved at this characteristically oblique reference to her earlier response to his kiss.

He smiled back. "Well, there you are. When I heard some rich exiles were planning a gesture in Budapest, I thought the Habsburg hereditary chamberlain ought to be there as well."

"I thought it was all your idea."

He shook his head, lithe body slumped, mobile face

reflecting every change of mood. "Perhaps I tried to add a little grace to a rather vulgar idea. But grace or not, Jenny, I wouldn't take your pearls to Budapest."

"At least they'd be worthy company for an imperial chamberlain," answered Jenny lightly. She wished now that she had left with the rest, although had the house been empty when she arrived, probably she would have been in bed with Sandy now. But quite suddenly she seemed to have taken all she could manage for a single day, her earlier near certainty over Sandy blurred by freshly niggling doubt: Sandor Havasi, the last hereditary chamberlain of the Habsburgs, was not the same as jet set Sandy, that lighthearted dabbler in daily toil and lunatic driver of fast cars.

She would have liked to discuss Pushkin with him, but if she did, then he would naturally see it as a plea for help. Sandy would love to outwit officialdom in Budapest, and the riskier an enterprise, the more he would enjoy it. Unfortunately, Jenny could imagine nothing more likely to provoke official interest than Habsburg-style flamboyance, whereas she planned to use the most finicking caution to make sure she kept herself out of jail. On the other hand, to refuse Sandy's help once she told him about Pushkin would be unthinkable. Most especially tonight, when he believed she was waiting for him to make love to her, and all she longed for was her own solitary, uncomplicated bed.

So she kept quiet and thought instead about how agreeable it would be to wear the Keszthely pearls, just once, in Budapest. Very modern Ms. Marshall, illegally seeking to profit from smuggled diaries, could indeed be romantic, too.

While she was still lost in a vague reverie about pearls and diaries, Sandy came over to sit beside her, speaking Hungarian for the first time that evening. "My love, would you ever believe me if I said this really is the happiest moment of my life? It is true, you know."

She stood up hastily, needing to tear out of his arms and

feeling horribly ashamed. "I'm leaving for Europe early in the morning. I simply have to go."

"*Kedvesem*—"

"No, Sandy, I'm sorry. I don't blame you if you're angry, but—"

"You say you're off tomorrow?" he said softly. "As I remember it, you weren't flying out until next Monday."

"I was, but now I have to stop over in London." She stared back into eyes that suddenly had darkened. "I know what you're thinking. No, it has nothing to do with Martin." But indirectly, of course, it did, since without Martin, Simon Druce would certainly have taken his script elsewhere.

"Then why London, for God's sake?"

"I'll tell you. There was this script I began reading only today, and it's terrific! Or it will be, once . . . Well, I guess for a start, maybe fifty thousand words need editing out, but I know that potentially it's a winner. But first I have to discuss where we go from here with the author; he's English and happens to live in London."

"You didn't know Rothbury might be in Budapest, you say, and now you're flying off early to spend the weekend around the corner from where the bastard lives—"

"I said, I only decided today I needed to spend some time in London on the way to Budapest. It's business, for heaven's sake. I changed my ticket on the way here."

"Then there's how you were not two hours ago when I kissed you, yet now you're all bright-eyed over London and only thinking about some goddamn book. A more suspicious man than me might say you didn't really give a shit for anyone but yourself."

"I'm sorry," she said helplessly. "Sandy, my dear, I'm so sorry. I know I've behaved badly, but it isn't how it seems. I really didn't know Martin might be in Budapest, and I don't expect to see him if he is. Or in London. We're washed up, finished, months ago. And I never pretended I was different to how I am: someone who has to love the person she sleeps with. Or not sleep with him at all."

Slowly his expression eased, mouth twitched into the shadow of a smile. "I guess you didn't. Has no one ever told you how much nicer life becomes when helped along by a few soft lies?"

"All the time! It doesn't work for me, that's all."

"Give it a whirl and you'd be surprised. Enjoy your weekend in London."

Jenny could see he would never believe she really wasn't somehow still in touch with Martin, felt irritated to realize her hands were shaking as she searched for her purse, shrugged into her coat.

Only as he drove her home in his old MG roadster did Sandy speak again. "You value the truth, you say. Okay, then. Will you tell me exactly why you decided in the end to take this trip to Budapest? You're short of cash and said before, you couldn't afford either the dollars or the time."

Jenny hesitated. "After the way I've behaved tonight, I guess you deserve to know. I'm going because for the first time in my life, I've begun wondering where the hell I belong. I thought it was here. All my life I took it for granted it was here. Hungary and past Keszthelys never entered my head except as bedtime stories Mother used to tell me. Then—" She gripped her hands on her purse; she hated telling anyone this, Sandy above all. "I'm not going to talk about Martin, but part of why we split up was because, one night in London, I suggested we eat in a smart restaurant I'd read about, and he answered he couldn't afford to be seen around with a half-Hungarian woman."

The MG shot through a red light, screeched on the wrong side of a traffic island. "Jesus, what a bastard," Sandy said with satisfaction. "But why, for God's sake?"

"He's official British to the spine, I suppose. I was furious, of course. I don't want to talk about that. What I was trying to say was, it started me wondering about the Hungarian half of me, which in America never seemed to matter. I began to think, maybe it ought to matter. Then I met you, at first not often but—"

"I guess I soon made sure you knew I'd like it to be more often."

She nodded, grateful for any help with this, a truthful answer why she'd accepted her mother's offer of an air ticket to Budapest. She could still keep quiet about Pushkin, since he'd come afterward. "You were born in Hungary, yet I've never seen anyone so easy, everywhere you go. Of course, as an American, but . . . Well, take tonight. In your house, those strange people felt instantly grafted back on their roots. I guess . . . once I began to think about us maybe together, having another look at the country my mother came from began to seem more important."

"You do that." He pulled into the curb, turned to face her. Not smiling, maybe still not quite convinced, but happier with himself and her. "To me, Hungary is still a great place for finding and taking what you want. You need to want it badly enough, is all. Sure, the communists have screwed up everything they've touched, but the old wild Hungary is waiting, out of their reach. That's why I love it there, and you will, too. Where are you staying, did you say?"

"With my uncle Janos Keszthely until I've found a hotel."

"I'm at the Korona. Promise you'll telephone?"

She nodded. "If you still want me to, after tonight."

"I want you to."

"And I bet the Korona has as much baroque gilt and turn-of-the-century plumbing as any romantic could wish."

"Now, there you would be absolutely right." He kissed her, deep and hard, while they both still laughed; but though he laughed, his mouth felt barbed and dangerous.

3

A WET WEEKEND IN LONDON. JENNY HAD LONG AGO become familiar with the two cities and innumerable interlocked neighborhoods that made up this sprawling capital, since London and New York between them monopolized English-language publishing.

She had telephoned ahead and arranged to stay with an editor she had come to know well during the year she had spent in the London office of a U.S. publisher, greedily went to the theater both nights she was free, and spent the Sunday working hard with Simon Druce. He was hard work, too, she reflected ruefully, incapable of discussing his script without descending into suicidal gloom or becoming entangled in so many ideas at once, it took hours to worry them into order. Jenny came away exhausted but even more convinced that if only she could help to guide such a prodigally faceted talent into addressing its own excesses, then *Let the World Die* ought indeed to become a classic of its kind.

She was, however, relieved when Druce eventually

emerged sufficiently from Dostoyevskian dejection to be left alone to brood on the iniquities of critical editing.

As she left, Jenny could not resist asking about his acquaintance with Martin Rothbury; several times she had scarcely suppressed a chuckle at the thought of Martin's reaction to such muddleheaded and mercurial genius.

"Rothbury?" Druce answered vaguely. "It's all quite clear in my head, you know; it's just that I fall behind where I'm thinking as I write it down."

"Martin Rothbury; he's one of your MPs and fiscal secretary to the treasury," said Jenny patiently. "You wrote in your letter he had suggested you should send your manuscript over to me in New York."

"Oh, Rothbury. I met him in the House of Commons."

"You *what*?"

Even Druce grinned at her astonishment. "I was taken there by a friend to demonstrate against something, I can't remember what, but then I wandered off to look at some splendidly hideous Victorian carvings, which were much more interesting. I think I ended up where I shouldn't, and when Rothbury asked what the hell I thought I was doing, we got talking and he showed me the Commons library. Now, that is almost worth being an MP for, I can tell you."

"I doubt it," said Jenny, laughing.

"My God, no. Too many bloody people wanting things." He returned to his cocoon of paper on the table.

Well, thought Jenny as she let herself out of Druce's basement flat, that was surely a meeting I should have liked to witness.

The next day she flew on to Hungary, and in spite of herself, a chill qualm cramped her stomach as the Boeing's undercarriage rumbled down on arrival, a checkerboard landscape reaching toward her out of a setting sun.

Ferihegy International Airport seemed enormous for its few aircraft squatting near the terminal building, guarded by slovenly green-banded troops carrying submachine guns. When Jenny came on her first visit to Hungary five years before, she had been disconcerted by both guns and empty space, an unease that only the relaxed atmosphere of Budapest had eradicated from her mind. Now bleak menace hit her over the heart. She had expected to find Hungary less Communist, and instead there were more guns and guards than before, perhaps because the financial conference was due to start on the following day. There was also a bitter wind blowing from the east, since this was November instead of June. Above all, her own covert intentions made each muzzle and icy blast seem directed straight against her spine.

But there stood Geza and Janos, Jenny's aunt and uncle, waving furiously from the roof of the terminal, pouncing on her with warmhearted bear hugs the moment she emerged beyond the barrier. Naturally they were indignant when she suggested they look for a hotel on their way into central Budapest from the airport, but Jenny, thinking more insistently now of Pushkin, was firm. "I'll come and see you often." She gave her aunt another hug. "But I have so much work to do while I'm here, I'll be more nuisance to you than I'm worth."

"You make words sound very strange," said little cousin Mari, wide-eyed.

Everyone shushed her at once, but Jenny laughed. "I expect I do. My Hungarian is a generation out-of-date, so you'll have to tell me all the rude slang your school friends use."

Mari giggled and sat on her knee when they crammed into a battered East German Trabant car for the journey into Budapest, thumping over uneven granite sets while everyone talked at the top of their voice.

Jenny answered almost at random, staring eagerly out of the window, not wanting to miss a thing. Her only other visit had been taken up with meeting so many unknown relatives that her head had spun with the effort of sorting out who was who. This time she had meant to savor the land itself and regretted very much that she must stay in a hotel instead of with Geza and Janos. But no matter what she said, they refused to listen.

"Of course you are staying the whole time with us," said Janos, his Keszthely mustache bristling, and short of offending everyone mortally forever, there was nothing she could do to overcome their insistence. "Until Wednesday, then," she said, in partial capitulation, and was hugged all round again while the Trabant nearly went under the wheels of a tram. Her appointment with Morvin was on Wednesday, and nothing was going to stop her from leaving Janos's home before she kept it.

She remembered Budapest as beautiful, but suburban rutted roads and occasional neon signs did not prepare anyone for the wide sweep of the Danube at the city's heart. On each side lay solid Habsburg buildings with the Buda Hills beyond, a happy mix of old and new reflected in swift-flowing water.

Much too quickly they were across the river and plunged into a tunnel before jolting up a steep, rock-lined road that led past Empress Maria Theresa's castle. Jenny wondered where the Havasi lands had begun and ended when all this was open meadow. "There are more banners around than I remember," she said aloud, and could have kicked herself for tactlessness. On her last visit she had gone everywhere she wanted and spoken of anything she wished, except politics, and Ferihegy Airport made her uncertain how much anything had changed.

"It's the financial conference," answered Janos after a pause. "Whenever we have an official gathering here, no matter whether it is Warsaw Pact or a chess congress, the banners come out. Even under Gorbachev, the Russians feel lonely without Lenin and red letters following their every move. Perhaps especially under Gorbachev, since we Hungarians have certainly learned that when you want to change things, it is more important than ever to pretend that nothing is really changed. But the day after our Soviet friends leave for Moscow, bunting and slogans will go back in store. This time it has been especially difficult for the city authorities; we understand these matters, but Western bankers will not like to look out of their hotel window and see Marx reminding them how capitalism is doomed. Particularly when they must be wondering how they could have been such fools as to lend so much money to Eastern Europe. We do not want to annoy the men who could send us back to jail for debt, but nor do we want to provoke the jailers."

His tone was bitter, and for a moment everyone in the car was silent, staring at giant, gimcrack portraits and extravagantly punctuated exhortations that disfigured most buildings in the center of the city. Jenny was born the daughter of an American because, thirty-three years before, the Russians had lost patience with Hungarian attempts to break out of their prison. Then this lovely city had been stormed in blood and fire. Probably it wouldn't happen that way again, but who knew with the Russians, paranoid over their own security? It wouldn't even need to happen that way again if the bankers panicked. The moment the West decided it had better things to do with its money than lend it to a hostile East, then Hungary's cautious return to freer ways would be blocked, her people forced back to labor on the Soviet economic treadmill.

The Trabant swerved so everyone inside cried out at once and drove into a courtyard behind narrow Orszaghaz Street. Most Budapest streets hid courtyards, but to Jenny this one was especially precious: ochre stuccoed walls, a single chestnut tree shedding crisp bronze leaves underfoot. "*Tessék!* Welcome home," said Geza, and everyone tumbled out on the cobbles.

Jenny had never forgotten the dark rooms where she stayed on her first visit to Budapest—crammed with carved furniture and cooking smells—and she was delighted to find that nothing had changed in a place where even the plants looked as if they must be heirlooms.

Two days. That was all the time she had to forget Pushkin and Marshall's Literary Agency, Sandy Havasi and the Keszthely pearls stuffed guiltily in her purse. Two days in which to remember that before Pushkin came, she had planned this trip as a voyage of discovery. In thought and instinct she was American, Western, but in blood half-Magyar, kin to Geza and Janos of Budapest. Granddaughter of Miklos Keszthely, who once owned two castles as well as a mansion on Budapest's most fashionable promenade, not to mention a hundred thousand Hungarian acres. Perhaps inheritance really didn't matter, wrapped up as she was in her New York life and taking American roots for granted, but after Martin, and now also because of Sandy, she needed at least to discover what that inheritance meant.

But the time raced past, and all she learned was how little anyone can discover in two days. Nothing new about herself, nor about any deeper reason for coming on this trip than buying manuscripts. Perhaps she, too, was falling into the same trap as Sandy's exiles, looking over her shoulder for something that wasn't there.

"What is troubling you, Jeni?" Geza asked her that evening. "Why did you come if not to see us and enjoy yourself?"

"I am enjoying myself, and I love seeing all of you," Jenny replied, which was both true and untrue. She was out of place in tiny rooms crammed with warm, fat humanity; and though she enjoyed learning to speak vivid everyday Hungarian, and the way Janos used poetry as if it was the obvious way to settle a dispute, she became very quickly bored by the hours of gossip Hungarians adored. "It's true . . . I came looking for something I'm not sure belongs to me, and I haven't found it yet. I shall be better when I'm working, I expect."

"And you insist on leaving us tomorrow?"

"I must. There are publishers and writers I have to see, manuscripts I must read, before I return to New York."

"You could do all that here," Geza said reproachfully. "We should enjoy to entertain writers for you, when Janos is so fond of poetry."

Janos chuckled. "Leave her, *kedvesem*. Jeni is too polite to say it, but she could not read manuscripts here. She has never learned the Hungarian trick of closing her brain to a family living in the same room where she must work. How could she flick through five hundred pages of tragedy and offer dollars for it next morning while Mari is curled beside her, and *Néni* Dodi spills coffee on her lovely American dress?"

"Oh, Jeni, I do hope the stain will come out," said Geza anxiously.

In the flurry of assurances an awkward moment passed, as Janos meant it to pass. Janos could make anyone feel at ease: Habsburg emperors from the past, Red commissars, anyone. He would have inherited all those Keszthely acres if history had worked out differently but seemed content as a semiretired professor of mechanics at Budapest Technical University.

Next day he drove Jenny to the Hotel Huszar, which he recommended as comfortable and run by a friend of his. It was also cheap and not too close to the Korona, where Sandy would have arrived by now. The streets were thronged, red banners flapping, yellow trams clanging, the River Danube like a bolt of unraveled cloth—actually blue today under a brilliant, late autumn sky. Brown, peeling buildings, green-uniformed soldiers strolling in the streets.

"It's strange," said Jenny thoughtfully. "In spite of so many reminders of the East, Budapest most of all makes me think of Paris. A brown Paris without the café tables."

Janos hurled the Trabant at a gap between two trams. "No Magyar compares Budapest to anything else. But Paris, now: I spent the happiest six months of my life there, in 1938." He looked at her sideways and narrowly missed a diplomatic BMW. "Perhaps I don't mind it just a little like Paris in your eyes."

Jenny stayed quiet after that, since she wanted to live to reach the Hotel Huszar. My Magyar blood must have been diluted by American traffic laws, she reflected wryly; she hated being frightened in an automobile and realized now that Sandy drove like a Hungarian when previously she had blamed his recklessness on sports car racing. Though she would not have dared say so to Janos, Budapest actually reminded her of a faded sepia photograph of old Paris, and not the modern city at all. The buildings needed scrubbing and repair; the trams roared like dinosaurs from a vanished age.

This strange, persistent sense of living in the past, which she had also felt among those strange guests in Sandy's house: the sooner she was here and now again, the better. At least there was no doubt that Pushkin and his diaries belonged most definitely to the modern world.

After Janos left in a bustle of hugs and worn gears, Jenny felt both forlorn and edgy, filled with nervous anticipation about meeting Pushkin's messenger secretly this same afternoon. Her hotel room was too hot and the window looked out on a dingy well, but at least she was some distance from the clang of trams. As soon as she was unpacked and had looked at her watch for the twentieth time, Jenny decided she might as well start walking to Morvin's offices. Anything was better than waiting and wondering how Pushkin would make contact. Wondering, too, whether she really could have been such a fool as to decide to smuggle diaries out of a Communist country, where convicted criminals were sent to drain the marshes.

She stopped on her way to stare in shop windows, which were mostly filled with tightly padded upholstery and unfashionable clothes. There was plenty to buy in Budapest, far more than in Moscow, so the Hungarians smugly said, but not much of it would tempt a Westerner.

But those diaries, now . . . She wanted very badly to shop for them; her mind hadn't changed on that. Abruptly Jenny's spirits rose. Ever since coming to Budapest, she had felt oddly depressed. Now her pace increased to her usual rapid dash, and her dark eyes snapped with anticipation. Sure, this was a risk, but provided she moved a step at a time, not too much could go wrong. Even the Hungarians couldn't do more than throw her out while she only looked at diaries; and until she did, she couldn't begin to decide whether to try and take them to New York.

Morvin's offices were painted a drab, absorbent green and filled with toppling piles of paper, but the editors were welcoming and kept plum brandy in their desk drawers. They also had a great many manuscripts they were painfully anxious to sell, as if the international bankers closeted in conference across the square made everyone aware how important exports were.

Jenny spent the afternoon trying to make some kind of selection from the mass of folders offered her, to talk dollars and translation rights through a gathering glow of good fellowship. *"Köszönöm! No, thank you,"* she said again and again, to both toasts and manuscripts. "I have enough to study now, I think. May I telephone you again in a day or two?"

Yes, certainly she could. May you find much there to enjoy, *Asszany* Marshall. Can we call a taxi? *Nem*, of course Morvin would be only too happy to deliver such a pile of paper to the Hotel Huszar if she preferred to walk.

Really, I would like to lie down somewhere dark until my head settles, thought Jenny ruefully when she reached the pavement again at last. Nothing had happened, no one had dropped the name of Pushkin into the conversation, even casually, though she had dragged Russian literature into the most inappropriate discussions just to give everyone the opportunity. Nothing; a great big zero. Feeling very much let down, she stood irresolutely by the curb, a headache niggling behind her eyes. She could do with a walk, and if she had taken a taxi, then Pushkin would have been denied this last faint chance of making contact.

Jenny shivered. At this time of year in Budapest an east wind blew almost constantly, stripping the last leaves from the trees. Vanquished occasionally by the sun but always returning to howl around ochre walls, pounce across the Danube, and whirl in dust from the plains. Next would come the rain, before the east wind came roaring back to bring the first deep falls of snow.

"Asszany, I think you dropped your newspaper." A Hungarian voice broke into her thoughts.

"Oh no, I—" Jenny broke off, staring doubtfully at a narrow, freckled face, tangled, graying hair, and blue eyes

as guileless and cheerful as a baby's. He did not look in the
least like her idea of a literary smuggler. "Unless—that is,
I did keep a copy which had an article on Pushkin I enjoyed."

"Baszom a Pushkin!" answered the other cheerfully,
which was quite exceptionally rude in Hungarian. "I'm
Andras Benedek, at your service. Shall we drink coffee
together, eh? Although I'd sooner talk about London or
New York than Pushkin."

He knew where she came from, so probably it was all
right. Jenny cursed Pushkin heartily now for having told
her so little about what came next.

The coffee was welcome all the same, as black as lico-
rice and hot enough to skin her throat. Benedek swallowed
his at once, without blinking. "Tell me, is it true that in
London it is easy to steal a car and not be caught?"

"Yes," said Jenny gravely. "Quite easy."

"Rolls-Royces?" The *R*'s were rolled like drumbeats.

"They're more difficult, I suppose, being bigger and
fewer."

"But possible?"

"Perhaps. I've never tried."

"I must go there sometime," said Benedek dreamily. "It
is difficult here to steal even a Trabant for long, and not
worth the trouble once you have it."

"Yet you don't see many police around." There were a
few patrol cars, but mostly they seemed to stay parked and
empty, and foot patrols only came out in strength after
dark.

"Asszany, that is true, the swine. I like police where I
can see them, but these are too often out of sight, living
like pigs in clover. Perhaps in London or New York one
more car parked in a courtyard would not show, but here it
does, which makes life very difficult."

"It must," said Jenny sympathetically. "Perhaps it might
be easier if you dealt in other goods instead. Plum brandy
or—or books, for instance."

He leaned back in his chair and beamed at her. "Yes,

asszany. Exactly. In the afternoons I deal in anything."

Jenny failed to resist temptation. "And in the mornings?"

"I earn my salary, of course. Not a good salary, because the party does not pay as well as it ought, but enough to form my concrete base."

"Concrete base?"

"I call it so because concrete is a safe foundation for whatever you wish to lay on it. Hard, businesslike, respectable stuff, concrete. People take it for granted and look elsewhere for interest."

Jenny stared at Andras Benedek, staggered by his candor. Surely no secret policeman would set out to trap her so clumsily? Unless she was much mistaken, Benedek was a thief who boasted of how he applied himself to some petty post in the Communist party during his working hours.

He had gone as far as she could possibly expect to identify himself; now she must judge whether to accept what a complete stranger said or not.

"If you are a party member—"

"A party organizer," he interrupted, positively radiating enthusiasm.

God, she must be mad not to leave at once. "A party organizer," she repeated. "In such a position you must handle a great deal of—of Soviet literature."

"Oh, propaganda, yes indeed. I find it very strange no one has told Moscow that we can buy toilet paper in our supermarkets nowadays. We were grateful when the Soviet people understood our need before, but even then the Budapest sewers department complained. Comrades, they said, we have a difficulty. Habsburg drains cannot digest shiny Marxist pamphlets as they ought; we would prefer something rougher if it is at all possible."

Jenny laughed. "But Russian books aren't all Marxist. Pushkin, Tolstoy, Chekhov; anyone would be pleased to receive their work as a gift."

"Nothing comes from Russia as a gift." Benedek's good humor hardened abruptly, and he looked at her out of the corners of acquisitive blue eyes. "Everything is paid for, many times."

"In rubles perhaps. In pounds or dollars, it might be different."

He leaned back, sighing. "I thought you would never dare to say it. Books from the Soviet Union indeed cost less if paid for in pounds or dollars."

"Three hundred dollars, Pushkin said."

"Five."

Jenny shook her head, smiling. "I don't know whether they are worth even one. I never bought anything unseen before."

"But of course you must eat with us tonight. Have you ever eaten *fatanyeros*?"

Jenny shook her head again, feeling slightly dazed.

"A specialty from where my wife was born." He kissed his fingers and belched carefully. "You will like it very much. Where are you staying?"

"The Hotel Huszar."

Benedek frowned. "And I live in outer Pest. I will ask Ferenc Karolyi to bring you out with him. He is a policeman, and they are very well placed to jump the queue for Trabant cars."

"A policeman?"

"Ferenc is to marry my daughter, Judit. He is dull but obliging, and I think they will do well together. Half past six, then, at the Huzsar? Ferenc will be there."

Jenny went over this extraordinary meeting a dozen times in her mind, torn between delight in absurdity and derision at her own idiocy in being so easily gulled. Eventually she came to the conclusion that she had not said anything that could not, somehow, be explained away. After all, if Benedek admitted quite openly that he used the Communist party for his own purposes, it wasn't so extraordinary to find him boasting a policeman as a prospective son-in-law. Especially a stupid policeman.

All the same, she felt apprehensive waiting for him in the hotel lobby. Step by step she was being drawn into a looking-glass world that was very much less simple than it had seemed in New York. There, the main question had been whether the diaries were genuine, and she had been able to tell herself that the risk of taking them out of Hungary wasn't really very great. Hungarians who traveled abroad were carefully checked, foreign tourists more likely to have their luggage searched at Kennedy than at Ferihegy. Now the situation appeared quite different. She had made contact with the custodian of Pushkin's diaries, but instead of dealing with some dissident as she expected, she was about to be whirled away in a police car to eat *fatanyeros* with a Communist party official. His word alone could send her to drain marshes for the rest of her life. Yet in a crazy kind of way, it all made sense.

If Pushkin was the son of a high Soviet official, a diplomat perhaps, his contacts would be very limited. Soviet citizens working abroad could not risk being seen with dissidents, and Andras Benedek was the sort of man who would try to make money out of anything. He might easily perform small services for the KGB, when no doubt he told them that American propaganda stopped up the city's drains. Pushkin could meet him without making himself in the least conspicuous.

Of course, he'd taken one hell of a risk.

As she must, too, if she trusted Benedek.

When Ferenc Karolyi arrived to pick her up, she found him unremarkably neutral: buff hair and indoor face, unexpectedly wide shoulders straining his policeman's uniform; dour, buff-colored responses, little more than grunts all the way from the Huszar to Benedek's apartment in the industrial suburbs.

Jenny saw what Benedek meant about his concrete image of respectability the moment she climbed to the eighth floor of an anonymous block of workers' apartments. Screwed to his door was a neat sign indicating that the secretary of the area branch of the Hungarian Socialist Workers' Party lived within, the minute passage between his door and the communal stairs almost filled with stacked-up pamphlets.

"I have an extra room allocated because of my work, but it is more convenient to use it for the family," Benedek explained, flicking his fingers at the pamphlets. "So I keep the paperwork out here. Come in and enjoy our *fatanyeros.*"

Jenny did thoroughly enjoy the wooden platterful of peppered meat served with dark, dry wine and sharp cheese. She had felt uneasy when Janos and Geza fed her lavishly, because as a professor who bore an aristocratic name, Janos had to be careful what he did and only earned an academic salary, whereas most Hungarians paid for luxuries by working at several jobs at once. With Benedek she felt no such scruples: whichever way you looked at it, he took care to earn as much as he needed.

His wife had clearly eaten whatever she wanted for a long time, another sign of success; her plump passivity softened several awkward moments when Benedek could not resist teasing Ferenc and his daughter Judit. She was a robust girl who looked as if she spent her time doing all the virtuous things the party wanted her to do and now could hardly believe her luck in finding exactly the kind of man she desired. It was painful to watch her yearn over taciturn Ferenc, the touch of her hands on his broad shoulders each time she passed, the quick fumble when she thought no one was looking. Jenny found herself hoping that the extra room was free for them, immediately after supper ended.

She also wondered whether she would ever be able to eat again, as dish succeeded dish. But when supper ended at last, it was Benedek and she who retired, leaving Ferenc and Judit to hug each other wordlessly on a hard sofa.

"He has a very fine chest," confided Benedek to Jenny as he closed the door on them. "You would not think so, but Judit told me it was his chest which threw her into a frenzy. So I looked, and it is true that he has a great deal of hair and muscle. Unlike me." And he roared with laughter, ushering her before him into a small room filled with imported stereo and electrical equipment, staggeringly expensive and difficult to obtain in Hungary. "I like gadgets," he added unnecessarily.

"And I like manuscripts which will sell in the West," answered Jenny, made reckless by the contradictions of her evening.

Benedek hauled a large cardboard suitcase out from under the bed. "You will find them too heavy to carry."

He flipped back the lid, and Jenny saw twenty or thirty thick volumes inside. "Heavens, are they all diaries?"

He grinned. "I nearly died, carrying them up the stairs. Russians are all the same; they never believe in anything small. Not small countries like Hungary; not short books. We had to learn Russian in school, and every accursed book we read was as long as an encyclopedia. Tolstoy!" He spat with devastating accuracy into an empty glass, which rang like a bell.

Jenny dropped on her knees beside the case, no longer thinking of risk. She was in Benedek's hands now; it was too late to have regrets.

The books were bulky, many quite old. Inside, the writing was so oddly varied that Jenny immediately thought they must be fakes since more than one person had written them. Then she saw the similarities, the haste, exhaustion, and secrecy that had shaped each page differently. The first book she held must have become soaked in some way, the entries blurred, pages crinkled. The next was quite modern, the quality of paper good, an official code stamped on the cover as if it had been filched from some ministry stores. With gathering excitement, Jenny opened one of the older volumes at random, shut the suitcase, and sat on it to study her trophy.

At first it was enormously difficult to make sense out of what she saw. The paper was yellowed and so fuzzy, the writer's pen often sputtered ink. The Russian was very difficult, too: full of abbreviations, lines tumbling into each other as if they had been written in the shadows. There were sketches, too, often no more than half a dozen curling lines, but surely recognizable to anyone who knew the subjects. Sulky jowls dripped resentment, malicious cheekbones sprouted around the number of a page; inside the cover a merry philosopher gesticulated behind some kind of scientific apparatus. Sad, crouched backs in a meeting; a double page free of writing where two peasant women walked silently across an empty landscape, one cradling a dead child: the only true drawing among a host of impressions. Jenny stared at it, a dryness in her throat. The man who drew that was no bloodless functionary of the state; these sketches were a find in themselves.

She flicked through the pages in mounting frustration. She spoke moderately fluent Russian and had thought she would be able to read enough to form a snap judgment of how much risk Pushkin's diary was worth, but these packed volumes needed experts with a great deal of unhurried time to interpret and annotate them. She picked up another book. It was newer, cleaner, but crookedly written, in pencil and spilling words like a torrent across the page, as if the writer felt too unsafe for the luxury of pen and ink, yet needed the purge of words as a drunkard might crave the bottle.

10 July 1952 . . . The old filthy nightmare has come again. Only seven years after all the sufferings of our people in the war and the *khozyain* again demands blood to make him feel safe. . . . I saw him yesterday. He watched me out of eyes like cesspits while P left me to explain our poor performance. When I came out I was sick on the doormat, yes sick with fear and the guard's boots were splashed. What ignominy . . .

The *khozyain*, the boss, Stalin. Jenny flicked more pages, engrossed. The writer was high up in the party now and terrified for his life. Initials, abbreviations; a splendidly abusive description of P being caught with a cryptographer, making love entirely naked except for his boots.

"Coffee?" asked Benedek.

"Thanks." Jenny swallowed automatically, her mind in the Russia of thirty years before. Then she spluttered, still unused to the fierce Hungarian brew.

Benedek glanced at the book on her knees. "I couldn't read them. I get along in Russian when it suits me, but the bastard who wrote all that must have been demented."

"No," said Jenny slowly. "I don't think so. He would have been if he hadn't written. Writing kept him sane, and he must have known it, otherwise he would never have risked his life keeping these year after year." Terror fairly leapt from some of the pages. She got off the suitcase and rummaged until she found what looked like the most recent volume. 1987. Well, fairly recent anyway. Probably he was still writing the next one; days or even weeks often went by without an entry, then something would happen and words were vomited on the page.

8 Dec At last a sensible decision but what an effort to reach it! . . . like Stalin, Ls has murder where his mind ought to be. Two days ago G never noticed his driver had changed and his car was deliberately driven into a tree near the dacha. . . . G lucky only to be shaken and cut. All our arms proposals have to be changed at the last moment because he cannot appear in public. [Gorbachev? thought Jenny, startled.] 19 Dec General Gh orders twenty million concrete tetrapods to be manufactured because he thinks they might come in useful but quite where or how he cannot tell us. Twenty million! So our targets are lost again, and for a wilderness of junk! What a price civilians pay for keeping generals one step back from power.

A sketch she recognized there: this time unmistakably Gorbachev at his cabinet table, caricatured nose-to-nose against KGB and military, a knife sticking out from between his shoulder blades. Dimly Jenny remembered exasperation when the Russians had changed their negotiating stance on missiles without warning at Geneva, when Gorbachev had been due to sign an agreement. "No, he's not demented," she repeated, snapping the book shut. "What a terrible life his generation of Russians has led."

Benedek shrugged, as if to say: Hungarians, too. She had not thought of it before, but Benedek must have been a boy when the German army was rolled back though Hungary in 1944, a youth when Soviet tanks stormed Budapest in 1956. "Do you agree to give me five hundred dollars for keeping them safe?"

Jenny stared at the case. It was half the size of a trunk and filled with heavy books. Alone, she wouldn't be able even to lift it. "I never dreamed there would be so much. How can I take a small library through the customs at Feri-hegy?"

"Five hundred dollars," repeated Benedek. Airport customs was not his business.

Pushkin had implied that three hundred would be owing to the custodian of the diaries in Budapest, but Benedek would always try to make extra profit. At this moment two hundred additional dollars seemed unimportant compared to her need for Benedek's goodwill. Subconsciously Jenny had already discarded any idea of forgery, although the possibility of a trap remained: she was not a scholar trained to skepticism but a romantic, though not in any way Sandy would have applauded. The man who had written these diaries was already real to her: she would have expected to recognize him in the street. It was her imagination insisting that these confidences were not fake, and judgment had very little to do with it.

"All right, five hundred dollars," she said clearly.

Benedek beamed and rubbed his hands, the idea of mere books being worth five hundred dollars a pleasant surprise to him. "I expect you would like to take the case as well. I'll get Ferenc to carry it down for you."

"Couldn't you keep them a few days longer?"

"When are you leaving?"

"My flight is booked for next Tuesday. I could try to alter it, but—" The sheer quantity of scribbled volumes was fearful; she hadn't the slightest idea how she might take them out of Hungary undetected.

"Don't alter anything," said Benedek briskly. "You never want anyone to give you a thought, not even an airline clerk. Take my word for it, that's the way to survive."

He ought to know, thought Jenny. "I have some manuscripts to read," she said slowly. "From Morvin, your State Publishing people. I was going to handle one, at the most two, and send the rest back. I'm wondering whether I could pretend to take more, and pack these in their place."

Benedek clicked his tongue disapprovingly. "You're making people look at you again. Give officials a crate of books to clear and they'll read every word. They're not educated, the pigs, so the first thing they'll do is bawl for someone who can read Russian. Then you'll be in trouble."

She would indeed. "So will you keep these a few days longer while I think?"

"No, *asszany*. I have done what I agreed to do. Tomorrow everyone in this block will want to hear about my American guest who came to find out how Hungarian workers live. Of course, as a party organizer, it is only natural I should show you, but not natural at all if you were to come again. For you, perhaps, since everyone knows Westerners are curious. For me, no. A good party man does his duty without allowing himself to be seduced by a pretty face into doing more." He pursed his lips, shaggy head tilted. "I've earned my five hundred dollars. To do more is a different deal, and I do not think any bargain would be worth it. I want to live safely on my concrete."

The warning was clear. Benedek gave notice that after tonight he would not stay bribed, unless it suited him. Which was honesty of a kind, Jenny supposed.

So Ferenc sulkily heaved the suitcase downstairs while Judit quarreled with her father in the background, much put out by having her evening cut short. As Benedek said, it wasn't easy to do anything unobtrusively in a Budapest apartment, and a great many people clattered past during Jenny's departure, followed eventually by Judit, commiserating with Ferenc amid a flurry of explanations.

Jenny stared down the bare stairwell, alone again with Benedek for an instant. "Whatever will Ferenc think about me taking a large case full of books back to the Huszar?"

"It's none of his business, and Ferenc doesn't often think."

"He's a policeman, for heaven's sake! Of course he must wonder—what if he should make a good story out of it for his buddies?" Jenny didn't like Ferenc much.

"He isn't a policeman tonight, but my daughter's lover. They will marry as soon as they are allocated an apartment," answered Benedek, as if that settled everything.

"How can you be so sure? Some policemen never consider themselves off duty."

"Do not worry, *asszony*. Everyone has to trust in something, and in Hungary you trust your family."

Perhaps that is what I came here to find, Jenny reflected on the journey back into the center of Budapest. In a shifting world everyone indeed needed someone to trust, and she envied Benedek's confidence in the strength of family ties, when this was something she had never known. But she hadn't been at ease with Janos and Geza, either, all tumbled together with a widowed daughter and her child in the courtyard off Orszaghaz Street, would have hated to inhabit Benedek's concrete box. If that kind of closeness was all her Hungarian inheritance offered, then the sooner she went home the better. Home. She stared out through the windshield at an alien land that suddenly seemed immeasurably strange and menacing. How delighted she would be to find herself taking Pushkin's diaries through the streets of New York City, rather than those of Budapest.

Ferenc drove fast, this capital populated by two million people almost deserted by eleven o'clock at night. Occasionally a greatcoated policeman turned to stare at them, but there must have been something special about the car's license plates, because several raised an arm in greeting. At night there were quite a lot of police about; they had long batons hooked to their belts and guns slung over one shoulder.

"Are you often on night duty?" Jenny asked, not because she wanted to know, but in the hope it might be safer if she could reach some limited understanding with Ferenc.

"Sometimes."

"Do you mind?"

"Sometimes."

Jenny sighed but tried again. "Last night when I crossed the Danube, I thought how beautiful the city looked in moonlight."

"I enjoy night duty if we find some drunks. A fight passes the time."

They finished the rest of the journey in silence, Ferenc simply heaving her case into the Huszar's hall before driving off with a perfunctory nod. Jenny had a disagreeable feeling that he was not the kind of man who worried about any woman long enough to let her tie down his loyalties where it didn't suit him. So, poor Judit. But if poor Judit, then what about the other, compromising things about the Benedeks that Ferenc also knew?

The hotel porter was more obliging but exclaimed at the case's weight when he picked it up for her.

"Did a large parcel arrive for me from Morvin?" Jenny asked, to divert his attention. "I am in Hungary to read your authors' works, so I can sell them to the West."

Which, as she anticipated, satisfied him at once, Hungarians being firmly convinced of their place in Western civilization and anxious to claim it, no matter what their politics.

When the porter finally went, after lingering for an age to talk about a poem he had read in the paper recently, Jenny sat on the edge of her bed and stared at the suitcase. Common sense told her that if she went out and bought another half dozen grips and cheap clothes to go in them, put some of Pushkin's diaries in each, hired a taxi to the railway station, and asked a porter to put her bags on the rack, she would be unlikely to be caught. Frontier officials would not be looking for books, but for drugs or illegal export of Hungary's antiques. Yet common sense also urged that any baggage would be opened, most especially large quantities of baggage, and a single glance inside those diaries would tell that they were written in Russian, a compulsory language in Hungarian schools. Once he saw them, any official would investigate further. Then the police wouldn't let her go for years and years and years.

So no matter how strong her desire to bolt at once, before it was too late, that particular risk was too great to take without very careful investigation of alternatives.

But after a restless night, Jenny was no nearer to a solution. She felt jaded and had come to hate hard beds covered with single rugs—too small to sleep under like a duvet, and too thick for comfort when the central heating was scorching hot. Hungarian beds are another part of my heritage I shall be glad to leave behind, she thought viciously.

The telephone rang while she was in the bath, and she padded across wrapped in a towel to answer it, expecting Janos. No one else except Benedek knew she was at the Huszar, and he wouldn't ring. Making people look at him, he would call it, and besides, they had nothing else to arrange. Only she had everything still to fix, like getting twenty-five damned thick volumes out of Hungary without being caught.

"*Ki-ez*?" she said crossly into the receiver.

"You don't sound in a very agreeable mood," said Martin Rothbury. "Perhaps I won't ask you to have dinner with me tonight after all."

4

J ENNY VERY NEARLY PUT THE RECEIVER DOWN STRAIGHT-
away.

She was finished with Martin and still bore him a certain grudge. Then, insidiously, the thought came into her
mind that he could very easily take the diaries out. She did
not know much about diplomatic bags, but had already
read in the Hungarian newspapers that Martin was indeed
in Budapest as head of the British delegation to the financial conference. Customs was unlikely to search his luggage. They would also expect bureaucrats to take crates of
paper everywhere they went.

She needed to think about that, so at the last moment
changed refusal into reluctant acceptance: no matter how
hard she tried, she couldn't infuse enthusiasm into her
voice.

To assert her independence and honor a promise, after
Martin had rung off, she telephoned Sandy at the Korona.

"Jenny!" His voice stampeded down the line as usual.
"Where are you? Janos wouldn't tell me when I rang."

"Why on earth not? I'm at the Huszar in Szolnok Street."

"Come over at once, love. Or better still, I'll fetch you and we'll go to Lake Balaton for the day."

"Oh Sandy, I'm sorry, but I can't."

"Why not? At this time of year we'll have it to ourselves."

"I'm working, Sandy. I can't go racketing off to Balaton at a moment's notice just because you think it would be fun."

"There's no better reason for going that I know of. In New York you told me you'd decided to come here to look at your Keszthely past, not work, as I recall."

Jenny stared at the suitcase she didn't dare to leave for long, the room as somber as her mood. Already she felt like a prisoner awaiting trial. "I'd like to come, but I can't today."

"Tonight, then."

"I've already accepted something else." She hoped to God he wouldn't ask what.

"Tomorrow?" He was beginning to sound angry.

"I'd love to..." If only I didn't have to spend every moment planning how to take a truckful of diaries out, she wanted to say, but changed her mind. Why shouldn't she take an evening away from worry? "I've something on in the day, but tomorrow night would be lovely."

"It's our celebration party tomorrow night."

"Then I'll come to that," she said irritably. A celebration party was the last thing she felt like now.

"You sure make it sound a chore," Sandy said sarcastically. "The Hungarians are putting on a special performance at the opera for the delegates to the conference, so both Schiller and Gyula Sebestyen have to go there first. Some of us thought we'd buy tickets, too, since it'll be as fashionable an occasion as you'd find in Budapest nowadays and give the ladies a chance to wear their jewels. One in the eye for the commies, as Zoltan would say. His wife is sneezing diamonds, just so no one misses the point. You didn't bring your pearls, did you?"

Jenny hesitated. "Yes, I did."

"I warned you not to."

"Well, I did."

"Leave them in the safe, then, but come with us to the opera. We've ordered a private room here for our supper afterward. Zoltan wanted to have it in the best restaurant we could find, complete with Gypsy orchestra, but—"

"I'm glad there was a but," said Jenny, laughing. Already Sandy had made her feel more cheerful. "All those diamonds are bad enough, but I can just imagine the kind of toasts he'll propose. At the top of his voice, of course."

The phone almost leapt out of her hand. "Christ, Jenny! You should have heard him last night at Pipac's, though Pierre Sorbaz was almost worse. He speaks better Hungarian than Zoltan, and that goddamn drawl of his carries like he was spraying acid. We were practically thrown out in the end. I haven't laughed so much for years."

"I wish I'd been there. I really mean it, Sandy. But I think perhaps I won't come to the opera."

"More work," he said tightly.

Not work, but Martin, she wanted to say. A special performance for the conference delegates meant that he would certainly be there, and she could do without another encounter between him and Sandy, when each had detested the other on sight in the past. Martin would be polite in public, but she couldn't guess how Sandy might react, especially now Budapest had gone spectacularly to his head, along with a good deal of plum brandy.

"Well?" repeated Sandy. "I should like to take you to the opera in Budapest, Jenny."

"And I'd like to go, but not tomorrow. I'll come in time for your party at the Korona."

"No Balaton today, no opera tomorrow. Is anything the matter?"

"Of course not."

"But you don't intend to allow yourself a single glimmer of pleasure in case Marshall's Literary Agency collapses from the shock? It's a wonder you've got any friends at all if you can't squeeze a single evening away from your infernal books."

Jenny stared at Benedek's case. She must sound drearily one-track but was damned if she would change her mind just because Sandy felt annoyed the moment she failed to fit in with his plans. Instead she threw the receiver back in its cradle and didn't answer when it rang again. She wasn't sure whether she felt angrier with herself or him; ridiculous to feel so overwrought because a case full of someone else's diaries stood on her carpet.

Pointless to watch it all day, though. Hotel maids weren't interested in books, and no one had any reason to search her room. Sandy would quite likely come rushing round to the Huszar, too, and Jenny didn't think she could face him at the moment.

So she went out to wander through the city, finishing quite late at the National Gallery inside the castle, and by then she felt rested, almost philosophic. If Martin and his diplomatic bag either couldn't or wouldn't help, then tomorrow she would just have to think of some other way to get those diaries out, even if it meant taking them across the frontier in a wheelbarrow.

The gallery rooms were spacious but not exactly restful. Jenny stared at the ranks of pictures, wondering and oddly stirred; faintly embarrassed, too. She liked the landscapes with their soft coloring and sense of Eastern space: she had never traveled far into the Hungarian countryside, yet in a strange way she did seem to recognize what she saw. But most of the other pictures dramatized Hungarian struggles against superior odds, so much emotion bursting from the canvas that, to her, they were as much propaganda as Benedek's Marxist pamphlets. Yet the Hungarians around her did not think so, as they proudly pointed out past heroes to their children.

I have found nothing here, she thought and, unexpectedly, yearned again for New York. It wasn't only Pushkin's diaries that had seemed simpler there.

Perhaps because of this feeling, she greeted Martin rather more warmly than she intended when he came to call for her at the Huszar. At least he was a product of a world she understood, and no nonsense about it.

Martin Rothbury belonged to a family more noted for its long nose than for intelligence, most of his ancestors having lived comfortably in northern England without much need for cleverness. Then his father made the mistake of marrying a brilliant and restless woman, and a greater one in trying to satisfy her whims. She left him in the end, and he returned, disheartened, to discover that the woodworking business that had kept the family in comfort for so long was foundering. He never made any serious effort to rescue it, leaving his only son, Martin, to poke around among discarded timber during solitary school holidays. Within ten years of this near bankruptcy, the company was thriving and Martin had become extremely rich; he possessed all his mother's drive and brains but a great deal more skill in managing his affairs. He was also, like her, very easily bored. Not restless in the same way, but quite simply bored when, by the age of twenty-seven, he had converted the Rothbury Woodworking Company into Rothbury System Buildings Ltd, with a full order book and a research department headed by one of the brightest minds in the building trade. Martin had head-hunted him, paid him handsomely, and saw no point in doing his work. So he went into politics. Rothbury System Buildings continued to expand and went public five years later, which was just as well, because by then Martin had become parliamentary secretary to one of Britain's treasury ministers.

At this point he met Jenny Marshall, who was working in London at the time. Martin valued intelligence and elegance, but found her disturbingly attractive, too, which was only the first of many contrasts that delighted him. The soft sensuality of her lips and the cool tact with which she handled the most unlikely contretemps; her sense of the absurd when set beside the seriousness of her regard for good writing; the reckless tilt of her cheekbones and the long time that passed before she allowed him to make love to her. Jenny was entirely modern but also confident enough to think relationships mattered, which meant she refused to fake emotion. Until Martin became important to her, friendship was all she would offer or accept.

Martin had worked hard since before he left school, and as he became rich, he enjoyed his money with the same single-minded determination. He had never before been quite simply happy, as he was during the time when everything went well between him and Jenny. But it hadn't lasted. Perhaps both of them were too exacting, too inexperienced in the tolerances of normal family life; whatever the reasons, his unfortunate remark about Jenny's Hungarian blood had only marked the end of a process of erosion.

A year had followed during which she had returned to the United States and then set up her own agency. At first they still met occasionally, and if Martin discovered more reasons to visit Washington than were strictly necessary, then Jenny never guessed it. During that year Martin had also jumped from the unpaid job of parliamentary secretary to one of the coveted junior ministerial posts at the treasury. He had expected to forget Jenny and was indignant when he failed. He was infuriated when, after a severe tussle with himself, he finally decided that the only way to resolve his difficulty was to marry her, and she instantly refused.

That had been six months before, and after the angry quarrel that followed, neither expected ever to see the other again. The only sane course was to forget the whole tangle —they were both busy enough, God knows.

Yet when Martin saw her waiting for him in a Hungarian hotel lobby, obviously pleased to see him, his rage against her vanished.

"Why did you ask me to dinner?" she asked as soon as they were seated in a restaurant. Typical Jenny to go straight to the point.

"Why did you come?"

She reflected. "Because I thought I might want to ask you to do something for me. I'm sorry if that sounds dreadful, but I didn't want you to think—I mean, after what happened last time we met, I never expected . . ." Her voice trailed away. With her mind taken up by diaries, she had not anticipated quite how awkward this meeting was likely to be.

"It's nice you want to spare my feelings," he replied dryly. "I also seem to remember that you are annoyed by people who fail to use the English language to express exactly what they mean."

She flushed and then laughed. "All right. Last time we met, you asked me to marry you and I said no, in italics, I guess. I didn't expect to have dinner with you six months later as if nothing had happened."

"Nor did I." He tasted the wine and nodded to the waiter. "I don't like being beaten, I suppose."

"It wasn't a case of being beaten. As you ought to have realized by now, you had a lucky escape. I should make Her Majesty's fiscal secretary to the treasury a rotten wife."

"I expect you would."

"You don't have to agree quite so easily." She felt unreasonably ruffled, then smiled reluctantly at the illogicality of her own reaction.

"I was agreeing to rather a different proposition to the one I actually have in mind. But don't let's spoil what I hope will be an excellent meal by going over old quarrels. You said you wanted me to do something for you."

"I said I thought I might." Jenny studied him in dim lamplight. Apart from the Rothbury nose and bright green eyes, his appearance was unremarkable, his manner definitely different from before. More how he might be with a civil servant in his department: direct, businesslike, and about as loving as a rolled umbrella. He also looked very tired. "How is the conference?"

"It's full of ill-natured wrangling and goes on forever.

Which doesn't alter the fact that unless we get some kind of agreement, the world will be an even poorer place. Literally."

Jenny frowned. "I thought it was about Hungarian debts."

"And by implication, those of the other East European satellites. Poland and Romania owe more than Hungary and possess much weaker economies. Yugoslavia has one hundred and twenty percent inflation. A few years ago banks fell over themselves to lend to the East, believing that if anything went wrong, then the Soviets would never allow their allies to go bust. Easy profits out of communism; what could be better? Or so the bankers thought."

"It seems to me that every country in the world owes money, but it makes surprisingly little difference to what happens," observed Jenny.

"Perhaps. But just think of this: If Russia now refuses to contribute to a rescue package, then the Western banks have to decide whether to lend so much more that some may risk their own stability, or to refuse to lend any more at all. Which very likely means they lose their existing loans, and confidence in the system would be ripped apart. Countries like Hungary would be forced back into absolute dependence on the Soviet Union. A slave economy again, with the prison gates padlocked shut."

We in Hungary do not want to annoy the men who could send us back into jail for debt, Janos Keszthely had said, and to be honest, Jenny had thought little more about it.

"Surely the Soviets couldn't allow its Communist allies simply to fall apart?"

"Why not?"

She groped among the ill-assorted pieces of her financial ignorance. "Pride, I suppose. Security, certainly. The Russians are nothing if not worried about their own defense. All the systems they've built up over forty years would be lost if their satellites collapsed."

"Not necessarily. The opposite, in fact. Hungary, for instance, would be far more securely tied to the Soviet

Union if its trade with the West was torn up by the roots, and Gorbachev has plenty of enemies in the Soviet system who would like to prove that reforming a Marxist economy will not work. But you may be right; I hope to God you are. It's the accepted view, and a good deal more comfortable than the alternative. The Soviets may simply be hanging out for the best bargain they can get; bankers are bankers everywhere and don't like uproar. The military are different, and there are too many political generals running loose around Moscow and Washington. I have the feeling that they at least wouldn't be too displeased if things went seriously wrong at this conference. The kind of economic collapse we're talking about could overthrow governments and put freedom fighters on the streets. Could we then refuse to help? Would the Russians stand by while their missile sites were overrun by rioters carrying flags? I don't think we want to find out, but then, I've never liked soldiers in high places."

Jenny was silent, thinking about her diarist's hatred of the military pulling political strings, his sketch of Gorbachev facing down a general. Common ground was found in the strangest places. "You don't make much distinction between Soviet and American generals," she said at last.

"I expect American ones understand money rather better, and I haven't any doubt about which side I should die on if I had to, if that's what you mean. But all generals are paid to defend a point of view, not haggle about it. The rest of us blunder about, wondering just what the hell we are meant to be doing most of the time, so I suppose their simpler view must occasionally look tempting."

A waiter came to change the plates, and Martin filled the time while he was close by remarking idly on the filigree of her necklace. It wasn't quite such an innocuous subject as he imagined, and Jenny waited until the fuss of serving braised boar meat was over before she explained about the Keszthely pearls. "I never liked to ask Janos what happened to the other family jewels," she added, "but my mother loved this necklet more for its workmanship than the value, so when she decided to escape from Hungary in 1956, her mother gave it to her. She wore it on her escape through the marshes and never undressed completely all the months she was in the refugee camp, for fear someone would see and steal it. She gave it to me on my twenty-first birthday."

"So now you're wearing it again in Budapest."

Jenny's dark eyes lit with half-derisive amusement. "Do you think that so ridiculous? We all need to come home sometimes."

"Yes," he answered after a pause. "We do indeed. It becomes you very well; I never realized it before, but you have a Renaissance face."

"Not the Borgia kind, I hope," said Jenny lightly. She knew now that she had been a fool to come out with him, after six months had dulled a little of the hurt between them. And yet, he'd needed her company badly tonight, must have asked her because he had to have a few hours of peace away from conference pressures and intrigues, where the pettiest wrangle held potentially disastrous consequences. Martin might be leading the British delegation because governments hadn't wanted to rouse fears of banking failures by sending their most senior ministers to bargain over Hungarian debts, but, from what he had said, he realized far more than most people what was at stake here. And at thirty-six he was young for such responsibility. "I'm glad you didn't try to warn me that the Hungarian police might try to seize a Keszthely necklace," she added to cover an awkward moment.

His eyes narrowed. "Who said that?"

Jenny experienced an unusual sensation of being outwitted. "It was just a general feeling that the Keszthely pearls were best left in New York."

"Oh?" He looked politely skeptical. "You say they belonged to your grandmother, and she gave them to your mother, quite legally, before they could be confiscated. The Hungarian government hasn't a shred of title to them that I can see."

"And I am American born after all, even if it is the Hungarian in me you dislike. I guess I'm favored a British minister feels he might just risk dining out with a foreign half-breed, so long as it's only in a place like Budapest." There it was again, the old resentment from the past, the impulse to hit back for the pleasure of seeing him flinch as she had done.

"Jenny, what I said was a fact, and nothing more. Or less. No member of a British government, nor the American, I daresay, can afford to figure in the gossip columns with a woman, half of whose relations live behind the Iron Curtain."

"So you were considering the problem quite impersonally," said Jenny silkily.

"No. Very personally, I'm afraid, although I ought to have explained myself better. I wasn't ready to, I suppose. You see, I prefer to make up my own mind about who I'd like to marry, which means before and not after the mine field of publicity is sprung. You may have noticed there have been some ugly messes lately when the private affairs of ministers on both sides of the Atlantic have been allowed to get out of hand. I didn't want it to be like that with us."

She thought how strange it was to have love discussed in such a coldly academic way. The Martin she remembered from when they lived together had not been in the least impersonal about love. "You talk about facts," she said tightly. "There's nothing to be done about where my mother was born."

"Is that a reason why you came here? To see if you want to live at least part of your life in Hungary?"

"Of course not." She was astonished he could think she might, completely forgetting that she had planned this trip because she hoped to discover in Budapest something she believed her life had lacked.

He laughed, the tight lines of his face easing for the first time that evening. "Thank God for that, because I shouldn't like to, either. The beds are too hard, the flats too small, and the fences too high. Which leaves my job as the remaining fact. I went into politics because I wanted to, and I can come out again for exactly the same reason. If I could marry you—if you wished to marry me—then I should be happy to come out. I wanted you to know."

"You would resign from your government?" said Jenny dazedly. No wonder he had expressed his meaning hurtfully, if this was the choice he believed himself forced to make.

"Under those circumstances, yes."

"Martin . . ." She looked around the restaurant, at checked tablecloths and busily screeching Gypsy orchestra. "Oh, damn!"

"Don't worry, I shan't behave like this again. The conference looks as if it will be adjourned for the weekend to let some judicious scuttling among the bankers take place; if you felt like driving out somewhere with me, I promise to be as impersonal as you like. It was just that I'd come to realize I didn't want to leave things how they were, all loose ends and resentment."

Jenny could never remember afterward how she answered, and he immediately changed the subject with a completeness that left her floundering. By the time she came up for air, he was talking about baroque architecture, about which, she decided afterward, his ignorance was quite as profound as hers.

It wasn't until they parted outside the Huszar that he added, out of nowhere, "You still haven't said what you wanted me to do for you. No, I remember. Might want me to do for you."

"I've changed my mind," Jenny said uncomfortably. "You have quite enough to worry about at the moment."

"I've brought a good many highly paid assistants to help me do it, most of whom are wasting their time. I expect, between us, we can offer whatever assistance you need."

She was very tempted. But if those diaries were as detailed as she thought, then they would provide invaluable background briefing material for British intelligence. Once she told Martin what she had found, then as a respectable delegation head, he wouldn't touch them himself, but within the hour capable young men would call at the Huszar to take them from her. And that would be that. Goodbye to dreams of fame for Marshall's Literary Agency, to Simon Druce and Pushkin's father, the quality of whose writing she also expected to admire. When she accepted Martin's invitation to dine, she had been looking for easy ways; after tonight she knew there weren't any easy ways left for her to find with him. If he was prepared to give up a more than promising career in politics to marry her, because he knew that with her as his wife he could never reach high office, then while he remained a minister his first loyalty would be to the government he served. Nor would she wish it otherwise.

Yet the British government was labyrinthine and secretive; if Martin's young men took Pushkin's diaries out of Hungary, probably she would never see them again.

She held out her hand. "Thank you for an evening I shan't forget, whatever happens to us in the future. I always did think there was a great deal to be said for tying up loose ends, and now I'm sure. I don't want to risk unraveling any more by involving you in something you're better kept away from. Incidentally, am I right in supposing it was Simon Druce who told you I was coming to Budapest?"

Martin grinned. "He actually had the grace to write and thank me for introducing him to such a bloody exacting editor she nearly drove him crazy, and I rang him back. Did the imbecile tell you I discovered him roaming around the members' lavatory in the House, and all he said was, Are the seats the original mahogany?"

Jenny burst out laughing. "Not exactly, no. Although I remember wishing I could have been around, watching you two meet. You must have realized he wasn't just some screwball, though, or you wouldn't have shown him the Commons library and then recommended that he get in touch with me. I guess I haven't said how grateful I am;

he's a tremendous writer." She frowned and added, "But the Huszar? I hope you didn't order your tame British spies to discover where I was staying?" That's all I need to make the Hungarians interested in anything I do, she thought anxiously.

"Your uncle, Janos Keszthely, told me. I remembered the name, and he's the only one in the Budapest telephone directory."

"That's strange. He wouldn't tell Sandy."

"Perhaps he doesn't like Sandor Havasi," observed Martin acidly. "Jenny, I can't make you tell me what you're up to, but if it has anything to do with Havasi, for God's sake, drop it."

"It hasn't."

He looked at her, brows drawn tight above his nose. Well-cut suit, well-brushed brownish hair, well-shaved expression: the framework that was Martin Rothbury looked ministerial enough, his beaked nose and unpredictable green eyes less easily categorized. "I have a distinct feeling that you are about to behave like a damned fool."

"Not with Sandy."

"You've better taste than that," he agreed. "What, then?"

"I'm not going to tell you. When we are both back in London perhaps."

They were standing just outside the Huszar, and he glanced at the thinning evening traffic, the everyday people hurrying past. "Don't be fooled, Jenny. This may seem a free country compared to most in the East, a place where the police prefer to watch and warn, providing that's enough. But once out of the safe ground, you would find there are still a great many dark places left."

"Yes," said Jenny. "I know."

5

After Martin had gone, Jenny felt annoyed she hadn't somehow managed to mention the party planned for the following night. It was true that Sandy had nothing to do with her deal with Pushkin, but if Martin subsequently heard her name connected with an émigré escapade in Budapest, and he quite easily might when Sandy and his friends apparently saw themselves providing an anticommunist giggle for the Western press, then he would conclude that she had lied to him.

Well, by then she would have taken the diaries out of Hungary and be able to explain.

She slept instantly that night, after nearly forty sleepless hours interspersed by strain, but woke early. Trams clattered past all night in Budapest; she could hear the clash of steel while the sky turned pale dawn gray. Today she must decide what to do; it was also the day of Sandy's party, and she regretted now that she had agreed to go. Without realizing it, she had begun to see the party through Martin's eyes. He would think it juvenile, a silly irrelevance at a

67

time when goodwill between East and West was important. Still, she had promised Sandy, and at least he'd changed the place to a private room. She was only glad she had refused to accompany him to the opera first.

All the same, she wished she had told Martin.

Martin. She would be crazy even to consider changing her mind and marrying a man made resentful by a wrecked career. He might not think so now, but surely he would never be able quite to forgive her. Subconsciously Jenny had always listened carefully if Washington gossip happened to touch on British politics, and she knew that Martin Rothbury was considered a coming man, only seven years in parliament and already in line for one of their top ministerial jobs. But of course, he was right. She must have been willfully blind before, but now he spelled it out for her, his choice was painfully clear; for the foreseeable future, no minister whose wife possessed a gaggle of foreign Communist relatives was likely to be able to sit in a British cabinet. Nor was Martin the kind of man who would be content to occupy lesser posts while others were promoted in his place.

Anyway, what about Sandy? Only the week before she had felt close to certainty with him.

Jenny turned over, and the suitcase full of diaries stared back at her accusingly from the shadows: Martin had faced his choice, and so must she. Make up her mind once and for all, then stick to her decision. She would never have lived with him for most of a year unless she'd more than liked him, nor been so distressed when they broke up. But marriage was something she wouldn't consider unless she believed they could make it work. And this wouldn't work, even if she loved him. Even if he loved her. How much of his determination had been sparked by the anger of a man who so far had been successful in everything he tried?

The diaries. First she had to decide something about the diaries.

Jenny padded across and took one out of the case, curled back under skimpy bedcovering to read, but this time she had chosen badly. The volume dated from three years previously, when the author was in some position to do with finance. Pages and pages of annotated ruble signs, thought Jenny disconsolately. There were still some wickedly amusing sketches, though. Huddles of miser-faced inquisitors sitting on tumbling files, a leering official pocketing bribes; each one drawn with the vitriol of rage, pen strokes dug deep into the paper.

Suddenly Jenny thought back to the previous evening, her heart thudding with excitement. What was it Martin had said about the Soviet delegation? After that first disturbing exchange they had talked mostly of trifles, as if afraid of further feeling, but toward the end of the evening she had said something about character in fiction, and he had answered . . . She racked her brain, trying to remember every word. He had said that trying to speculate about the private people behind official masks was occasionally the only way of enduring time, when hours could pass in arguing over a single point. And then had gone on to describe the constipated faces on the Russian side, which only sometimes offered the illusion you might understand them. One of those faces was Pushkin's diarist; she was sure of it. The other books she had opened covered a multitude of topics, but this one made it clear that by 1986 the author was high up in some financial ministry. Of course, Soviet officials were promoted at an age when most Westerners were retired, but Pushkin's father must be considered old by newer Gorbachev standards, that promotion likely to be his last. And Pushkin had said his father would defect through Budapest: if she had thought to question Martin, probably he could have identified the man she wanted.

The newspaper wasn't enlightening when she bought one after breakfast, but by careful reading, Jenny narrowed her choice to three names: Comrades Berdeyev, Adhuzov and Lyazin seemed the leading members of the Russian financial delegation. It didn't really matter; this diary would kill its author, whoever he was, if it was published before he came out to the West, and when he did, she'd meet him face-to-face.

The day lagged past so slowly that soon Jenny was longing for the evening. At least Sandy's party was something happening; a relief that it should be lighthearted nonsense when everything else she thought of seemed so menacingly dangerous. After long and careful consideration, she had come up with no better idea for taking the diaries out of Hungary than to hire an automobile for a few days to explore the countryside: when she asked the State Travel Bureau about crossing a frontier if she felt like it, they had been reassuring. Without a visa she could not visit Czechoslovakia, Rumania, or the Soviet Union, but of course, she didn't want to. The important thing was that they foresaw no difficulty if she decided to spend a day in Austria.

"You would have to leave your passport with the frontier guard, and they will give you a day pass which the Austrians accept. Hungarians quite often cross for a day, to look at the shops, you understand. But you cannot stay across the border while you are driving a car hired in Hungary." The girl clerk had shrugged and laughed. "A commercial precaution, *asszany*. We don't want to lose our car, that's all."

So this must be her best chance. If Hungarians often crossed for the day, probably the border police would be more interested in them than in her. All she had to do was hope they wouldn't worry about a single suitcase, and once she was out, leave it in the nearest Austrian baggage deposit before driving back into Hungary to pick up her passport. Simple, really.

She chose the cheapest car on hire, a Russian Lada, money already a worry after paying Benedek two hundred dollars more than she expected. Tomorrow she would drive west, sleep the night near the border, and cross over the following morning, which would be Saturday. It would seem more natural to cross in the morning, she decided, and more likely there would be plenty of Hungarian trippers on a Saturday to keep customs and police well occupied.

The hotel had a locked garage, so Jenny decided to

spend the afternoon bringing the diaries down a few at a time. Though she preferred to have them under her eye, they ought to be safe in the Lada's hatchback, Hungary being a country (as Benedek had mournfully remarked) where car theft was not good business. Far better to smuggle the books downstairs a few at a time than risk remark when her cases were carried down in the morning. Most police forces relied on information from hotel porters.

It was unexpectedly nerve-racking to make half a dozen journeys downstairs with books clutched under her coat, some of them leaking loose pages. Fortunately, not many fellow guests were around in the afternoon, but several times Jenny had to wait, feeling remarkably foolish, until the porter left his hut at the entry. She wondered whether spies ever felt as she did, more afraid of looking demented than of being found out. Even so, she felt triumphant once all the diaries were locked into the Lada. When she returned upstairs, it was as if an accusing eye had been exorcised from her bedroom, and for the first time she was able to concentrate on reading some of the Morvin manuscripts.

She read for several hours, steadying her mind by cramming it at a familiar task. Nothing would lead more surely to a search at the frontier than any impression of unease. Eight o'clock. Nine. The opera should be over about ten, Sandy had said. We'll call for you on our way back. Jenny began to dress slowly, spinning out time and only now admitting to herself how great a strain it had been to keep her mind harnessed away from contemplating risk. She wondered how many other Keszthely women had looked in the mirror before leaving for balls or dinners in Budapest and seen the same pearl and gold filigree necklace glinting against their skin. Each tiny pearl flower was set on tendrils so fine, they quivered when she moved, the workmanship exquisite.

Since Jenny was careful about her appearance, yet unconcerned about the impression she made, she did not pause to consider how well the necklace became her. A Renaissance face, Martin had said, and though the necklace was nowhere near as old as that, it performed the same

function as fine brushwork in a portrait: attracting attention, which, once caught, would be kept by Jenny's curved
and delicate lips, strong bone structure, and dark eyes.

Sandy came alone to fetch her, saying that the others had
taken a taxi directly to the Korona. "I'm starving," he an-
nounced with relish as he threaded a hired Trabant expertly
through the tramlines. "I hate opera, and all those stout
women singing made me think of fish and french fries." He
opened and shut his mouth, blowing out his cheeks, and
succeeded in looking remarkably like cod on a slab.

"I'm hungry, too." Jenny had only eaten some breakfast
rolls since her dinner last night with Martin. "I hope the
food won't be cold by the time it reaches a private room."

"I told them to leave everything in heated trolleys; we'll
do better without waiters hovering all the time. What have
you been doing with yourself? You were out when I called
yesterday."

"Enjoying Budapest and reading manuscripts. Since
four o'clock this afternoon I've read a novel about a com-
bine harvester, something very symbolic about the Danube,
and a slapstick sketch."

"My poor love. Were they any good?"

"No. I think they were well written, although my Hungarian isn't really good enough to judge style, but not one
of them would sell a hundred copies in the West."

"Their fault or ours?"

"Both," said Jenny slowly. "Do you know, Sandy, I
didn't expect you to see it wasn't only them. I thought you
hated Communists too much."

"Oh, I do. I hate them because I can't live in Hungary."
He spoke with such suppressed venom that Jenny flicked a
glance at him and then away, as if it would be prying to
look closely. "The odd thing is, one reason I want to live
here is because it's been Communist for forty years. Can
you understand that?"

"Yes, of course. Communism is the aspic which has kept a
great deal else unchanged, some of which we would try to
preserve in the West if we were lucky enough to have these

same forty years again. But you can't live here. Not because they wouldn't have you, but because you couldn't breathe."

"You haven't met Schiller yet, have you?"

Jenny shook her head.

"He's as rich as only bankers can be, his wife wearing rubies the size of my front teeth. I dislike both of them, but I don't think he's a liar. He told me he preferred East Germany to West."

Jenny laughed. "I bet he doesn't live there."

"God, no. What he means is, the East is more like the Germany of his youth."

"I thought you said he was Hungarian."

"Half, like you. But his wife is pure-blood Esterhazy, all corseted bones and pride. My sweet, I've just thought. You'll have to curtsey to her: even Keszthelys couldn't sit when there were Esterhazys around."

Jenny thought he was joking but was less certain when they joined the rest of their party in a private room. In his role of ex–imperial chamberlain, Sandy certainly bowed very gallantly to Frau Schiller, and there seemed a distinct tendency among the other guests to speak to her only when she spoke to them.

Oh, fiddle, thought Jenny impatiently. It's going to be an annoying evening after all. But at least Sandy only shrugged when he saw her pearls, although she expected him to be angry; he had never been a man who liked having his advice disregarded.

There were twelve guests altogether. The Romans; Pierre Sorbaz and his wife; the Zakonyis and the Schillers; a very much painted and rather drunk woman who was Gyula Sebestyen; Sandy, Jenny, and an American-Hungarian film director called Miller.

"The name was Marosz," he confided to Jenny. "But when I lived near the Zakonyis, I changed it."

She laughed; Zakonyi was certainly enough to give Hungarian-Americans a bad name. "It's fun to be at least part-Hungarian tonight, when there's such a splendid setting for our dinner."

"Oh, sure, I'm told even the commies love an Ester-hazy," Miller said disparagingly. "The opera was wonder-fully sung, but not one of them listened to it. You didn't come, did you?"

Jenny shook her head, looking around at her ill-assorted fellow guests. The Korona was an old hotel, and red dam-ask curtains were drawn across long windows, gilt settles stood in each corner of the room, and ponderous candela-bra glittered above the elegantly decorated table. The at-mosphere was sultry, and champagne had never been her favorite drink.

"Well, Miss Marshall, that sure is a pretty necklace. Sandy tells me it's been Keszthely for hundreds of years." Excitement made Zakonyi shout even louder than he had in New York, but he was also rather nicer, like a difficult child temporarily satisfied by an expensive present.

"Yes, for quite a long time. Did you enjoy the opera, Mr. Zakonyi?" She saw Miller wink at her from where he was listening to a monologue from Schiller's Esterhazy wife.

"Christ, no. Those singers are like seals at mating time. They ought to be banned, I guess."

"I like seals." Jenny was beginning to enjoy herself. "Could you open a window for me? It's awfully hot in here."

She escaped to talk to Gyula Sebestyen while Zakonyi stirred up a great commotion among the waiters, who swore the windows couldn't be opened. She would back Zakonyi every time and was not surprised when a wel-come, if chilly, draft began to blow through the room.

"Who are you?" Gyula Sebestyen asked morosely.

"Jenny Marshall. My mother was Hungarian and I'm over here on business, so Sandy asked me tonight."

Gyula opened her bag and took out cigarettes. "I'll smoke my own," she said unnecessarily. "Jesus, I need a meal after that fucking conference."

"How is it going?"

"Conferences don't go, they come and come and come. I've had a bellyful of conferences. At least this one is in

Budapest." She swayed, perhaps more drunk than her voice suggested, her skin turning almost green under Jenny's fascinated gaze.

They were an uneven number, so Jenny was able to make sure she sat next to Gyula when the move to the table came. She wanted to talk about the Soviet delegation to the conference but was disconcerted to discover she was beginning to feel almost as dizzy as Gyula looked. The windows were shut again, and the room seemed hotter than ever.

She toyed with delicious stuffed mushrooms, listening distractedly to Miller on her other side and beginning to wonder where the bathroom was.

"You don't look so good," said Miller solicitously. "Come to that, I don't feel good myself. Maybe the champagne was off."

Jenny had a notion champagne didn't go off, but it seemed too much effort to explain. Perhaps it was her imagination, but talk seemed to be lagging all around the table.

Sandy stood up soon after the waiters withdrew, holding his glass. Nothing the matter with him, apparently. "Ladies and gentlemen, a toast. To our return to Budapest, the city of our fathers."

They stood and drank, their eyes on the patriotically red, white, and green flower arrangement in the middle of the table.

Zoltan Zakonyi gave a belly laugh. "To a Hungary free of Reds." He drained his glass and threw it at the wall.

There was also glass breaking closer at hand as Gyula dropped hers on the table. By now Jenny was feeling so strange that she tried to put hers down, too, unharmed, but the table seemed to have moved. Drinking a toast had been a bad mistake and made her head spin faster; she turned, gasping for air and oblivious of manners, intent only on reaching the bathroom before she vomited. Instead the floor spun dizzily away, then snapped back, fast, into her eyes, but by then the impact was so distant it might have happened to someone else.

* * *

Faces swam back toward her through waves of nausea, their lips puckering and filling anxiously. A voice, very loud and close, was blaring Hungarian in her ear, but when Jenny opened her eyes, all she could see was a man standing by the door with an official cap pushed back on his head. You are being noticed, she thought muzzily, but Benedek's warning remained too far away for her to worry about it.

She was conscious next that someone close to her had a quite unbearably awful headache. If only the person with the headache would stop moaning and go away, she would be able to drift into sleep again.

With an enormous effort Jenny rolled over to see what the tiresome person wanted and discovered that the headache was her own. After several moments, dazedly, she sat up, head in her hands, wanting to hide in shame. How could she have got so drunk? She had only been drunk once in her life, as a sophomore. She peered between cupped hands, squinting against the light, and saw Sandy lying unconscious on his back, and beyond him Zoltan Zakonyi slumped in a chair with his face resting on a plate of food.

"Stay still." A man's voice, speaking Hungarian. "A doctor is on his way."

"What happened?" Her tongue felt too large for her mouth.

"We don't know yet. Keep quiet, I said."

"I can't remember a thing." She was worrying now and unable to keep quiet, the light drilling into her skull.

"We'll find out." A rough voice this, determined, not in the least concerned about her.

Quite how long she sat semiconscious with her head on her knees, Jenny couldn't have said, while hustle and confusion increased around her. Then hands felt her neck and stomach, and she was made to lie back while a doctor examined her.

He straightened. "Drugs. Definitely not food poisoning, the manager will be glad to hear."

"Will he indeed? I don't know what he thought he was

doing, hiring out a private room for Westerners to drug in. He'll be in trouble whatever happens."

Jenny opened her eyes again and saw black scuffed shoes planted squarely on the carpet near her nose, gray official trousers sloping into the distance, a gun holstered in a leather belt; the rest of him too far away to bother with. Police. She'd been noticed, all right.

She licked her lips. "We weren't . . . It was a perfectly ordinary supper party after the opera."

"It doesn't look ordinary to me," said the policeman skeptically. "Perhaps it's different where you come from."

There was food and champagne everywhere. Several glasses were broken on the floor—Jenny remembered toasts. A full plate lay upturned under Pierre Sorbaz's legs, bottles had fallen over on the carpet, Frau Schiller was vomiting noisily in a corner. No wonder the police were hostile; it was the most degrading scene Jenny had ever seen.

More and louder moans were coming from elsewhere in the room, people moving, trying to stand after the doctor finished examining them, unable to believe what they saw.

"How many of them are staying in this hotel?" demanded the policeman.

"I don't know," wailed a different voice, the manager presumably. "How can I tell what guests get up to in a private room? The Korona is a very respectable hotel."

"My pearls," said Jenny clearly, her hands to her neck. "They've gone."

Everyone except Sandy was half-comatose by then, and her voice cut through confusion.

"My diamonds!" screeched Madame Sorbaz.

"My rubies which were Esterhazy," sobbed Frau Schiller.

"The dirty slobs have taken the lot." Zoltan Zakonyi stared around him belligerently. His face was smeared with spiced gravy, and he looked like a hippopotamus just crawled out of a swamp. He heaved to his feet and swayed there, grunting. "You goddamn Reds drugged us so you could take the Esterhazy rubies and Jenny's Keszthely necklet she had from her ma." He swung his fist at the nearest policeman and sent him sprawling across the table.

"*Nem szabat!*" squealed the manager, and darted forward to save his mahogany from being splintered. Zakonyi helped him on his way with a kick, and the table collapsed under the combined weight of manager and policeman, depositing all the remaining dishes and bottles on the floor.

"Now," said Zakonyi, turning with the light of battle in his eyes. "Who wants to be next?"

Curled tightly around her throbbing head, Jenny began to laugh. She was appalled by what had happened, anguished by the loss of her pearls, but she simply couldn't help it.

"I do not want to shoot you, but I shall unless you sit down before I count five," said the policeman standing close to her. He sounded neither amused nor outraged, merely like a man used to handling drunks. "One."

"You Red bastards have stolen our girls' jewels," yelled Zakonyi. "Christ, you've even taken my gold pen. I suppose you'd gotten tired of plastic commie ballpoints, huh?"

"Two."

"Sit down, Zoltan." His wife lifted a tearstained face.

"Three."

"The Reds have stolen your diamonds, honey."

"I know, dear. Sit down and maybe they'll give them back."

Zakonyi sat sulkily. "I bet that guy with the gun has them in his pants pocket."

The next few hours made up a time Jenny preferred to forget. Policemen, waiters, and doctors were summoned and dismissed and reappeared as if through rotating doors. Everyone except Jenny was staying at the Korona, so she had to change into some of Gyula Sebestyen's clothes, because no one was allowed to leave; statements were taken, witnessed, contradicted, torn up and taken down again. It soon became apparent that the Hungarian police, however skilled at other tasks, were completely inexperienced when it came to a jewel robbery. They exclaimed and marveled over it, swore there was not a single receiver for such goods in the whole of Eastern Europe and probably no jewel thieves, either. In a people's Socialist state, jewels of value do not exist outside museums, you understand, so how could thieves expect to make a living from stealing them?

All the champagne in the Korona's cellars was taken away for analysis, the waiters arrested, and the kitchens torn apart while the distraught manager begged the police to remember his other guests.

"But how did the thieves get away?" demanded Miller. "It mightn't be too difficult for someone to drug our wine, but even after the waiters left, there must have been people about in the passage outside our room."

"Certainly it must be one of the staff; the police should arrest them all," snapped Pierre Sorbaz. His wife's diamonds were insured, and he hoped the police would not recover them, since shopping for replacements in the Champs Elysées would keep her happy for months, but arresting anyone who might have been concerned in a robbery was a matter of principle, after all.

"I tell you, it was the Reds themselves," said Zakonyi angrily. He had been warned he would be charged with assault and was temporarily handcuffed to a chair.

Sandy came over to sit beside Jenny; because he had been the last of them to recover, he still looked wretchedly ill. "I'm so sorry about your necklace, love. I know how much . . . Well, it wasn't just their value, was it?"

"You warned me not to bring it."

"I don't believe this nonsense of Zoltan's. The Hungarian government wouldn't do it like this; they'd be polite bastards and take it off you at the airport. I never expected robbery. For Christ's sake, Budapest must be one of the safest cities in Europe. A virgin could walk from the Buda Hills to Csepel, and the only risk would be from tourists."

"So could it maybe have been a non-Hungarian jewel thief, since the police don't seem to have heard of any here?"

He shrugged and winced at the same pain Jenny still felt from her throat to her eyeballs. "Whoever laced the drink, I'd like to make sure he swallowed a whole bottle by himself. D'you know what I think? Hungary is just finding her way into the real live naughty world and has bred a new generation of crooks without the police here even noticing. As for getting away afterward, there were four doors into that room. But Jenny—I really am sorry."

I bet you are, she thought. "Sandy—"

"But now let's look on the cheerful side! It can't be easy to get stolen goods out of a Communist state; the frontiers are tight enough, God knows, when they're not looking for anything in particular. And I love the way you call me Sandy."

"Everyone calls you Sandy, including me, for months."

"Not the same way as now, like a houri plotting mischief."

"Perhaps your head is made differently from mine, but I shan't be able to worry about how people pronounce my name until I've had a bath and slept for a week."

For some reason this disconcerted him, and he left her alone.

Tests on the champagne proved positive, and traces of at least one man's footprints were found on the ledge outside the window of their private dining room, but more hours went by before they were released. "I want your passports, and then you may go back to your rooms," Inspector Nemeth said at last. He disapproved of Westerners with money to spare for jewels and was polite but very curt.

"You've already taken mine," shouted Zakonyi.

"You will have a charge made against you in the morning. The rest of you go quickly with my men to fetch your passports."

"What about telling our embassies?"

"You may inform whoever you wish. They will no doubt advise you to cooperate fully in our investigation."

"*Mon Dieu*, for how long? I am due to return to France tomorrow." Sorbaz had dipped his wife's scarf in an ice bucket and wrapped it around his head, apparently in order to help him keep up a nonstop barrage of speculation about the robbery. If there had been any drugged champagne left, everyone else would cheerfully have poured it down his throat.

"As to that, I cannot say. A few days perhaps. Except for you," Nemeth added bleakly to Zakonyi.

"My passport isn't here. I'm staying at the Huszar." Jenny uncurled from her sofa. Apart from feeling as if she had been processed with the trash, she was better. But the frontiers are closed, she thought in dismay. Starting now, they'll search everything. Nor would she have a passport until the police chose to give it back, and long before then she would need to find a safe hiding place for the diaries.

Nemeth nodded. "I will take you myself to fetch it. I must return to my office now anyway."

"What has happened to the waiters?" Jenny asked him as he drove her through the streets in a green and white police car. She felt horribly conspicuous and thought of Benedek again.

"Nothing. Why do you ask?"

"Well . . . you arrested them, so you must think they know something, perhaps about the drugged champagne."

"We intend to find out who did it, and maybe one of them will tell us."

"But you said—"

"Nothing has happened to anyone yet. They are being questioned. If no one cooperates, then we will see."

Jenny bit her lip. There are many dark places left in Hungary once you leave safe ground, Martin had said. "What if none of them knows anything?"

"We believe at least one of them does. This necklace you have lost, it was a Keszthely necklace, I think Mr. Zakonyi said?"

"A Marshall necklace. It belongs to me, and I was born in the United States."

"But in the past it was Keszthely. He also said the German woman wore Esterhazy rubies, which I find interesting when Esterhazy property was long ago forfeit to the state. I have a good memory for many things."

"Let's hope it comes in useful for investigating our robbery, then," retorted Jenny sharply. "The waiters," she repeated, after a long silence. "You can't—"

"*Asszany* Marshall, I suggest you follow the example of your friends. Go to your room and leave us to continue our investigations."

"I never follow examples," said Jenny tightly. "Of course I'm worried if you've decided the quickest way to gather evidence is to lock up every Hungarian we've happened to meet, and for as long as you choose!"

"That is our affair," said Nemeth dismissively. "Some of these stolen goods, now, those might be for you and Frau Schiller to explain. I shall be making many reports, and one of them will go to the Ministry of Culture, telling how some of Hungary's historic jewels must long ago have been smuggled to the West. Then another perhaps to the public prosecutor's office." He pulled up outside the Huszar. "Now I come with you, and you will give me your passport."

Jenny could only be thankful that the diaries were not stacked on her carpet, for him to consider while he waited.

6

It was still dark when Jenny stirred sluggishly out of sleep, and instantly thoughts swarmed like bees into the empty spaces of her mind. Ever since her arrival in Hungary, she had slept and wakened at odd times, and at first she couldn't remember which day it was or work out how long she had slept. The hands of her watch said ten to four, so after a struggle she decided it must be early Saturday morning: if all had gone as planned, she would have been crossing into Austria in a few hours time.

She stared at the shadowed ceiling, hearing trams clanging and shrilling up the Rakoczky Ut. You have to hand it to Sandy, she thought. For sheer razor-edged nerve, if nothing else. The question was, what ought she to do next?

A dozen times during the past interminable day, she had been on the point of demanding an interview with Nemeth to tell him her suspicions. While returning with him to the Huszar, she had been freshly torn with doubt as she began to feel afraid that he might lock up not only the waiters, but her aunt and uncle, too, once the ownership of the Keszthely pearls were in question.

At first she had rejected her wonderings about Sandy as absurd. Then, as suspicion began to harden into a pattern, she thought her brain must be scrambled by the aftermath of drugs. She wasn't even clear exactly when suspicion had begun, because in New York she remembered thinking it odd that Sandy, an exhibitionist if ever there was one, agreed so easily he was not the guiding spirit behind the Budapest dinner. But by that time Zoltan Zakonyi already accepted the idea as his because he believed all worthwhile ideas were his, but Jenny's memory, like Inspector Nemeth's, was extremely good. At that supper in Sandy's brownstone, Zakonyi had said . . . She frowned. Zakonyi had said that without Sandy, they would all be vacationing in Budapest at different times. He himself had intended to go big-game fishing until he heard of Sandy's scheme.

It was Sandy who had decided on a private room for their party, too, although while safely in America, he and his friends had laughed over the gesture they would make by celebrating their capitalist successes where everyone could see. Yet once they were in Budapest, the change seemed sensible enough, after Zakonyi and Sorbaz had shown they couldn't be trusted to celebrate in a restaurant without getting everyone into trouble. Sandy had also tried to persuade her to leave her pearls behind; *I expect he prefers to rob people he dislikes,* Jenny thought sourly. But once she ignored his warnings, presumably he considered his honor satisfied and any subsequent loss entirely her own fault.

As for herself, she had spent most of the previous day unsuccessfully trying to crawl out from under the shock of realizing that a man who said he loved her—and almost certainly believed it, too—had simply shrugged and continued to carry through his plans once he learned they would cause her great distress. Yet she had liked him. She had liked Sandy Havasi very much.

Jenny sat up and drank great gulps of mineral water, her

mouth still scaled like reptile skin. Once she laid them end to end, her suspicions didn't amount to much. So had she been indulging in mere fantasy? Inspired perhaps by Martin's dislike of Sandy, and to avoid facing an irreplaceable loss?

No, she really did not think it possible.

As she had said to Nemeth, she didn't follow examples. Sandy was different, and his difference amused and intrigued her until that moment when he looked in her eyes and said how sorry he was her pearls had been stolen; if he'd said nothing, she would have found it easier to forgive. Sandy belonged to a different time, that older and wilder Hungary whose loss he bitterly regretted, where his ancestors had behaved as they pleased and were forgiven for it, because that was their nature. It required entirely modern hypocrisy to call her his love in the same breath as he mouthed regret that she had lost her necklace.

How he'd stolen it, she wasn't sure, but that somehow he had pulled off a barefaced double cross, she was nearly certain.

He had remained unconscious much longer than anyone else, which suggested he must have avoided drinking the drugged champagne until sometime after everyone else was lying senseless. Perhaps it was that extra time he remained unconscious that had fueled her suspicions. One of the waiters might know something, but if she was right, then Sandy could have drugged the champagne himself, so long as he found a trustworthy accomplice to wait below the window and take the jewels away.

So what was she going to do?

Tell Nemeth what she thought she knew? Neither she nor Frau Schiller would ever get their jewels back if she did, and Sandy could easily spend the next twenty years of his life in a Hungarian prison. Sandy, who loved speed and excitement, rotting in marshes until he went crazy or was shot trying to escape. And tell Nemeth what, anyway? She hadn't much fact to offer out of a jungle growth of suspicion. She could be wrong.

"I'm so sorry about your necklace, love. Well, it wasn't just their value, was it?"

No words could describe what she had seen in Sandy's eyes as he said that, but no, she didn't think she was wrong.

What she needed now was proof, however fragmentary, before she told anyone anything. When she did, she intended that she, not Nemeth, would challenge Sandy, and while witnesses listened to what she said.

And once she had recovered her pearls, she preferred him to escape.

Jenny climbed out of bed, feeling quite cheerful again. The diaries were a hideous complication but, however difficult it might be to corner Sandy now he'd nearly won, that was what she had to set about fixing, if she could.

An hour later, she felt more cheerful still. The Budapest telephone directory revealed only one Benedek, Andras, his name followed by the magic letters HSWP: Hungarian Socialist Workers' Party. As she reached for the receiver, Jenny just hoped he wouldn't be organizing the comrades on a Saturday. Then she paused, thinking. Nemeth could have ordered her phone to be bugged by now.

She couldn't risk using it, especially when Benedek knew about the diaries and would not hesitate to save himself by protesting innocence at her expense.

She needed to contact him, all the same.

It was still very early when Jenny finished a leisurely breakfast and went out for a stroll, but after half an hour she still wasn't sure whether she was being watched or not, since nerves alone gave the sense of eyes following everywhere she went. Her inexperience, too, meant she didn't know what to look for.

Therefore, she mustn't use a public phone in case there was a watcher, because then Nemeth would realize she had something to say that she didn't want him to hear. Eventually she went into one of the hard-currency tourist shops and asked, in English, if she could use their phone. It was an innocuous place for her to visit, and conveniently empty at this season; if anyone should be watching, he would wait outside for her to reappear.

"There are telephones in the metro station at the end of the street," answered the assistant.

"I don't understand how to use Hungarian phones. I thought perhaps you would help if I came here." Jenny dug five dollars out of her purse and gazed at her helplessly.

Foreign currency was available only in minute and occasional amounts to Hungarians, although they were allowed to travel; consequently, even American dollars were eagerly accepted. "What number?" asked the girl.

Jenny scribbled a state tourist number, and rang off as soon as the girl's back was turned. The telephone was on a shelf beyond the counter, the assistants giggling among themselves. Carefully, she dialed Benedek's number.

"*Kicsoda?*" Judit's voice.

"Is Andras there?"

"Who is it?"

"A comrade. He is meant to be attending a meeting at our canteen this morning."

"Are you sure? It's Saturday."

"Quite sure. Get him, will you?"

A pause followed by distant quarreling; Jenny chuckled to herself.

"Benedek here. What the hell d'you mean, a meeting at your canteen?"

"There ought to be a meeting. It's very important," said Jenny carefully, hoping he would recognize her voice.

"Oh, *baszom*," he said rudely. "I remember now. Can't you manage without me?"

"No."

"Well, I've promised to take my wife up the cog railway today. We're going in an hour. This time you'll have to make speeches on your own." He slammed down the receiver.

"Did you get the information you wanted?" asked the girl as Jenny bought a bottle of Tokay to account for her visit.

"I'm not sure," answered Jenny truthfully. "I hope so."

The cog railway in an hour, Benedek had said, if she had grasped his meaning. The Budapest cog railway ran steeply into the hills behind old Buda and was much used by skiers in winter and tourists in the summer. On a damp November Saturday the station would be nearly empty, and Jenny decided the best place to lose a possible watcher would be Moszkva Square close by. Trams, buses, metro trains, and cars tangled kaleidoscopically with each other there, and even under ordinary circumstances a pedestrian feared for his life while dodging across its disorganized spaces. In drizzle it was worse, and worse still when she intentionally cut her chances close. After five minutes of artlessly changing her mind under the jaws of ravening machinery, Jenny was reasonably certain that if anyone had been following her, then he was recovering from the experience over a bottle of plum brandy in the nearest bar.

She glanced at her watch and left the doorway where she had been standing for several minutes out of sight, walked down some steps, and turned a couple of corners to reach the street that led to the cog railway terminus. In an hour, Benedek had said, and she had cut the time as closely as she dared.

There was no sign of him at the station, and her heart sank. Perhaps he'd meant what else he'd said, and stuck to his decision she must manage on her own.

Jenny sat on hard plastic seating, staring out at thickening rain as red carriages slowly hauled themselves up the steep track. Apartment blocks spread out on either side, everything looking its worst in mist and wet.

There were several stops along the way, and at one of them Benedek got in, talking amiably to a soldier. Jenny looked away hastily, letting her breath out in relief. The run to the top took twenty minutes, and on a wet day there was nothing to do when you reached there: grit-covered paths wound through dripping woods, kiosks were shuttered, childrens' slides deserted.

"We might as well go down again," said Benedek when the soldier had disappeared.

They walked casually up and down the platform together while waiting for the train to leave, under the indifferent stare of a woman knitting in the ticket office.

"Well?" demanded Benedek. "You'll get me noticed, you will."

"I was very careful, but I want you to do something for me."

"How much?"

Typical, thought Jenny, that he should ask the price even before he knew what she wanted. "Fifty dollars. I haven't much money left."

He shook his head. "You can't get anything for fifty. It has cost you that to bring me here this morning."

"Listen, then." The train started on its downward journey while Jenny swiftly summarized everything that had happened at the Korona.

"*Baszom!*" he exclaimed, astonished. "And you dared to bring the police with you to meet me?"

"I'm sure I didn't."

"They would be watching. It is something our police know how to do from the time they were born."

"I thought they might be. I couldn't see anyone, but I spent quite a time in Moszkva Square."

"Oh, Moszkva," he said, and grinned. "Anyway, you are here, so I will just have to think of a good lie if anyone asks. What do you want?"

Jenny looked at him speculatively. He was much more cooperative since she mentioned jewels. "I think I know who the thief was."

Benedek scratched his chin with his thumb; since it was Saturday, he hadn't shaved. "You didn't tell the police?"

"No."

"Why not?"

"Because I'm not sure. Because I think it is the Sandy Havasi I mentioned, and I don't want to put a friend in prison for the rest of his life. Because I want my necklace back, and if the police find it, they'll probably keep it."

"Why?"

The train seemed to be going faster down than up, not many minutes left to explain about Keszthely and Ester-hazy jewels.

"You're a Keszthely?" demanded Benedek when she had finished. Jenny nodded. "Well, I'm damned."

"Does it matter?"

"Not to me, *asszany*. I'm a Benedek; so what?"

"I don't want to talk to the police if I can help it." He nodded, this being a point of view he entirely endorsed. "This—this man I think took the jewels; I haven't any real evidence, but I'm sure. My passport, too . . . I have to get those diaries out of Hungary soon; it's horribly unsafe to leave them in Budapest as things are now. And if Nemeth should find them, well, I'd do my best, but I've never been questioned by Communist police. I don't know whether I would be able to keep you out of it. I think you have to help me, not for money, but for your own sake now."

Benedek looked down at his sinewy workman's hands. "If you told our police the smallest suspicion, they would listen. They're suspicious bastards themselves. Then they would question this Sandor Havasi and kick something out of him."

"He's a naturalized U.S. citizen, and there's a confer-ence going on at the moment in Budapest where Hungary hopes to obtain a great deal of money from the West. I don't think Nemeth's masters would let him beat up an American on mere suspicion. And Sandy's tough. He wouldn't say anything under normal grilling, and if he did, it wouldn't help me. Once the police recover jewels they regard as state property, they'll keep them."

Benedek grunted. "You want me to beat up Havasi for you?"

"No! By now someone else will have the jewels any-way," she added, belatedly realizing that unless she offered some sound reason against such a course, then Benedek would probably beat up Sandy anyway, on his own account. "I want you to have him watched. He must have passed the jewels on immediately to an accomplice, arranged a safe place to hide them, I don't know. But one thing's certain: even he wouldn't be crazy enough to try and travel them out of the country himself."

"Hm," said Benedek thoughtfully. "If you know how, it isn't too difficult to get out of Hungary. Not like East Germany. That's a ten-thousand-dollar place."

Jenny understood this to be the cost of an illicit border crossing. "How much here?"

The train was roaring and squealing down toward the terminus; not long to go now.

"Two, three thousand if you're lucky; even our border isn't easy. People get shot there every year. The point is, such jewels as you describe must be worth many times that. You would have to be very sure who to trust while carrying goods like that, and how could an amateur coming here on vacation from America learn such things?"

"That's what I mean, so I've been thinking. I think Sandy plans to carry out a trade with someone here in Hungary. Probably a Westerner who knows the illegal market well, including how to get goods out." Her fingers tightened on her lap. Only superb craftsmanship gave her necklace value, unlike the Esterhazy rubies; she hated to think it might be broken up for trifling amounts of gold. "How payment and exchange will be arranged, I can't imagine, but I want to know who Sandor Havasi sees and where he goes. I'll do my part by sticking close to him when I can. If he shakes me off, you'll know he's worth following."

"He may have made contact already." Benedek rose and turned his back on her as the doors slid open.

"I think Inspector Nemeth is still too close for him to risk it yet," answered Jenny with a ghost of a laugh.

"Then he may not try for weeks."

"The same answer, surely. Nemeth detests the pack of us, and very soon he'll throw us out, knowing we'll have to come back whenever he asks. If we hope to recover our property, that is. Sandy needs to have everything fixed before then, so he can leave innocently with the rest of us and pick up his payment in the West."

Jenny caught a bus back to the Korona, where she meant to latch on to Sandy like a burr, feeling confident and excited. She might not succeed in getting her pearls back and in other circumstances would have chosen never to see him again, but she possessed the kind of temperament that overcomes its losses best by fighting back.

Sandy remarked at once on her cheerful looks. "I thought you'd be pretty upset today," he said, looking at her keenly. "All of us were too frazzled to take much in yesterday, but Frau Schiller and Sadie Zakonyi spent this morning in tears."

Hastily Jenny explained that she'd decided her necklace would probably be recovered eventually, since alone out of the jewel robber's haul, it could not be recut or reset without losing nearly all its value.

Sandy's eyes flickered. "I hope you're right. Nemeth asked me where I thought you'd gone."

"I woke at four and couldn't concentrate on manuscripts. I've been everywhere. Where else shall we go now?"

"Don't you ever feel tired?"

"Well, one thing I definitely don't want to do today is sit and think. I know; let's go to City Park. I prefer the simple life after that disgusting dinner."

"Jenny, for God's sake, it's pouring with rain! Anyway, Nemeth said we must tell him if we left the hotel."

"He didn't tell me."

"I don't suppose he expected you to go out at dawn. He was pretty quick asking where you'd got to, though. He also admitted he hadn't discovered anything new."

"So they'll start beating guilt out of the waiters soon."

Sandy shrugged. "The most they're likely to know is that a stranger maybe offered one of them ten dollars if they'd doctor the champagne as a joke."

"You sound as if you know," said Jenny lightly.

"Common sense, love. Which Hungarian cops don't possess, or so it seems. Okay, if you're determined, I'll ring Nemeth's office and say we're going for a walk in City Park."

Jenny had not realized how much of a strain it would be, staying close to a friend she now believed had robbed her. She never caught a glimpse of Benedek and supposed he must have helpers who would watch people for a fee, but all the same, it was difficult to be natural. She laughed too easily at Sandy's jokes and hated him to touch her; said firmly that she didn't want to discuss the robbery anymore, although it filled her mind every moment she stayed with him. She was also terrified of saying or doing something that might reveal suspicion, even while Sandy himself chattered as he always did. Whether he noticed anything amiss or not, Jenny could not guess.

"I never knew a park could be so amusing," he said at last.

The rain had stopped, and children ran squealing under bare-branched trees. Above all, because Jenny's senses were stretched so tightly, she sparked interest or amusement out of everything they saw, so that Sandy's high spirits also slipped their leash.

"I didn't, either," answered Jenny after a pause. "Where shall we go tomorrow? I meant to fly home on Tuesday, but I don't expect Nemeth will have given our passports back by then."

"I shall start demanding mine if it isn't back soon. Not that I mind when all Hungary is on my doorstep, and I've done better with you in a single afternoon here than I did during six months in New York. Too many books and politicians there, I suppose." He shot her a look as if he intended to say more, but changed his mind when Jenny did not answer. She had always refused to discuss Martin with him, and the distasteful charade she was now playing made everything worse. "I can't take you anywhere for the next two or three days," he added. "How about Szentendre next Thursday if we're all still here?"

"I hope we're not! I'd enjoy to if we are; I've heard Szentendre's lovely. So where are you escaping to tomorrow that Nemeth doesn't mind?"

"Boar hunting," he said with satisfaction. "I've a cousin who lives near the Soviet border, and he promised a long time ago to take me hunting the proper way. Nemeth agreed at once when I asked him: he knows I wouldn't start fooling around on the Soviet border, with or without a passport."

"Boar hunting," repeated Jenny. "So how do you do that the proper way?"

"With spears. At this time of year Hungary is full of rich Westerners—Germans, mostly—who come to butcher trophies to put on their walls at home. Sheer vandalism, of course. What chance has a boar got against a good marksman using telescopic sights? Our grandfathers would have ridden at them with a spear, and that's what we're going to do. On foot instead of horseback, though."

"I'd like to see it," said Jenny untruthfully. She had never been hunting and hated the idea of killing animals.

"You'd hate it, love. A cunning old boar who has outwitted years of trigger-happy Germans is really mean. He'll weigh six hundred pounds or more, and there are only two places you can kill him cleanly with a spear: straight through the eye, or between the shoulders. Since I shan't reach either while he's coming at me like a truck, I'll aim to weaken him first, and that's not a pretty business." He threw back his head and breathed deeply, as though he scented blood already. "If you miss, then he weakens you instead. A slash from a boar tusk can lay your leg open to the bone, but it's the last true hunting left in Europe, and no sport like it."

"You've been before?"

"Once, to learn. This time I shall be trying my own skill."

"I'd like to see it," Jenny repeated. "Of course, I wouldn't expect your cousin to put me up, but couldn't I drive out? I'd hired a car before the robbery, hoping to see something of the country. Now I don't want to sit and brood alone in Budapest."

"Jenny, even in Socialist Hungary, boar hunts are all-male affairs. Well, perhaps not the tourist kind, though even there I'd guess women aren't too welcome. We shall stink of boar and get drunk afterward, I expect."

She couldn't persist without arousing suspicion, so changed to a more oblique approach. "I never knew you enjoyed hunting so much. You'll have to ask Zoltan to take you big-game fishing sometime if you really like trying different things."

"I like danger," he said simply. "I only bother to hold down a god-awful government job at all because it gives me six weeks vacation a year and enough of a salary to pay for what I enjoy doing the rest of the time."

Jenny doubted whether Sandy ever gave more than per-functory attention to desk work and had already revised her ideas on where else he obtained the cash he needed for risky living. The Sandy Havasi she was now discovering might easily regard a really stylish robbery as recreation rather than crime. "What are you laughing at?" he demanded.

"You," she answered frankly. "For heaven's sake, Sandy. You ought to have been born a hundred years ago. Then you could have speared boar and held some kind of decorative position as a hobby, without anyone thinking it odd."

"A pity, isn't it?" he said with a gleam of a smile.

"The point is, you weren't born then, but now. Why tramp for miles in the hills so you can spear boar as far from medical help as possible?"

"Istvan's place isn't in the hills, but in a swamp beyond Tokay; he has gallons of the most marvelous wine hidden underneath a barn and knows the habits of all the craftiest boar for miles around. It's no good, Jenny. We would never agree on this. From where Istvan lives you can hear Dutch and Germans gunning down boar by the dozen, driven out of the trees to slaughter. It simply doesn't compare with a whole day spent stalking one old tusker, when, if you should happen to corner him, it'll be on ground of his choosing, not yours, which with a spear, makes it a very equal fight."

"All I can say is, I hope you stay lucky."

He stared at the clearing sky over Budapest. "I feel lucky."

7

JENNY WAS EXHAUSTED BY THE TIME SHE RETURNED TO the Huszar after dining with Sandy. In fact, she pleaded tiredness as the easiest way to avoid spending the night. Because she had confessed in New York that meeting him was one of the reasons her Hungarian heritage had begun to seem more important, to him spending the night together would be the natural climax to a harmonious day in Budapest. To her, the strain of deception had become increasingly unbearable, made worse by the taste of treachery. She was furious with him and determined to get her necklace back if she could, but she did still find Sandy attractive. Nevertheless, if she had not suspected him before, she would certainly have done so after twelve hours in his company. Under the influence of her false spirits he became quite simply drunk on triumph, but being Sandy, delight in his own cleverness was made to seem amusing. Perhaps no one else there knew him well enough to recognize his elation for what it was; even so, Jenny was astonished the rest did not comment on his mood. Possibly they were too tired. In the aftermath of drugged wine, shock, and humiliation, the Zakonyis and Sorbazes picked glumly at their food and found fault with everyone, especially Inspector Nemeth, who saw no reason to tell them anything at all. The rest of the party did not appear, Schiller and Gyula were back at the conference, the others eating in their rooms.

The same mood of gloom descended on Jenny as her head began to ache with the effort of matching Sandy's vivacity for hours, the many skills needed to guide conversation in directions where she might glean some information, when, as exhaustion grew, she would have liked nothing better than to snap everyone's head off.

But when she was back at the Huszar at last, she couldn't sleep. It was still quite early, and the old hotel echoed with feet and chatter while the events of the day flipped wearily but persistently in her mind, like landed fish.

The phone rang, making her jump. Surely Benedek wouldn't be such a fool as to ring her here if he had anything to report.

"Hullo?" she said cautiously.

"Jenny? I've been trying to reach you all evening."

Oh God, Martin. Martin sounded extremely angry, which was worse. "I've been out."

"So I realize. I heard a very odd story from a German banker called Schiller this afternoon."

"I'd forgotten what dreadful gossips men are." Jenny was alarmed by her failure to grasp that at his conference Martin was sure to hear rumors of so exceptional a happening in Budapest as a jewel robbery.

"You told me you weren't mixed up with Havasi."

"I'm not. It's none of your business if I went to a dinner where he was present."

"The hell of a dinner, by the sound of it."

"Yes, it was," Jenny agreed wearily, hoping that Martin was enough of a politician not too blurt out over an open telephone line that two days ago he had suspected she was about to make a damned fool of herself, and not with Sandy Havasi, either.

"So what happened?"

"Everything you heard from Schiller, I suppose. My necklace was stolen, among a great deal else, and the Hungarian police have retired to read up on how to investigate jewel robberies." I hope Inspector Nemeth enjoys that in transcript, she thought irritably.

"You will be glad of police help if you're ever to get your belongings back." The warning in his voice was clear, and Jenny sighed with relief. Martin Rothbury was indeed enough of a politician to understand that on a telephone, words needed to be used with care. "Jenny?"

"I'm still listening."

"You remember I said the conference might be adjourning for consultation? Well, it has, and I'm free for a couple of days. Would you like—" He paused, still sounding angry rather than understanding. "I thought you might feel better out of Budapest for a day or so."

Jenny thought fast, possibilities spinning quicker than she could grasp them. "You needn't make it sound such a penance."

"It's a pity women are always so bloody unsporting," he replied coldly, and Jenny promptly felt ashamed of herself. Martin seldom swore, and she knew better than he did the explanations that care for her prevented him from demanding. "Do you want to come, or are you fully occupied with your Habsburg acquaintances?"

Jenny chuckled involuntarily. "No, I'd like to come. I have to ask the police, though. They've taken my passport, and I'm not allowed to leave Budapest without permission."

"I see. Perhaps it would be better if I had a word with them, when the circumstances might make some difference."

The circumstances being Hungary's need for loans, Jenny supposed. "I wish you would. You need to ask for Inspector Nemeth of Budapest Third District." A quite different thought struck her. "I've got an automobile wasting money in the lockup here. I asked the car rental people, but they won't give me any refund, so we could use that if you like. Or do you have to drive Rolls-Royces from the embassy?"

"I should think Inspector Nemeth and I will discuss your shortcomings very amiably together," he observed. "I'll call for you about ten tomorrow."

Jenny sat hugging her knees after he rang off. Ten o'clock ought to be just about right, she thought, and set her alarm for six-thirty. Sandy had said he would be leaving, by train, early in the morning.

Before seven next morning she was strolling toward the East Railway Terminus, enjoying crisp morning air. The streets sparkled with frost after the previous day's rain, and there was very little traffic; she was almost sure she wasn't being followed, since early on a Sunday morning there was little cover to hide a watcher. All the same, she did nothing to rouse suspicion; loitering and window-shopping as anyone might after a restless night.

Sandy hadn't hired an automobile, mentioning last night that his boar-hunting cousin would meet him off the train. Jenny could only hope Benedek might overhear his exact destination, since she herself didn't dare go where Sandy might catch sight of her. All the same, she wanted to be close enough for Benedek to be able to reach her in a hurry if he should discover anything of use. After checking out various hints in Sandy's cheerfully unguarded descriptions of boar hunting by a careful study of maps and tourist brochures, Jenny had decided he must be going to one of three areas, all in the northeast of the country and all within a few kilometers of luxury state establishments run for foreigners who wanted to hunt in Hungary. The trouble was, to have any chance at all of following, she needed to know which one.

It was lovely in Budapest that morning, sauntering under a sky polished by a keen steppe wind. She had done the best she could; if Benedek did not appear, she would be disappointed but not downcast, feel freed to give her full attention to the diaries. Which were more important than any necklace, after all.

Except perhaps to her.

Instinctively she quickened her pace. Jenny wasn't used to sauntering for long, and whatever she told herself, she did not take easily to the idea of defeat.

Only a few trains left the East Terminus on a Sunday morning, and soon after eight Jenny saw Sandy paying off a taxi. No one seemed to be watching him, either, but then, Nemeth knew where he was going and why, so his whereabouts could easily be checked. Unless Jenny was wrong in all her guessing, then Sandy had no intention of giving a false destination, and once there, all his actions would be calculated to disarm suspicion.

He was carrying something long wrapped in paper; a spear, Jenny supposed and shivered. Suddenly it seemed barbaric to find pleasure in spearing boar, and the understanding she had felt yesterday for him abruptly disappeared.

She strolled on slowly as he turned away from the taxi and walked into the station concourse. Benedek couldn't miss her on these empty sidewalks, or Nemeth, either, if he was interested in her movements. Damn Benedek; perhaps after all he had decided to leave her and her schemes alone.

A few of the bleaker kinds of coffee shop were beginning to open, and she selected one and went in, glad of something hot. Ate and drank slowly, glancing often at her watch. Martin was always punctual. Nine-fifteen. Nine-thirty. Strange how she had been convinced that Benedek would never resist the lure of jewels. She decided to wait five minutes more, and they flicked past like leaves blowing down the empty streets. Pretense vanished, and she had to face the fact that now there was nothing more she could do to recover her pearls, she was bitterly disappointed. Sandy had been right under her eyes, and she'd lacked the nerve to go up to him and say she'd come to wish him luck. And by the way, Sandy, why not have coffee together while you're waiting for your train? Then she could have discovered where he was going for herself.

But deep in her heart, she knew she hadn't hung back only because prudence suggested that if he was indeed going to meet an accomplice somewhere in Eastern Hungary, then however carefully such a meeting was arranged, the smallest thing would alarm him. For the sake of her own self-respect, she had gone far enough along the path of double-dealing. If Sandy had simply been a thug, she would have tricked him any way she could, but she did not fancy trading any further on the affections of a man whom, despite everything, she still liked.

A stranger brushed past her as she came out of the café, his single sentence almost whipped away by the wind: "He took a ticket to Komoro."

At the last possible moment Benedek had done his part.

When she reached her room at the Huszar again, it took quite a long time to find Komoro on the map, a wayside stop less than ten miles from the Soviet border. Which was a surprise, since that district had seemed the least likely of her possibles. From the map it appeared both flat and marshy for considerable distances in every direction; she'd never visualized Sandy doing whatever it was he planned in wetlands, where he might be visible for miles. No wonder Nemeth didn't mind him going to such a place, when even Jenny was shaken by fresh doubt. It had all seemed so logical once she worked it out; now she was swept by uncertainty again. And yet . . . Sandy was doing more or less what she had decided he was likely to do, if he was indeed the thief. He was traveling to a place that looked innocuous even to the police, and quite close to Komoro was a castle run by the State Tourist Board as a hunting lodge for rich foreigners: men who bought stolen jewels for a living were likely to be rich and presumably could shoot boar if they wished. So what would be more natural than for Sandy to encounter a stranger somewhere in the green flatness shown on her map? Also, he was staying with hs cousin, and blood ties were the safest of all in Hungary. Even Benedek thought so.

Jenny pitched the map aside in exasperation and finished packing a suitcase. You couldn't tell much from small-scale maps, except that Komoro was too close to the Soviet border for comfort. Not even her Keszthely necklace was worth an enforced stay in Siberia.

Martin was waiting for her by the time she went downstairs, and gave her a singularly considering stare while remaining distantly polite. Oh, bother! thought Jenny resignedly. She would need to put forward some very persuasive explanations to win assistance from so obviously reserved a judgment.

Since she had the automobile keys in her handbag, there was no argument over who should drive, and therefore be in a position to decide their route. Jenny simply sat behind the wheel and started up. "Are you any good at reading maps?" she asked.

"I expect you know which way you want to go," he answered noncommittally.

Which might be shrewd or rude, depending on which way you considered it. "I thought it would be fun to go east. The old Keszthely lands are up that way. If you can direct me to the right road out of Budapest . . ."

Half an hour later they emerged from the suburbs, and Jenny put her foot down. The Lada was not a lively car, but they had reached a three-lane highway that carried very little traffic: there were few speed restrictions in Hungary and a steady seventy miles an hour wouldn't look as if they were in an unnatural hurry. Sandy was a long way ahead, but Jenny had discovered that he needed to change trains twice in order to reach Komoro on a Sunday and wait three leisurely lunchtime hours at a junction called Nyíregyháza. Only one train a day ran from there to the Soviet frontier, and Komoro was on the frontier branch line. With fast driving and a good road, they could arrive there first.

Martin said very little, sitting beside her and staring through the windscreen with a frown between his eyes, as if he took a mildly unfavorable view of Hungarian agriculture. Which would be unfair, thought Jenny with an inner spurt of laughter; the highway sliced across the great Magyar plain, and the land was both rich and intensively farmed.

"I should have asked," she said at last. "Inspector Nemeth didn't mind me leaving Budapest for a couple of days?"

"No, but you have to check with the police wherever we are this evening."

Now, that might make Nemeth think, when she and Sandy separately checked in from places embarrassingly close together.

"He also agreed that unless he turned up something unexpected, he wouldn . ue justified in keeping your passport very much longer." Martin turned in his seat to look directly at her for the first time since leaving Budapest.

"You mean you told him. How much longer, then?"

"I expect to be leaving at the end of the week. I said I should be unhappy to do so unless you were free to accompany me."

Jenny swallowed. "Martin—"

"There's a town called Szolnok coming up soon. Are you in too much of a hurry, or can we stop there while you decide how much you want to tell me?"

"I'm in too much of a hurry." Jenny gripped the wheel as if he might snatch it from her. "Martin, I haven't been fair to you. There will be a quite dreadful fuss if things go wrong; now Nemeth can suggest that a minister of the British government is mixed up in—"

"I must confess I should prefer to know exactly what it is I have walked into. As to fuss, I imagine it is my masters rather than Nemeth's who will make their annoyance entirely clear. The Hungarians want a loan and will keep their mouths shut if it suits them. Her Majesty's somewhat sanctimonious governments generally prefer to leave their dirty work to subordinates. But since I hope to be resigning soon, I daresay that's unimportant."

The car swerved. "Which was your idea, not mine."

"Well, I've got an even better one just now. Let's change over and I'll drive; after all, I only have to listen."

Jenny laughed reluctantly and pulled up as soon as the road was clear. She certainly needed to give the whole of her attention to deciding how much to tell him. The robbery was simple, and once she had described her suspicions and offered such scraps of evidence as she possessed, it was up to him to decide how far he could become involved. The diaries came into a different category and she hadn't intended to breathe a word about them, but somewhere along the road from Budapest, her mind had changed. It would be despicable to ask any man in Martin's position for his help in recovering a necklace without also revealing that the most cursory search of their car would place the government he represented in a very embarrassing position. On the other hand . . . if it came to a pinch, she would give up any hope of recovering her necklace rather than lose the diaries. Or then again, perhaps she wouldn't, when the Keszthely pearls remained the only part of her Hungarian heritage she felt was entirely hers.

Martin stayed silent during the considerable time during which reluctance, scruple, and doubt tumbled together in her mind, for which she was profoundly grateful. Several miles sped by, and Szolnok came and went. But on some things there could be no compromise if she was to live with herself when this was over. Her decision made, she told him everything. First about the robbery, about why and how they were here, swooping through Kisújszállás now, then settling down again to scorch across more miles of flat plain: Martin was maintaining as high a speed as she had done. He listened without interrupting, hands loose on the wheel, eyes on the unraveling spool of road. His long face, high forehead, and beaked nose reminded Jenny of the Concorde, droop-snooted and full of sophisticated systems.

When she finished, he asked at once why she thought Sandy might be meeting some third party so dangerously soon after a successful robbery.

"Successful so far," Jenny pointed out. "But if we assume, as I think we may, that his only help comes from a cousin who must be even crazier than he, then he's still facing the biggest hurdle of them all: how to get rid of his haul. He's amateur, you see."

"You don't know that."

"I suppose I don't," she said slowly, taken aback. Because she had assumed for some time that Sandy was a gambler, she had simply accepted that he had decided to try a different kind of risk in Budapest. It had never occurred to her that he might have habitually financed his expensive tastes from the proceeds of theft. "Of course, he is fairly well-known on the New York social circuit; he could have used the women he met to . . . Well, I suppose if you're right, it would help to explain the slick way this was planned. I don't think it changes much. He's not professional in the sense of blowing safes twice a week, and this time he's got hundreds of thousands of dollars' worth of jewels to shift out of a country where the only people he can trust are his relations. I guess the police will double-check everyone who attended that party when we're eventually allowed to leave the country. Sandy can't cross a Communist frontier carrying anything himself."

"So you think he's arranged for a professional to buy?"

She nodded. "It's guesswork, but I figured it that way. Of course, he'd never part with a thing until he's been paid, but an open draft would do. I imagine he'd chance taking a single piece of paper through the customs. If I should be guessing anywhere near the truth, then he's needed to set up a fairly complicated deal, and Komoro could be the place he planned to do it. There's a government hunting lodge for rich foreigners close by."

"Hm." Martin looked neither surprised nor skeptical, merely contemplative. Attention apparently concentrated on his driving, the only sign he might believe her that they were traveling even faster than before, the little Lada vibrating as the road deteriorated.

She had finished the easy part. Whether Martin agreed

with her or not, and she knew she had strung enough circumstantial evidence together to make a kind of sense, there was no particular reason why he should refuse to come far enough to test the most straightforward of her speculations. Jenny took a deep breath. "Martin—"

"Yes," he said quietly. "I'd like to hear the rest."

It was annoying to discover that he realized there was more, when she had needed to fight so hard against her baser self before deciding to tell him. "Will you come to Komoro?" she demanded, nettled.

"Don't spoil it, Jenny. You are telling me because you want to, not because I've agreed to fall in with your plans."

"Oh Jesus," she said crossly. "Listen, then." And in a dozen bald sentences she told him about Pushkin, the diaries, and Benedek, at last succeeding in startling him out of his calm.

"Where are they now?" he demanded.

"In the trunk," she said with relish. "Would you like me to drive? I've only got to listen, after all."

Helplessly he began to laugh. "Jenny, you devil."

And suddenly she was laughing too, the Lada joining in with undisciplined leaps of its own until Martin pulled himself together as another town straggled off the plain, its streets narrower and more untidy so far from Budapest.

"Well, do we turn back?" She tensed, waiting for his answer.

Characteristically Martin did not question her about the diaries' authenticity; he was used to handling experts and accepted that she was as certain as it was possible to be under unfavorable circumstances. Nor did he indulge in recriminations: what was done was done, and politicians spend much of their time burying mistakes.

"I think it may be too late for that," he said after a pause. "Don't look round, but we've been followed for several miles now."

Who? Jenny's lips shaped the word, but no sound came. It could only be the police. "How do you know?"

"Either they're not very skilled at their job, or don't care whether we see them or not. They turned out behind us about ten miles back. Of course, I'm not sure, but each time a road junction is signed, they close up a little, in case we make a turn." He adjusted the driving mirror. "You watch."

The road was no longer completely straight but snaked between clumps of woodland and undulating farmland. Side turnings were few, but when the next came, Jenny watched in the mirror as a gray automobile grew from a speck to a silhouette, heads bouncing like popcorn inside, stayed there until the turning swept past, and then drifted back again. "What fools," she said aloud.

"They must be saying the same of us. After all, we're doing their work for them by pointing suspicion at Havasi. Or at ourselves, of course."

"What do you want to do?" asked Jenny, studying the map.

It had to be his choice now.

"You've no idea where Havasi is going, except he planned to leave the train at Komoro?"

"No. Although if I had to guess, I'd say further east. The government hunting lodge is that way, by the River Tisza. He told me he'd learned to hunt boar while staying with his cousin last year; perhaps finding other foreigners in such an unexpected place gave him the notion how to carry through a highly unusual robbery."

A sign flashed past them: Kisvárda 10. Kilometers, of course, and Komoro wasn't far beyond. They would have to decide within minutes whether or not to abandon Sandy to his schemes and scuttle for safety while they could.

"We have to try and shake off our escort," Martin said. "I'm sorry, Jenny, but I can't afford to be stopped while we're carrying the kind of diaries you describe. I'd like to get them back to the embassy in Budapest if I could, but—"

This was exactly what Jenny had feared. "They're mine."

"I daresay they are; we'll fight over possession later. At the moment I'm much more concerned that when we stop or turn off, that lot following have orders to pull us in."

Jenny thought about it for a moment. "Because they will have made up their minds by now that somehow we're mixed up with Sandy going to Komoro, so if we turn, they'll believe there's nothing more they can learn by watching?"

"I wish to God some of my hired help at the conference had a literary training. Yes, exactly. They know we've come as fast as we can, stopping nowhere, from Budapest very nearly to the Soviet frontier. If we're reported as turning off now, Nemeth will realize it must be because they've frightened us, guess perhaps we've something on board we can't explain away. So they'll stop us and look. They've enough excuse, even if they found nothing and I made the devil of a fuss. But they will find something, not jewels, but diaries written in Russian. And I've a nasty hunch that, in fact, the police have been just out of sight all the way from Budapest. This lot may be clumsier than the rest; their job is certainly more difficult when we might turn off at any time. If I'm right, then it's us rather than Havasi they're interested in. They'll be wondering about Havasi now, of course, but only because we're heading for the same place as him."

"They couldn't have discovered about the diaries." All the same, Jenny's stomach jolted with alarm.

"You know better than that. No matter how well a secret is kept, once it's there, it can be discovered."

Whether he was right or not, they simply couldn't chance being stopped. "Kisvárda four," said Jenny aloud, and looked down at the map again. "This highway skirts the town to the west; if you take the turning into the center instead, then there's a maze of lanes the far side of the town."

"Hold on to your seat, then." Martin showed no sign of slackening speed, sending the Lada hurtling down a slight gradient, slicing an uncambered curve so fast that for a moment Jenny thought they must plunge into the field beyond. Lada cars tended to drift on corners at the best of times.

"There," she said, dry-mouthed.

The turning for Kisvárda gulped toward them while the following car was still accelerating hard to catch up, taken unaware because they were surely going too fast to turn. Five hundred yards to the turning, four . . . Outraged machinery squealed, the chunky saloon bounding like a runaway beer keg before they were round, two wheels up the bank throwing them back on the tarmac with a jaw-rattling lurch.

Jenny whipped round in time to see the following car overshoot the turning by fifty yards.

"Sorry," said Martin. "It's got too high a center of gravity for this sort of thing."

No time to wonder whether he could be serious, Kisvárda's narrow streets already reaching out toward them. As soon as they reached the first corner, Martin trod on the brakes, turned right, and threaded past some unhitched carts. In the middle of a November Sunday afternoon, Kisvárda was nearly deserted. Left and left again. "You'll be back on the road we came in on soon," said Jenny.

"Yes, I know. I'd like to let them go by if we could. We passed a petrol station on the way in and ought to fill up before we take to the lanes."

Jenny glanced down at the gauge. They had been traveling at high speed for a long time, and the needle showed the tank was nearly empty. Martin pulled in behind a parked truck, and as he did so, the gray car that had been following them went past the end of the road like a squall. The four men inside were in uniform, and Jenny had an excellent view of the front-seat passenger.

It was Ferenc, Benedek's prospective son-in-law.

8

THERE WASN'T A MOMENT TO SPARE. AS SOON AS THE police following them realized they had lost their quarry and summoned the courage to admit it, they would call in help to seal off the area.

But they had to pick up more gas. In Hungary, fuel points were scarce enough to be marked on the map, and once they left Kisvárda, there wasn't another before the Soviet frontier.

"Ask them to fill us up, and see if you can buy something to eat," Martin said as soon as they pulled up by the pump.

Jenny hadn't told him yet about Ferenc; time for that when—if—they won clear. Ferenc here meant the police knew about the diaries, must already have put Benedek in jail, where she would join him as soon as they were caught. As they must be caught, pulled up beside the road while a friendly pump attendant dawdled over fuel, trying out his English on Martin. Jenny had not expected to feel so panic-stricken, had always considered herself reasonably reliable in a crisis. But she had no experience of crises two hundred miles east of Budapest, where the penalty of failure was years in a labor camp.

A woman in the kiosk behind the pumps sold packets of crackers and a basket of apples willingly enough, although she clearly thought them crazy not to search out cream cakes in the center of Kisvárda. "The shop is open," she kept insisting.

But at last the pump attendant finished, a couple of slaps on the roof to say the fuel cap was on. "If they don't catch us here, they don't deserve to find us at all," Jenny said shakily as they pulled out, hardly daring to look down the straight stretch of road that led back into the town.

It was clear except for a horse-drawn cart, but the only way out into the tangle of lanes Jenny had seen on the map lay through the suburbs of Kisvárda. Martin hesitated and then pulled in behind the slowly ambling cart. "I think we'll take our time."

Jenny saw his point, since the Lada was almost hidden by an overflowing load of cornstalks. Even so, it needed a real effort not to yell at him to hurry when all the time Kisvárda must be closing against them. Crawling along like this behind an ancient cart, they weren't so much sitting ducks as paralyzed dummies waiting to be shot. She stole a sideways glance at Martin, conscious that she had behaved badly to place him in such a compromising situation, irritated, too, that he should remain so calm. Her own nerves raw enough for her to reflect that he could afford to be, since debt-haunted Hungarians would never dare to send a British minister to drain marshes, before she felt ashamed of herself for being so unjust.

Without speaking or taking his eyes from cornstalks filling the windshield, he held out his hand—tentatively, as if unsure of her reaction—and her fingers closed on his. Tightly, until they hurt; until that infernal crawling cart reached a corner where they could turn, and he had to twist the Lada through a maze of tiny streets. The police could be anywhere, Kisvárda small enough for every corner to be a trap. Houses gave way to brightly painted cottages; an onion-domed church, a tiny cobbled square, the mound of a ruined castle just beyond. Then leaves flashed yellow against dark earth and they were out of the town again, having avoided its dangerous center, forced to follow a lane across plowed ground so flat they could be seen for miles.

"Left," said Jenny. "There ought to be a turning soon which will take us toward that wood."

Martin put his foot down again, their only safety in such open country lying in speed that would take them away from Nemeth's police long enough for them to decide what to do, but these narrow roads were so rough-surfaced, it was like traveling inside a tumble dryer. Jenny breathed out in relief as trees closed in on either side, but relief lasted only a few minutes. Almost immediately their lane deteriorated into a cart track leading to a huddle of buildings. "There ought to be another turning quite close, which brings us into a tangle of back roads along the river." Jenny hoped to heaven the map was right.

Martin did not argue—no point arguing with nowhere else to go—but set the car to lurch and sob down the track.

The farm was freshly painted yellow; a woman whose face was as rutted as the land about her stood to watch them as they splashed past her door. When Jenny called to ask about a turning, she didn't answer. The track was wet and becoming wetter, reeds growing on either side, the plain already turning into marsh as they came closer to the Tisza River. Martin glanced at her and then away. "Will you drive for a while?"

Jenny nodded and got out to take his place. The sun was dropping toward a vast red-brown horizon and wind slapped at her face, as if to emphasize the extraordinary remoteness of their situation. She was glad to get back in the car and allow driving to take the edge off her thoughts. She soon discovered why Martin had wanted the change, as he repeatedly asked her to pull up while he climbed to reach any suggestion of a vantage point—an occasional

wayside tree, a hummock, the edge of a drainage ditch—
in the hope of obtaining warning if there should be a police
checkpoint ahead. Only when he left his seat for the sixth
or seventh time did it strike Jenny how incredibly their day
had changed. And how, after six months without seeing
Martin, and more time before that when misunderstandings
had soured their relationship, his image in her mind had
imperceptibly become as flat as a photograph in the press.
A public figure, two-dimensional. Now he was acutely real
again; the lover she had very nearly loved and who loved
her still. An ordinary man scrambling in ditches, whose
instinctive reaction had been laughter when she told him
about Russian diaries in the trunk. How shaming that she,
with all her imaginative grasp of literary emotion, should
have fallen into the most common delusion of all: that of
believing public people weren't flesh and blood.

As Jenny had hoped, eventually they reached a tangle of
tiny tracks, most of them little more than unsurfaced
bridle-ways, as open plow-land gave way to scrub-
woodland and marsh on either side of the River Tisza. Twice
they pulled aside just in time to let another car go past: both
looked innocuous, the drivers rocketing along in what looked
like a haze of Sunday afternoon plum brandy.

The way was now absolutely blind; if Martin walked to
the next bend, then he seldom saw more than thirty yards
ahead. "We'll have to lie up," he said at last. "God knows
we need a break and time to think."

Jenny guessed what he was already thinking. In this wet
country they could be rid of Pushkin's diaries forever, and
then it wouldn't matter if the police did stop them. As they
must, very soon.

All the same, finding a safe place to lie up wasn't easy.
The tracks were sodden and bounded by deep ditches, the
woods spongy underfoot. Another nerve-racking quarter
hour passed before they reached a fractional rise in the
ground, marked by a trail that led to some old wood cut-
tings: beyond these the ground fell again, forming a miniature bluff above a mere and giving an excellent view to the

north and east. Martin immediately went back to cover any tire marks that might show where they had left the road, while Jenny stretched luxuriously, breathing deep gulps of cold dusk air. And as she stood there quite alone, silence came roaring in with the wind; all she could see was orange light from the setting sun slicked over wetness, a glimpse of swift-flowing water that must be the Tisza, and misted emptiness beyond, most of it probably inside the Soviet Union.

She felt tired after driving so far and fast; discouraged, too, because in justice to Martin, she didn't see how she could refuse to sink Pushkin's diaries in Hungarian swamp. All the excited interest she had felt in her unknown diarist curdling into guilt as she looked around at marshes where his dangerous scribblings would be left to rot.

A flash of light from beyond the mere showed where a car was coming fast; the bluff offered a good vantage point. Daylight was fading too rapidly for her to be able to see inside as it passed, but tied to the roof was the same narrow package she had seen that morning, outside the East Railway Terminus in Budapest. The evening was so silent and the land so flat that the noise of the engine took a long time to fade; in fact, it didn't fade completely, but seemed to turn where Jenny remembered seeing a farm track leading toward the river when they were looking for a place to lie up. Then the engine changed note again, coughing on rough going, before cutting out just on the edge of hearing.

"That was Sandy," she said when Martin reappeared, and she shivered as darkness brought the woods in closer. The thought of boar living here, creatures made cunning by the hazards of their survival, added another twist to the fierce tensions of a day made up of hard traveling, exhausting evasions, ferocious uncertainty. It was an effort to speak calmly, to turn and smile instead of weep. "I suppose it isn't surprising to see him, really. We've come in a half circle, and Komoro can't be far."

"Was anyone following him?"

She shook her head. "They won't think they need to. He had to tell the police where he was going; they will have checked when he left the train and who met him at the station."

Martin must have caught the false note in her voice, because he came over, the last of the light glinting from the green of his eyes. "What did you buy us to eat?"

Jenny showed him crackers and apples. "That's all, I'm afraid."

"What, no plum brandy? That's what we need."

"I hate it."

"So do I, but sometimes less than others. Biscuits and apples it is, then."

"Martin—"

"Eat first," he said, and she felt that he was smiling. "We shall quarrel all over again if we try to argue now."

"I suppose that's why conferences spend so much time eating," Jenny said spikily. She had expected him to kiss her and this time very much wanted him to; when he didn't, she felt let down and annoyed. A quarrel wouldn't be unwelcome.

"If so, the idea hasn't been very successful." Suddenly he sounded weary, too, and she remembered how tired he had looked when she went to dinner with him; since then he had spent two more days in his conference, seen Nemeth for her in the middle of the night, and driven much of the way today.

"I apologize," she said. "You've been very good. . . . You must be furious at the fix I've put you in, and you haven't said so once."

"Oh Jenny. Only you could say, 'I apologize' like that, without excuse. Don't make things any harder for me."

She looked at him dry-lipped, a laugh half gulped in her throat. "Because anything we do together in a Hungarian wood seems more final than it was in a comfortable Westminster apartment?"

He gripped her shoulders, hard. "My dear, yes. Ridiculous, isn't it? As if it made any damned difference, and you'll freeze if we stay apart." He kissed her then, and she would never have known there was anything wrong except his hands were shaking so badly, the breath rattled in her lungs.

"Martin," she said as soon as she could speak. "It was you I wanted, and not just to be kept warm in a Hungarian wood."

"Leave it, Jenny, will you?" An unexpected edge to his voice, as if Martin Rothbury, politician, already regretted disclosing any weakness. Which wasn't surprising really, reflected Jenny as they chewed dry crackers in awkward silence. Considering he had twice asked her to marry him in the safety of New York and Budapest, and she had twice refused.

"You'd better show me these diaries," he said at last, and turned on the dash light to study the volumes she selected. He couldn't read Russian, so Jenny translated a few passages, but in such difficult light, the scrawled words swam under her eyes. She roused herself at once. "Ferenc. I haven't told you about Ferenc."

He listened as he usually did, without interrupting, his face all planes and hollows in faint under-lighting from the dash. He must be a good negotiator, Jenny thought. "Well, that settles any doubt," he said when she had finished. "Poor Benedek."

Jenny stared out at the blackness of the wood. Poor Benedek indeed. The Hungarian police might hesitate to beat the truth out of her, wouldn't dream of beating it out of Martin, but once Benedek lost his cover, he would be destroyed. "He trusted his family completely; because, he said, in Hungary you can't rely on anything else. I suppose Ferenc and Judit could have quarreled. Easily, really. She was very possessive."

Jenny dozed off soon after that, her mind staggering among images of prisoners lost forever in marsh-floored cells. Cold and horror woke her eventually, quite how much later, she did not know. The wind had risen, and she could hear rain darting against the car roof; Martin was still turning papers under a gleam of light, and looked up as she stirred. "I can understand why you can't bear to lose these."

"I guess I haven't a choice anymore, since the police must have the whole area surrounded by now." Both she and Martin would be in different kinds of appalling trouble if they were caught with Soviet diaries, but Benedek would certainly die as soon as he could be confronted by hard evidence of treason.

"I think I could name your author for you." Martin stared at a drawing meditatively. "Berdeyev. Head of the Soviet delegation to the financial conference at Budapest. That's him." He held the book so she could see a grave, bespectacled gnome perched cross-legged on a pile of folders.

"How do you know?"

"You said he was very likely with the Soviets in Budapest, and Berdeyev's the right age. He's also an annoying, querulous gadfly of a man, a firm Gorbachev supporter and the only Russian I've met who negotiates by trying to get behind my mind."

Jenny nodded. That was Pushkin's diarist to the life; she was impressed that Martin had summed him up so well without being able to read his text. "Are you surprised to hear he's planned to defect to the West and live in comfort off his royalties?"

"Astonished. No, more than that. I don't believe it. Berdeyev must be over seventy and told me only a few days ago that he was worried about his wife, who is ill in Moscow. They've been married fifty years, and he spoke of her with the affection of an otherwise lonely man."

Jenny looked at him sharply, realizing that only some quirk of fellow feeling could have led an elderly Russian who understood other men's minds to confide so personal an anxiety to a stranger. In spite of his gifts, perhaps because of them, Martin, too, was a lonely man. "Then—"

"If your Pushkin is indeed Berdeyev's son, I think he

must have stolen his father's diaries without his knowledge. For money, presumably."

Jenny flicked over the pages on her knee, remembering the almost tangible passion to kill which she had sensed when she suggested exactly that to Pushkin. If Martin was right, at least Pushkin's fury meant he felt a certain guilt, even though guilt hadn't stopped him from selling his father when it suited him. "What would happen to him if his diaries were published while he still lived in Russia?"

"To Berdeyev? Shot for treason, I'm quite sure. Where selling scurrilous political reminiscences are concerned, the Soviets wouldn't pussyfoot around trying to serve injunctions."

Jenny huddled deeper into her jacket. "How horrible. Not so much being shot at the end of a very full life, but being shot because your son saw a quick way of making money. I shan't mind losing his diaries so much now."

They spoke only occasionally after that, but as Martin had said, it was too cold to stay apart. They did not make love, his body impersonal as they huddled together on the backseat wearing all the clothes they had brought, but as a pale moon floated above the trees, Jenny slept deeply in his arms, a glint of light struck from open eyes her last glimpse of his face.

He was awake when she stirred, too.

"Didn't you sleep at all?" she demanded. She felt rested, but horribly stiff and crumpled; he was still holding her and must be set like concrete in his seat.

"I'm used to kipping in the House of Commons," he answered lightly. "Jenny, I've been thinking. I think we should hide those diaries and not destroy them yet."

Her heart leapt. Last night she had been all self-sacrifice and nobility, trying to think about the consequences to others if she was caught; but what she really wanted was to take those diaries back to New York in triumph, devise a way to negotiate publication without killing the man who wrote them, and enjoy every moment of the excitement.

"Do you think we could find somewhere safe enough to leave them?"

"Finding somewhere dry will be the problem, I imagine. Enough trees here to lose anything you want." He heaved himself out of the car. "We both brought weatherproof jackets; we'll have to do the best we can with one of those."

They found a fallen tree not far from the bluff where the ground was a few feet above the marsh, and lined the space beneath it with spare clothes. Then they packed the books into such cover as the tree provided before banking earth and leaves against it.

"You'd have to bring dogs to find them if you didn't know where to look," said Jenny when they finished.

Martin looked round, eyes narrowed, committing a pattern to memory that would, with luck, guide someone else to this spot. "They'll be indecipherable within a few weeks, and snow must lie several feet deep hereabouts quite soon. Still, we've won a respite while some of the uproar fades."

The mere was well screened, and they both washed hastily in icy water. Martin insisted on shaving, too, and Jenny kept watch while she waited for him. There was plenty of activity on the road beyond the bluff; at first she thought it was simply Monday morning traffic, although the Tisza marshes were not the kind of place you'd expect many people to travel far to work. Then the hounds began to bay.

"It's the boarhunt," she said when Martin reappeared, looking chafed around the jaw. "And there isn't any reason now why we shouldn't try to watch what Sandy does. I suppose it might be better if the police didn't see us, but if they did—well, I doubt whether we could think of a better explanation for the strange way we've behaved than telling them some of our suspicions about the robbery."

"No. I'm sorry, Jenny, but I have to be back in Budapest early tomorrow morning, preferably without creating an international incident with the Hungarian police. Fine fools we should look anyway, haring around country like this trying to keep experienced hunters under observation without them noticing."

"Well, I'm not tamely giving up, but if you have to go, then it oughtn't to be too difficult to thumb a lift back to the station at Komoro," Jenny said sharply. "Then when you see him, you'll be able to explain to nice Inspector Nemeth that I'm still looking for my pearls in the Tisza marshes. With luck, it'll take his mind off Pushkin's diaries long enough for British intelligence to ooze around searching for fallen trees."

"You know perfectly well I can't leave you here." Martin jerked open the car door for her, adding: "And that is the first time I've been glad you didn't fancy the idea of marrying me."

She did not answer, wondering why Martin so often brought out the worst in her. She wasn't usually a bitch, yet with him she too often tried to score cheap points. Nor could she apologize again, when yesterday apology had been something he loved in her. She also needed to be clear about one thing in particular: Martin was a tough, well-armored man, not easily hurt except by her. As she was a sophisticated and ambitious woman so absurdly sensitized by him that every trifling mistake burst like shell fire in their faces.

Because of it, she had decided six months ago that they must finish with each other, after a mistake of his caused her more hurt than was reasonable.

Because of it, he wanted to marry her.

The difference between them was that he knew what he wanted and was willing to gamble on winning, while she admitted defeat and withdrew. She hadn't thought of it like that before and hated thinking of it now, especially when she had always believed she enjoyed taking risks. And yet, as they both in their different ways had realized, no compromise between them was possible: double or quits, no other answer.

"I've changed my mind," Jenny said. "We'll leave Sandy to stew and go back to Budapest."

"Why?"

She laughed. "I don't want you wondering for the rest of your life whether I married you out of gratitude, after I forced you to stay behind in the Tisza marshes."

He stalled the engine, slewed in his seat, and sat staring at her, eyes narrowed. "You changed your mind, you said."

"Yes."

He gave a grunt that might have been amusement. "Just like that."

"No. Like a lot of things I've come to see about you. If you still want to do such a crazy thing as wreck your career for me, then I've just decided that I can be crazy, too. Although I still think I shall make you the devil of a wife."

"My love . . . at least life won't be dull, if these past two days are anything to go by. You are sure? Or ought I to start explaining what an opinionated bastard I am, so you can take fright again?"

"I know you are," answered Jenny, smiling, and as he kissed her, subconsciously she acknowledged, not without derision, that after all, it had only taken the extraordinary events of the past few days to jolt her into behaving like a romantic. To give up any hope of recovering her Keszthely necklace because Martin mattered more; most probably she would also be forced to transfer Marshall's Literary Agency's rocky fortunes to the even more uncertain chances of London. A fateful decision taken and a colossal gamble now begun, because once love comes, then gambles are quite commonplace. When had love come? A love that was altogether different from, yet also part of, the sensual joy she and Martin had shared before; deeper than tenderness and more enduring than shared interests, yet would draw strength from both . . . Oddly enough, she knew the answer exactly. It had been born in the moment when Martin thought so little of his own importance that his first reaction had been laughter when she told him the diaries were hidden in the Lada's trunk.

Its cramped front seat resisted prolonged romance, however, and quite soon they also became aware of noise coming nearer: hounds barking, men calling, undergrowth crunching. Engines revving, too, and in both directions on the track, which meant they couldn't simply drive away until after such an unexpected concentration of traffic passed.

"The hunt, they're coming this way," breathed Jenny.

"Out, quickly. Don't slam the door." Martin whipped out the keys. "A car pulled off the road shouldn't rouse too much curiosity when most of the neighborhood seems to be beating up boar today. With luck, they'll miss us if we cross into the undergrowth and wait."

No time to discuss alternatives, and the logic of crossing the road was obvious, since by the sound of it, the hunt was keeping to drier ground, where hounds could pick up scent more easily than along soggy riverbanks. If they could keep out of sight somewhere closer to the river while beaters and huntsmen passed, then they ought afterward to be able to drive away undiscovered. Offer their suspicions of Sandy Havasi to the police as an excuse for bad behavior, and profess ignorance of everything else.

The moment they crossed the road, the going immediately became very rough. The ground was tussocked, and saplings grew between reed-choked pools, although too scantily to provide much cover. If it hadn't been for the inconvenient fact that the diaries' hiding place was too close by for safety, soon neither of them would have minded much if they had been discovered. Flies bit and crawled over their faces; neither of them was dressed for the wilds nor used to such punishing effort.

The hounds continued to sound uncomfortably close, however, and a great many voices were whooping them along. Only as Martin and Jenny plunged into ever wetter ground did noise begin to diminish slightly. Then, as the trees thinned, they saw a cold, wide river; several ramshackle landing stages were dotted along its bank, and two men stood talking under the cover of a clump of trees. One of them was Sandy, wearing leather and carrying a thick-hafted spear over one shoulder, the other a well-fleshed, good-humored-looking man dressed in checked knicker-bockers and slapping at flies with a plumed Bavarian hat.

"We're not the only ones who thought water would keep the hounds off a scent," whispered Jenny. She felt triumphant; never, even in imagination, had she believed that her intuition over what ought, somewhere, to be going on would quite so resoundingly be proved right. And at the very last moment, too, when they weren't looking for Sandy anymore. She chuckled to herself. It would be too much to hope that doing what Martin wanted would always bring her such swift reward.

Yet now they had reached within sight of the one spot in all Hungary where she wanted to be, they were too far away to hear what was being said. If Sandy and the other had been valuing jewels, then that part of their business appeared to be finished; if a bargain was being struck, then she might as well have stayed in Budapest for all the good she was doing here.

She could feel Martin watching her; he knew how much she wanted to risk everything on the chance of getting closer. The undergrowth was alive with small creatures, too—frogs and rabbits and a great deal else besides—all scurrying to escape from hounds and beaters in their woods. The sounds they made might help to cover stealthy movement.

"What do you think?" Her lips just framed the words. She knew darned well what he thought: it was time for respectable citizens to retreat and start searching for the police.

Certainly there was too little cover for them to reach anywhere near where Sandy stood without being seen, and Jenny herself felt at a loss over what more they could do. Then she remembered how, a little further back, they had crossed a narrow path that followed a bank of drier ground, probably linking the scattered settlements along the river. Both Sandy and the stranger would need to pass that way,

Sandy to rejoin his fellow hunters, the other to saunter back wherever he was staying. Now so much had turned out as she guessed, Jenny would have laid a handsome bet that Bavarian Hat was staying at the government hunting lodge a dozen miles off by road, less than four perhaps along the river. It would be worth waiting by that path to check and perhaps with luck to overhear some final instruction or remark.

Then she and Martin would have to decide what to do next, although really Jenny was beginning to feel quite reconciled to the police, now she possessed a good deal more than supposition to offer them. It was horribly wet and cold scrambling around in scrub, and providing they could put some distance between themselves and the diaries' hiding place before they were stopped, then with Martin's official position to make the Hungarians watch their step, there must be a reasonable chance of bargaining with Nemeth: information in exchange for the Keszthely necklace back. And no questions asked about any alleged illegal export of national treasures, either.

By the time they reached the path, the beaters had gone past somewhere closer to the road, barks and shouts already fading into the distance while an ancient peace flowed back where they had been. There was more cover here in which to wait, a tangle of thicket sprouting out of old drainage ditches on either side of the path. Sandy would never discover them there, and after they had seen and heard whatever there was to see and hear, they could return unmolested to the Lada: Jenny nearly laughed at Martin's expression when, in murmured exchanges while they waited, she agreed to withdraw as soon as it was safe. He had expected a fight and wasn't sure what else she might still have planned.

"No traps this time," she whispered. "Call it an engagement present if you like. You would have come further than you wanted with me; so I'll agree to leave quicker than I'd choose. Compromise, the secret of successful marriage."

"You're going to find it all a terrible strain," he answered dryly. He also smiled and held her while they shivered together, waiting for Sandy to go past.

The small creatures of the marsh were settling back into their routine; Jenny watched two squirrels climb leisurely down from their refuge in a birch, the larger looking round at its mate before both flicked their tails in self-congratulation. Like Martin turning when I stumbled in wet bog, she thought, amused, then stiffened as the squirrels, after a moment of panic, scuttled swiftly back up the birch. At first she couldn't see anything, only darker undergrowth and softly moving branches, but when she looked again, something more solid than leaves and darkness stood to one side of the squirrels' tree.

Moving quite slowly, an old boar was snuffling along the ditch.

Jenny was amazed by its size. Without thinking clearly about it, she had supposed wild boar would be a wirier variety of farmyard hog, but this one must have eluded the hunters for a long time, developing more cunning and muscle with each year that passed. Its hide was scarred and looked like asphalt; red eyes flickered warily. Its tushes were curved and dark yellow above a wriggling, suspicious snout. It must have measured nearly four feet high at the shoulders, solid gristle poised on delicate small feet.

Jenny breathed out carefully, feeling Martin's hands wire-tight on her shoulders. She thought she had held her breath ever since she first saw the boar, still coming slowly toward them while rooting nonchalantly below those swiveling eyes. Perhaps it hadn't seen them, the wind blowing boar stink in their direction while keeping their scent away from that questing snout.

If they stood absolutely still . . . perhaps the boar would never see them.

They hadn't a hope in hell of doing anything except stand still, weaponless as they were.

Draggingly, the minutes passed, and Jenny began to think all would be well. She sensed that the boar knew they

were there, but it had come fast and far to escape the hunt
and seemed willing to accept a truce. Then, without warning, too many things happened for an edgy boar to accept.

Sandy and his friend came walking noisily from the direction of the river, the scent of tobacco alien on the wind.
A rabbit started out of the undergrowth ahead of them,
almost immediately scented boar and still more humans,
and tripped into a pool in its terror to escape. The boar
started round and paused, head swinging from Jenny and
Martin to this new set of enemies, which this time cut off
its escape.

Sandy said something and laughed, turning to face his
companion with his spear carelessly sloped over one
shoulder, and the boar's senses, already unsettled by the
hunt, were triggered by such gratuitous disturbance. Shaking his hide, he pawed the ground for an instant and then
launched straight into a charge, experience having taught
him that chances at unsuspecting enemies seldom lasted
long. Jenny and Martin shouted a warning in the same instant, no calculation left except to save a life. Sandy shied
in astonishment at such a totally unexpected interruption
and leapt round, only to see six hundred pounds of boar
already hurtling toward him.

He was very quick. The spear snatched from his
shoulder and the butt grounded to accept a shock he
couldn't hope to hold alone, but he lacked the handful of
seconds he needed to brace and poise himself. A creature
of such weight delivering a charge at a standing man must
be taken with thighs and spine and upper arms precisely
balanced, or its sheer power would overwhelm him.

Jenny felt Martin shove her roughly into the bushes as
he scrambled to reach the path, shouting to distract the
boar. With terror compacted from throat to stomach, she
picked herself up just as Sandy was flung backward by the
charging boar, the spear ripped out of his hands.

The boar dipped its head almost contemptuously as it
passed, the slashing blow with upthrust tusk so quick that
for a moment Jenny thought Sandy was only trampled.

Then blood burst through his leathers where he knelt moaning on the path.

The boar turned and waited, watching them.

The boar, still very close. Beyond it, Sandy knelt on the path while his companion stared, jaunty hat still in his hand. And Martin, frozen where he stood between Jenny and Sandy, his hands empty, shouts dried on his lips. It had all happened so fast that only the boar grasped exactly where its best chance of survival lay.

It grunted and charged again, the spear flapping in its side.

How Sandy came to his feet, only the gods of strife might know, and also perhaps the men who worship them, of whom Sandy Havasi was one. Buckle-kneed, somehow he avoided the boar's charge and grasped the spear as it passed, wrenching it clear of flesh and bone. The boar squealed and swerved sideways, tusks and man a melée of blood-soaked mud.

The spear was tossed aside, and through a mist Jenny saw Martin stoop to grasp it. A scream filling her mouth, because only pride could drive a man without a single hunter's skill to try and save an already forfeit life, with the almost certain loss of his own as the price. As she blundered down the path with heart flailing against her ribs, she saw Martin drive the spear awkwardly underarm but fast at the boar's flank, and in terror remembered how Sandy had said there were only two places where you could kill so grossly armored a creature with cold steel. But this boar had been hurt: twice by Sandy and now driven off the rags of a man by slicing pain. It retreated a few paces and stood, considering.

"Martin," Jenny croaked. And saw Sandy's hunting knife lying in the blood beside his body, darted forward to snatch it. Before she could straighten, the boar charged again, its eye caught by her movement.

With the low, snuffling moan of its kind, spurting blood but with its head still held ready to slash, it came straight for her. Jenny had an instant nightmare sight of stained tushes and smeared snout; breathed in its stinking breath. But this boar was much slower than it had been, and her desperate, instinctive leap somehow took her clear: she felt a glancing blow on her leg in the same instant as the boar's head turned aside, deflected by a wild stab from Martin with the spear.

From where she lay winded on the path, Jenny watched dizzily while the boar turned again, very weary now, its grotesque legs shaking. And charged once more, directly where Martin stood. He could not dodge for fear of Jenny, when he didn't know where she was behind him; so he drove the spear with the power of desperation into those slobbering jaws, a tearing but not a killing or a stopping blow. The boar came on, and then, less than a pace from where Martin stood, the red eyes bleared, legs shook, and it fell shapeless on the path.

"*Er es verrückt!*" said a voice, speaking German. "And that is the fifth bullet I put in him, too."

Jenny scrambled up on pithless legs, she and Martin holding wordlessly together, scarcely able to grasp that they were unhurt. Both shaking with reaction, filthy, so enormously relieved that nothing else mattered at all.

"This lucky day," said Jenny, close to tears she normally despised.

And Martin smiled, one hand gripping her wrist, understanding exactly what else she meant. Lucky not only for their lives, but because she had not waited to tell him of her love. Then he might always have wondered whether it was only instant gut reaction from death and courage that had made her want to marry him.

Sandy's companion stooped over his body, a silenced automatic held in one hand. "He is dead, of course." He straightened. "Sigismund Winckler at your service."

"A brave man," answered Martin, declining the opportunity to offer names. Ministers needed to be wary over identifying themselves to men who carried guns. "We shall have to tell the police what has happened, but I don't think they will find anyone to blame."

"The police? *Mein herr*, I beg of you! What business is this of theirs?"

"A man has died."

"Everyone dies sometime," answered Winckler reasonably, reloading his gun. Five shots he said he'd put in that boar, thought Jenny vaguely, and still it nearly killed us.

"So you would leave a man's body to rot on the path?" said Martin sarcastically.

"If it was me, I would prefer it to a police morgue. *Ja*, I leave him to rot; why not?"

"Don't be a bloody fool."

Winckler snapped a slide shut on his gun. "Not I, but you perhaps. So let us go together, and you will tell me why you are on this path. An Englishman and a woman on the banks of the Tisza, at this moment out of all the rest—" He shook his head and laughed. "You are lucky I have not shot you both already."

Our lucky day, thought Jenny, and shivered. Winckler's laugh belied the man completely; the laugh of an idiot, very high and shrill.

Nothing else about him offered any suspicion of idiocy. He looked like one of the plump businessmen you saw pouring off trains from the richer suburbs, with smiling lips and clever eyes; out of place in a forest, but not particularly out of place holding a gun.

"Walk ahead of me," he added. "You first, *mein herr*, then the woman. And remember, I am curious about you, but I do not mind too much if I have to shoot."

9

BEFORE THEY LEFT, WINCKLER TOOK SANDY'S BILLFOLD and a flat, blood-splotched packet off his body, too small to contain the jewels, which must still be elsewhere.

But Jenny wasn't thinking about jewels, walking with a gun aimed at her back and her mind scarcely capable of moving past the fact of Sandy's death to this new and infinitely more threatening situation now facing them. All she could see was bare branches tossing in the wind and Martin out of reach ahead. "Keep several paces in front, *mein herr*," Winckler had said. "Do not look round, and remember the lady will be shot first if you try anything foolish." And he laughed again, the same asinine neigh that redoubled menace.

"Stop there," said Winckler after they had walked perhaps a mile without once speaking, and not even the bark of a dog remained to tell which way the hunt had gone. "Turn round but stay apart. I want to hear what you were doing on the banks of the Tisza today."

He was standing slightly sideways, hat pushed back on

his head, the gun pointing so exactly at Jenny's stomach that she felt her muscles cringe. She had never imagined death only the twitch of a trigger finger away and could not have answered Winckler even to tell him the time of day.

Martin's voice sounded strained, too. "We came to try and recover my wife's property. A very beautiful necklace; perhaps you have it in your pocket."

Jenny shifted at the unexpectedness of the word *wife*, and saw . . . Christ, she saw the hairs lift on the back of Winckler's hand as his finger tightened on the trigger. She stared petrified at the black hole of his gun muzzle while her stomach turned to glass.

"Don't move, I said." Winckler's voice was expressionless. "*So*. You came like a pair of *idioten* to recover your property. How unwise. But why come here, eh?"

A pause, as if Martin, too, needed to grope through shock in search of words. "I was not at the dinner where the robbery took place, but various circumstances suggested that Havasi was the thief."

"Why?"

"I would have thought that—now—time was more important to you than explanations of the past."

"It is safer to wait until the woods are clear of hunters. Continue, *mein herr*."

Slowly Jenny was patching thought together again, and she grasped that Martin was trying somehow to stall this new enemy, arouse his interest, because otherwise he would kill them without a second thought. How ironic that they should be held up by some back-streets gunman, a hazard any modern politician feared, yet Winckler did not know the value of the man he held.

"Havasi was careless," Martin said now. "He enjoyed himself and showed it when his robbery succeeded. He liked my wife sufficiently to try and dissuade her from wearing her pearl necklace where he would have to steal it; he also recovered from the effects of the drugged champagne much later than the rest. To us this suggested that he had only drunk it after everyone else was unconscious. He said, several times, he was not responsible for arranging the party which met at the Hotel Korona in conditions favorable for theft, but we recollected that in New York everyone had applauded it as his idea."

Wife. We; our. By every means possible Martin was linking them together in Winckler's eyes, quite why, Jenny still wasn't sure.

Winckler shook his head disapprovingly. "That is bad. Did you tell the police of your suspicions?"

"No."

"Why not?"

"Do you think they would have believed us? Hungarian police are scarcely convinced that jewel robberies exist, let alone detective stories."

Winckler gave one of his jackass laughs. "*Mein herr*, you are right. Havasi said Hungarian police do not understand modern crime, which is nice while it lasts. If it is true."

"We are also in the same line as you," added Martin softly.

"What is that?"

"We came to Hungary intending to take something very valuable out."

"Martin—" Jenny half turned, spun back in instant reflex as his voice ripped at her: *"Don't move!"* She had a blurred impression of his white face with lips distorted by urgency, and then was facing Winckler again, who giggled.

"Very wise, *mein herr*. As for you—" Deliberately, he fired into the earth between Jenny's feet, so grit sprayed against her legs. "Men can do crazy things if you kill their wives, or you would be dead already. But remember, if I must take risks, then I shall take them with your life, not mine."

Jenny stared numbly at torn earth where that shot had struck, and all she could think of was: Martin knew I would be safer if he called me his wife.

". . . worth perhaps half a million pounds." She missed

what he said next, but he must have told Winckler about Pushkin.

"*Herrgott!* Where are these diaries?"

"About a mile away. Our purpose in coming to Hungary was to liaise with the operation which brought them out of the Soviet Union."

The fact that the frontier was so close made such a tale more believable, panic imperceptibly rolling back as Jenny tried to figure out what Martin hoped to achieve by telling Winckler lies. The diaries were worth money, yes, perhaps as much for the sketches as for their descriptions. Sketches of politburo meetings or KGB confrontations were unique, many of the others journalistically or historically fascinating, pathetic, intriguing. But money would also have to be spent on editing and translating the text; when Martin asked her the night before, Jenny had answered that the author might receive two or three hundred thousand dollars in royalties over five years, more only if he was lucky, depending on the whims of public interest.

"I am not concerned with books," said Winckler.

He was interested in half a million pounds, though, she could tell. A thumping round figure that a dealer in stolen property understood.

"You've never had the chance to share half a million so easily before. I told you, those diaries were smuggled out of the Soviet Union. That means no author's rights, no copyright, nothing. Clear, legitimate profit out of worldwide sales once we can get them to the West."

"How do I know—"

"That they are genuine and worth what I say? If I can show them to you hidden in a forest by the Soviet frontier, then it's proof at least of hellish risks taken to get them this far. No one takes that kind of chance for worthless goods."

"I handle books from the East as part of my business in New York. As he told you, I came to Budapest on the chance of this coup, but then Sandy Havasi stole my necklace." Jenny added her contribution.

Winckler pulled at his lip, eyes darting from her to

Martin. Probably he sensed there was more they hadn't told him, hat and knickerbockers merely a flashy ostentation that helped to hide a ruthless and experienced operator. "Very well," he said at last. "When I am ready, you can take me to these books, and I decide. Turn round again and we will continue."

Victory, victory of a kind, since he had not killed them. Yet. Jenny caught the flicker of a glance from Martin as she turned, the only comfort he could offer as, obediently, he turned, too.

They left the path quite soon and floundered across wet scrub, Jenny glancing covertly about her, praying for police. Now, and not later, when those infernal diaries would incriminate Benedek and Berdeyev as well, who had nothing to do with this particular mess. No sign of anyone besides themselves, though, only bare birch branches tossing against a hollow sky. The Tisza came in sight again soon after, a boat moored out in the stream with a man fishing from its stern. Jenny's heart leapt for a moment as she believed this must indeed be the police, using an obvious trick of surveillance, but hope was killed by Winckler. He called out at once as the figure turned, and stopped where they could be seen. "You," he said to Martin. "Walk slowly to the bank and tell him what has happened. He is Havasi's cousin and waits for payment once terms have been agreed. Say he may have the same amount of dollars as he was promised, in exchange for the jewels he kept while our deal was struck. The other payment Havasi would have had—" He pulled out Sandy's billfold. "He can see it if he likes, to show I kept my part of the bargain, but I think a Swiss bank will not like their draft anymore, all covered in blood and made out in Havasi's name."

Martin hesitated. "I don't speak Hungarian."

He jerked his head at Jenny. "You?"

She nodded.

"You go, then. Tell the clod that, for him, everything is the same as when Havasi was alive. All he needs to do is hand over the jewels." He tossed Jenny the packet he had

taken off Sandy's body and jerked his gun into Martin's
ribs. "There is his payment we agreed, in dollars. Persuade
him any way you choose, but keep hold of the money until
you have the jewels. And make sure you succeed, eh?
I-don't-like-people-who-fail." Martin winced as the gun
stabbed harder with each word, but Jenny also saw the
slight shrug and shake of his head, the intentness of his
eyes on hers.

Two hundred yards of sodden ground stretched between
where she left Winckler holding Martin, and the riverbank.
It was during that interminable walk that Jenny worked out
how Sandy had planned to bargain with a man as unsafe as
Winckler. All the advantages had needed to stay with him,
since Winckler would double-cross anyone the instant
money and jewels came together. Exchange of the draft but
not the dollars fixed to take place in the woods, the jewels
kept out of reach on the river until Sandy returned to tell
his cousin to release them. And if Winckler should be
tempted to shoot the oarsman, now or earlier, then he
would soon realize that the current would still whirl both
boat and jewels out of his grasp.

Jenny stood on the last patch of marsh and called to the
boat. Absurdly she couldn't think what to say.

The man stared back at her; he was black-haired and
thick-boned and didn't look in the least like Sandy. "Heh?"

"Can you row inshore?"

"I was told not to."

"By Sandy—by Sandor Havasi?"

"What's that to you?"

"I have a message from him."

"He said someone might try playing tricks, but to stay
where I am until he comes back."

"He's dead. Killed by a boar." She discovered that she
could only think in essentials, was appalled by her own
passionless words describing what had happened. Only
later, if she lived, would she be able to mourn Sandy, quite
genuinely and without caring much about his sins.

Even across fifty yards of water Jenny could see shock

and confusion. Sandy led and others followed; if he was truly dead, then this man would not know what to do. And if it was difficult to explain how Sandy had died, it seemed monstrous to shout it halfway across a river, and then add that she had brought payment all the same. Such deals were whispered, and not yelled at the highest pitch of the lungs.

A long silence followed while black figure, glinting water, and small boat sank into Jenny's consciousness. What would Winckler do if she couldn't persuade this man? Had that shrug of Martin's meant that he agreed there came a point when they could no longer attempt to purchase their lives if it meant risking others?

It took a moment to realize the boatman was hauling up his anchor, rowing slowly, and then backwatering against the current before he reached the bank. "Tell me again what you say happened."

She wanted to scream at him but instead explained, yet again, as calmly as she could. ". . . so Winckler told me to bring your packet of dollars. He said to say that, for you, the deal is the same as before." But Sandy's cousin was a man who did not love words, or trust them. He stared at her, thinking hard about dollars but incapable of accepting what she told him. Somehow, surely, she had to win a fraction of his confidence. "Are you Istvan Havasi?"

He nodded, eyes wide, his mouth pulled tight.

"Sandor told me about you. I liked him, too, you know."

"He brought me the chance of dollars."

How sad, she thought fleetingly, if the new freedom Hungary is beginning to enjoy means only a better chance to covet dollars. "All right. If you put the jewels on the bank, then I'll leave the dollars, too, and we'll exchange."

"Sandor said I mustn't part with anything until he signaled."

Impatience, fear, and fury rose like bile in her throat. "Sandor is dead."

"I think maybe Sandor was killed for his share," said

Istvan slowly. "Anyway, how can I tell whether all you told me isn't a lie?"

"You can't, until you find Sandy's body beside the boar. Except you must know better than I whether an old boar hereabouts is cunning enough to do what I have said. It isn't a story a stranger could invent."

"Old Smartie!" Istvan answered at once, pleased to be back on ground he understood. "He's killed two men, and many hounds over the years."

"There you are, then," said Jenny desperately.

"No." Istvan gripped his oars again. "I couldn't hand over Sandor's property and take my dollars just because you say so. Maybe he is dead like you say, but I don't know, do I?"

"Row out quickly into the current, then, keep down in the boat, and let the river take you out of range." Jenny spoke almost gently, as if relieved that in the end, money had proved less important than the immemorial tie of blood.

Istvan simply gaped at her, unable to grasp so sudden a change of mood and words.

"Go! Hurry, lie flat!" she screamed at him. Winckler would kill rather than see a rich deal row tamely down the river and out of sight, each second of delay a jabbing gun in Martin's ribs as well.

She did not hear Winckler's silenced bullet strike Istvan Havasi, only the splash as impact spun his body over the side of his boat. He must have been dead before he struck the water, because he never struggled once, even when an inshore eddy snagged him facedown against some reeds. Long before then Jenny was floundering back over bog, frantic to reach Winckler in time to make him believe she had done everything she could, but when she reached him, she was so out of breath from terror and exertion that at first she was only able to claw his arm. "Martin? What have you done to him? Where is he?"

Winckler swatted her aside like an insect, hand slapped hard against her head, and by the time the tears of pain had cleared from her eyes, he was standing with his back to a tree, gun in one hand and a crackling handset radio in the other.

"Where is Martin?"

He jerked his head. "Still alive if you are good." He scowled at the river and added, "Because of your bungling, jewelry worth two million deutsche marks is adrift on the Tisza. No, stay where you are." He grabbed her shoulder, driving his fingers into bone.

Jenny could only twist helplessly in that grip, trying to peer into the undergrowth where Martin ought to be. Where he would never be left to lie alone, unless he was helpless. Then she heard sounds: a voice, boots slapping through marsh, a whir of wings from startled birds. Hope flared as she thought it must be the police at last; inconceivable that so much violence could continue undisturbed when most of the police in eastern Hungary must be out looking for them. But Winckler remained relaxed, gun steadily held in his free hand while his head turned to greet the newcomers.

As soon as they were close, he swore at them: three men squelching out of swamp, and she understood that he considered they'd answered his summons on the handset far too slowly. Jenny spoke German, but badly, and only grasped the sense of what they said. One pointed to his soaked trousers and was knocked down for insolence; by the time he had scrabbled up again, plastered in slime, the others had been sent down toward the river.

Winckler transferred his grip from Jenny's shoulder just long enough to hurl her through some bushes and snap handcuffs around her ankle and Martin's, where she had not seen him lying against the darkness of some roots. Then Winckler was gone, leaving his wet and sulky henchman to watch them.

"Martin." Jenny grasped him tightly. "Are you all right?"

"Yes," he said thickly. He was sitting with his head in his hands, and what she could see of his face was green-ish-yellow; so far from all right, the question was absurd, though she couldn't feel blood anywhere on his clothes.

So she sat quietly, giving him time to recover, so utterly exhausted by shock on numbing shock that she failed to think of anything at all beyond relief that he was alive. Dimly she could hear splashing and curses from the river, and after a while Martin stirred, his skin now white rather than green, which probably meant improvement. "You?"

Jenny nodded. All right, she supposed.

"What happened?"

"I'm not sure. I couldn't persuade the man in the boat to take the dollars. I told him—you meant me to tell him to get out if I had to didn't you? Martin—"

"Yes, don't worry. I didn't think a stranger he'd never seen would get far with a marsh peasant, and he deserved a chance to escape. Winckler shot him?"

"Yes, and I'm sure he's dead, although I didn't wait to see. I was afraid he'd kill you, too."

"He hit me as hard as hell across the kidneys. A shrewd man, Winckler. He wanted me out from underfoot, but fit enough to walk afterward. I've always understood that hitting people over the head is a chancy business." His voice was flat but sharp, a man who did not like his woman to watch him being easily defeated. A man used to relying on his brain rather than his muscles, and finding neither of much use against a gun. "Which doesn't matter now," he added. "Listen, Jenny. When Winckler comes back, he'll separate us again at once. If we do go to find the books, we ought to walk into police somewhere along the way, so take any chance of escape that comes. Any chance at all. If we wait for each other, we shall both get shot."

"What a fool you must think me," observed Jenny.

"I mean it. If you see the slightest opportunity, then go, and don't hesitate. We shan't have another."

"I don't suppose we shall, which is why you want me to take the only one there might be."

He wiped his face; he was sweating badly, although it

was becoming colder as the afternoon drew on. "You'll prevent either of us from getting clear if you persist in seeing this in terms of nerve and guts. Somewhere along the line there will be a moment when we might break free. I'll take it if I can, but if not . . . well, you speak Hungarian, and I don't. You'll be quicker explaining something which really has become extremely complicated."

"It has, hasn't it?" Jenny agreed, and laughed. When everything was so close to death, how much better to laugh than weep. "Darling, you may be the hell of a good performer in a conference, but you're not so hot on the banks of the Tisza. All those sensible sentences when going first isn't something which can be argued over. You don't intend to, and I'm not, so that's that."

"My dear," he said, shaken, and kissed her under the mocking eyes of their guard, who spat something rude that both ignored. "How easy conferences would be if you were there."

Both of them were laughing when Winckler returned. "Don't you realize that two million deutsche marks' worth of jewelry is adrift on the Tisza?" he demanded, so much like a priest facing the fact of sin that they nearly laughed again. Except that the spite on his face killed laughter in their throats.

"All the more reason to be interested in a million dollars' worth of books," answered Martin after a pause. A deliberate lack of emphasis this time, but his original half million pounds casually inflated by conversion into dollars.

"Not yet. I told you, I don't like failure. We need you to do some work, that's all." He unlocked the cuffs joining them. "Get up."

To Jenny's surprise, Martin stood quite easily. He straightened carefully and his color was still bad, but of course, Winckler would know best how to paralyze a man with pain while it suited him, and still leave him fit to do what he wanted afterward.

They walked side by side down to the river, with

Winckler covering them from behind. No chance at all with him. There was a great deal of churned mud where Jenny had talked to Istvan, his body hauled out of the water and facedown on the bank.

"I thought he would have kept the jewels on him somewhere," said Winckler, poking the body with his toe. "He didn't, so they must still be in his boat. Fortunately it has not drifted too far away, but we do not see why we should freeze trying to tow it in while you stay dry."

The rowing boat had been swept downstream and away from the bank, but then had snagged on a spit of reeds, the current grabbing at its bows.

"Well, *mein herr*?" Winckler said ironically to Martin. "We have not got all day, or would you prefer me to ask your wife to strip?"

His sidekicks would certainly have preferred it, Jenny thought, feeling their eyes undress her; but first things first for a single-minded man like Winckler. A woman would keep for later.

Martin stared at the river; it must be icy, and the current just beyond the boat looked dangerously fast. "I will try on one condition. If the jewels are there, then my wife keeps her necklace. You'll remember it, pearls and twisted gold, which won't sell easily."

For heaven's sake, thought Jenny, startled. He really is a politician in blood and bone, when all I could think of would be that freezing water.

Winckler merely gave a pitying shrug and fingered his gun, his eyes straying back to Jenny as if such foolishness made him reconsider ordering her to help. "I see you are a born loser, *mein herr*, since I am not in the business of striking bargains."

Jenny watched Martin with a kind of anguished exasperation as he attempted to argue. How could such a clever man be so unwise? Be such a fool, if she was candid. He simply did not seem to grasp that these were people with whom no deal was possible, that only survival mattered when you were stripped naked to face enemies holding guns, as well as the woman you loved as hostage.

Because that was how it was.

Winckler disliked prisoners who attempted to assert themselves, and though he did not recognize the Whitehall manner, Martin's cool detachment had grated on him from the start. Now the chance for humiliation had come, and he did not stint on it.

Common prudence would have forced Martin to strip before he went in the water even if Winckler hadn't, so Jenny was forced to watch a body whose intimacies she knew flounder through bitter shallows, gasping and grunting while their captors jeered.

Perhaps disenchantment is also part of loving, Jenny thought despairingly; at least thank God those bastards do not know it is one of Her Majesty's ministers they have there, the final, unendurable joke.

Not many men would show to advantage in freezing river water, and Martin was no exception. He reached the boat with difficulty and nearly upset it trying to support himself, already far too numbed to consider attempting to climb on board; called back through chattering teeth that it was empty anyway.

Winckler snapped his gun and swore. "They must be stowed there somewhere. Tow it in; there is a rope."

This was an even more arduous task than the outward journey, and in the end Jenny could not bear to watch. Then, when the boat was hauled to the bank at last, it was quite definitely empty.

No packet of jewels. No oars. Nothing except fishing tackle.

A great many diamonds, her pearl necklace, and the Esterhazy rubies, all had vanished forever into the muddy Tisza.

"That dolt of a peasant must have kept the package loose on his knees," said Winckler when they finished scrabbling over timber as if they couldn't believe the evidence of their eyes.

"If you hadn't shot him, you could have asked," said Jenny acidly. She wanted to help Martin dress, rub warmth into purple flesh, but he had turned his back, and she knew intuitively that her help now would be unforgivable.

"If I hadn't shot him, he would have escaped." Winckler sounded as if, for the first time in his life, he wondered whether he had made a mistake to shoot a man. Reluctantly he turned away from the river. "Those books, now. You said they were worth a million."

"Dollars. Yes, more or less. They are bulky to get out, though." Martin sounded breathless, as if ice had formed in his lungs. He was also trying to fumble with the knot of his tie, which Winckler's henchmen thought hysterically funny.

"And you will show me where they are, won't you?" Winckler spoke almost banteringly, his mind still on lost jewels. He no longer took Martin seriously; treated him like the gutted fish he looked while floundering in the shallows. But books! Winckler was out of his depth with books. Like Benedek, he could not visualize them being worth big money. Perhaps because he couldn't visualize it and therefore any figure they were worth would have been extraordinary to him, a million dollars seemed no more extravagant than any other. Merely tempting. Very tempting, when he had just lost jewelry worth several times that much.

So the dismal procession re-formed. Two men ahead and then Martin, still shuddering convulsively from cold. Jenny, Winckler with his gun, and his third henchman bringing up the rear. They seemed to have been trailing through pools and under puny trees with a gun in their backs forever; and behind them two men lay dead already.

Jenny hadn't spoken since Martin came out of the river, but she walked with her eyes fixed on his back, wondering whether he had needed to earn contempt in quite so bitterly hard a way. Filled with dread, too, ever since Winckler's changed manner made her realize that earning contempt was exactly what Martin had set out to do. Now he must mean to use it if he could, to conjure a chance out of nothing. Two of them against four armed men, and contempt the single, frail advantage they had so far won.

10

"WHICH WAY?" WINCKLER DEMANDED AS SOON AS they reached the path again. It seemed an age since they had come to the river and seen Istvan in his boat: an hour perhaps, at most.

"Up to the road," said Jenny quickly, afraid that anything Martin said would immediately provoke Winckler into further rage.

Soon they reached a wider track full of puddles and ruts, which made walking quite as difficult as by narrower but drier paths. None of them was used to wilderness; obstacles and wetness combining with the enormous solitude to make everyone uneasy, their nerves even more tightly strung than before. As a result, they received no warning of danger at all. The two men ahead of Martin had just stopped to wait for the rest to catch up, captors and prisoners alike bunched on the track before moving off again. As they did so, two policemen strolled out of an unseen side path, chatting together and with their automatic rifles pointing at the sky.

To Jenny, the gray uniforms and stupefied faces seemed to leap out of nowhere. Her muscles splintered with shock and a warning cry torn from her throat, the reflex urge to take her chance and run exploded by the certainty that it would be instant death to try. Then, without knowing how it happened, she was nose-down in the mud with a great silence in her ears. "Get up," said Winckler.

She stood, and Martin stood beside her; whether he or instinct had flung her flat, Jenny wasn't sure. There was mud on her lips and black hatred in her heart as she stared at the two policemen's bodies sprawled lifeless on the track.

They had never had a chance, slaughtered by Winckler's ever-watchful and silenced gun before they could loose automatic fire that would have alerted everyone for miles. One of Winckler's men, whom his companions called Loris, was holding his arm and cursing: he must have been winged by a bullet intended for the police, since they hadn't fired at all.

"See what is wrong with him," Winckler said curtly to Jenny, and jerked his head at Loris.

She went, still giddy from shock. Behind her she heard sounds that suggested the policemen's bodies were being dragged into the undergrowth, the stamping sound as blood was kicked out of sight in mud. She did not look round.

Loris's arm was broken, blood pouring into layers of cloth she couldn't reach. Jenny knew nothing of wounds, only that such a gush of blood must be stopped, and fast. She fumbled in his pockets and found a handkerchief, but he screeched like a skidding truck as soon as she tried to tie it above grating bones. It needed every scrap of will she possessed to try again, to concentrate on handkerchief and knot and close her ears to screams.

"For God's sake, make him stop that noise," said Winckler.

She didn't look up, refused to have any dealings with Winckler that were not forced on her. "His arm is smashed. He needs to go to hospital, quickly."

"Will he be able to walk?"

"Yes, perhaps. If he is helped." She was suddenly terrified that if he couldn't, then Winckler would kill him, too.

Winckler snapped his fingers at Martin. "You help as well."

But Loris howled each time his arm was jarred, and Winckler soon stopped their stumbling progress. Jenny sank down beside the track, utterly worn out. At first, when she realized Martin was holding her, she was simply glad he was there; as awareness drifted back, she grasped that Winckler now considered him of so little account that he had ceased to bother about keeping them apart. Which was the first small victory contempt had won.

The injured man continued to moan; the rest of them sat on wet ground in silence to wait for Winckler, who had gone ahead to reconnoiter the way to the road. Two against two now, and Winckler had not even handcuffed them. There ought to be some chance of escape in spite of the guns held by both their guards. But the men watched them all the time, too uneasy to drop vigilance for a moment. When Martin stood, pretending to stretch, one of them immediately tripped him in the mud.

"I think that tourniquet oughtn't to be left on so tight," Jenny said after a while. "I don't know much about it but seem to remember that circulation shouldn't be cut off for long." She wished her German were better, fumbling for the words she wanted.

"We would have to bandage him properly before you loosened it, or he will start losing blood again." Martin spoke English, and she translated, haltingly. Surely, surely, while they bandaged and rebandaged Loris, they could make a chance from somewhere.

After a moment, the younger of their guards, whom Jenny mentally called Ginger because of his orange hair, nodded and produced a penknife, said something about slitting seams. He also stood back and out of range of quick movement, his gun leveled.

Jenny swallowed. She had no idea how to begin to care

for a shattered arm, felt hideously sick when Martin used the knife to cut cloth, revealing bone sticking through torn mauve flesh. By then Loris had stopped moaning and looked semicomatose.

"What do you think, Hansi?" said Ginger.

The other guard touched Loris's cold lower arm. "I think we have to take the tourniquet off."

They stared at each other, enmity forgotten for an instant. "How much cloth have we between us?" asked Jenny at last. "We'll need a great deal, surely."

They hadn't much, they discovered. Everyone was filthy, their clothes torn on undergrowth. In the end they used the men's shirts cut into strips, and Martin's tie to secure the bandaging: but still there wasn't the fraction of a chance to run, Ginger and Hansi juggling guns between them and leaving the unpleasant business of bandaging to their prisoners. They finished as Winckler returned. Although watchful, Ginger and Hansi had not been aggressive while he was away; now they retreated into hostility again, gesturing with their guns and sniggering about Martin standing tieless and shirtless in the mud.

"The road is clear," said Winckler, his eyes darting from one to another as if he smelled something false. "I found the track I think you meant; it is not far."

"No police?"

Winckler's eyes narrowed. "Why should there be?"

"We just met some, didn't we?" said Martin reasonably. "And our car was left quite close to the road. Rental cars have a different license plate in Hungary, and if a police patrol noticed it, they might very well have wondered about a Budapest rental car so far out in the country. Apart from anything else, it isn't far to the Soviet frontier."

"So we find these books before anyone does too much wondering, while Hansi fetches our car. We'll leave Loris here to rest and pick him up on our way out." Winckler even managed to sound quite amiable about the nuisance of having to come back for a wounded man. He looked bleakly angry, though, a useless liability of no concern to him. On the other hand, he did need to reassure jumpy followers that they wouldn't be abandoned if they, too, should be hurt.

Hansi was going to pick up another car. Jenny didn't dare look at Martin to see if he understood rapid-fire German, but he had seemed to grasp the gist of it before. One by one their captors were being thinned out; soon only Winckler and Ginger would be left. Of course, two guns were more than enough to keep them prisoner, especially when one of them was held by a man like Winckler.

Nor did he believe in taking chances. When he went next to check the road, he took Jenny with him, her right hand handcuffed and the slack of connecting steel chain twisted around his knuckles. "Shoot the man if he gives you any trouble," he said to Hansi. "We don't need two of them to show us what they've got." And translated this into English to make sure Martin understood.

Then Winckler went, taking Jenny with him. He moved silently for so bulky a man, the brash checks of his knickerbockers blending like dazzle paint into the undergrowth. He showed no consideration for her at all, nor did she expect any; metal jerking and chafing at her wrist as they threaded through bushes to the road, her arm nearly broken when he thrust her unexpectedly behind a tree. Something was coming up the road, now close to where they stood.

Two vehicles coming, very fast, clashing and rattling over rough surfaces, flying past so their occupants were no more than glimpsed noses and blue-banded caps.

Winckler tightened the turn of chain around his fist, and twisted. "Now tell me what you think about so many police on this one small road. Whatever your stupid *herr* said, I do not believe they are here by chance. Me, I only found your car because you told me where to look. So I don't think the police are here because of some drivel about Budapest plates on rental cars. But they are here. Too many of them, driving on side lanes and looking for something."

Red and violet dots spiraled in front of Jenny's eyes, breath writhed in her lungs, as twisted steel doubled her arm high and higher behind her back. "I don't know! But I've been thinking since . . . since you shot those two police in the wood. They could have suspected Sandy Havasi stole our jewelry, just as I did, and followed him here. Sandy and I were both at the dinner when the robbery happened, and then we both came here. I would think that suspicious if I was a policeman."

Lies were no good against a man like Winckler; half-truth, changed truth, remained their only hope. If he realized the authorities knew about Soviet diaries near the Tisza, then he would understand that no effort would be spared to get them back. The Hungarian police might look for jewel robbers; for smugglers of Soviet documents they would call out troops if necessary: roadblocks, tanks, everything. And the moment Winckler grasped just how much skill and luck he would need ever to get away from here, he would free himself for action by killing his prisoners first.

Imperceptibly the pressure eased on her arm as he thought about what she had said. *"So,"* he said softly, and turned to signal the others up to the road. "We go on now. Then I discover how things really are before I try to leave."

He stood for quite a long time muttering to Hansi once they crossed the road; probably instructions to reconnoiter while fetching Winckler's own automobile from wherever he had left it. As soon as Hansi vanished back up the road, they turned and walked cautiously the other way, Jenny with Winckler still holding the chain that fastened the cuff to her wrist, Martin out of reach behind her with Ginger's gun in his back.

Jenny discovered in herself an enormous distaste for touching Winckler. They touched all the time, but her whole mind seemed taken up by the effort of trying to prevent her hand or sleeve from rubbing his.

"Here," called Martin softly from behind. She and Winckler had passed the path up to the bluff, only one of many muddy ways into the scrub. Once into the trees again, they soon discovered the Lada. What a lifetime had

passed since she provoked Martin into coming with her to
look for Sandy instead of catching the train back to Budapest. And then she had decided, quite irrationally really,
that she would gamble all she had on loving him. Only this
morning that was how she felt: double or quits, all or nothing. An attitude that seemed unbelievable now, when she
loved him for so many reasons she'd never even considered
before, like kissing her in front of a jeering guard. For a
reserved and formal man, that must have been more difficult to endure than taunts provoked for purposes of his
own.

Winckler locked the loose end of Jenny's handcuff on a
sapling as soon as they reached the bluff, which made her
an onlooker to the disasters that followed. She knew,
watching Martin, that he was nerved for whatever he intended but could do nothing to help. Knew, too, that everything was going wrong, because he must have hoped that
Ginger would be left to guard her while he and Winckler
went alone to find the books.

When they turned to go, Jenny began to weep; helplessly, noisily, uselessly. Winckler and Ginger laughed;
Martin stood expressionlessly between them, this time with
two guns in his back. Then they turned and walked away,
leaving her alone.

She understood then exactly how Martin had felt by the
banks of the Tisza, doing futile things because only the
lowered guard brought by contempt might possibly help
them. She felt hysterical, God knew, but had wept in the
hope that Ginger would be left behind to make sure a hysterical woman did not scream. It hadn't worked, and she
realized now that nothing was going to work; Winckler was
quite astute enough to know that while Martin remained
under his gun, she would not dare to scream. And, almost
certainly, there was no one to hear her if she did.

This lucky day.

This fouled and terrible day in which both their lives
would end.

Jenny stared around her at trees and bluff and mere,

where the white mist of early evening was beginning to form, and discovered she was praying. She was not formally religious, but prayed that when death came, it would be quick and both of them together.

She knew she was close to crumbling under repeated shocks and, partly to steady herself, began to try and twist her wrist out of the handcuff; but her skin was already bruised and broken from Winckler's handling, and she only succeeded in making it bleed again. After a while she stood quite still, listening.

Voices and the sounds of movement were coming back toward her through the trees.

"Martin!" she said, her lips slipping helplessly on her fear.

"Yes, Martin," mimicked Winckler viciously. "You didn't think to tell me there's a library of books up there, and not just one or two, did you?"

They disappeared down the track toward the Lada, Martin carrying a pile of books, Ginger and Winckler holding guns.

Ten minutes later they were back, Martin's feet dragging over tussocks. If he felt remotely as she did, he wasn't shamming exhaustion. His pace slowed further as he passed her, and she saw the glint of green as his head lifted slightly, his mouth softened for an instant. Neither Winckler nor Ginger noticed; only she could sense his meaning: I love you, though I may never again have the chance to say it.

This time, no matter what the odds, he meant to launch himself at Winckler. Who, had he not been a supremely careful man, would surely have brought the diaries down in one load, and thereby have burdened Ginger sufficiently to put him out of the reckoning for the vital instant when Martin grabbed at a gun. Which Martin must have hoped and planned for and yet again been frustrated.

As the minutes lagged past, the whole of her life was in her ears as Jenny strained to hear what was happening, unable to believe it when the same beat of feet came back through the trees again. So unutterably relieved that her sight blurred. When it cleared, she saw that Martin was again leading the way, carrying the remaining diaries; Winckler next and Ginger last. Then she saw the fury on Winckler's face and how awkwardly Ginger held his wrist.

"We take these accursed books down to the car and then I shoot you both," yelled Winckler as soon as he saw Jenny. "You first, while he watches. Do you realize the crazy fool tried to kill us both?"

And, quite suddenly, Jenny struggled free of shock, left terror behind because it wasn't important anymore. Wanted to laugh instead at such a ludicrous reaction. Only this last handful of life mattered now, to live it well and die with love on her lips. "A pity it wasn't you instead of your sidekick who got hurt," she said coolly, and smiled at Martin where he stood with his face in shadow. "I suppose you always make sure others are closest to a risk."

Martin dropped the diaries, carelessly, where he stood. Jenny still couldn't see his face clearly, but his voice sounded rough. "You can't kill us. Wait until Hansi comes back, and you'll discover you need us still."

"Pick up those goddamn books!" Winckler's knuckles whitened on his gun.

"No. Listen to me. When Hansi went to fetch your car, you told him to have a look around, didn't you?" Winckler didn't answer; gun, arm, and eye one deadly line, the range ten feet. "I'll tell you what he's discovered. A roadblock not too far away, and there'll be others in any direction he decides to try. The police followed us here, not for the jewels but because they had received information we might be carrying these diaries, which is why we hid them. You assumed they were smuggled across the Soviet border, but they weren't. They came from Budapest."

Jenny wasn't sure what Martin had in mind, when any disclosure was likely to make Winckler even more anxious to kill them than before, but added her mite of gloom just the same. "They only followed us so far as this because they wanted to know where Sandor Havasi fitted in. Now they've lost us since last night, they won't let anyone move out of here without a search."

"I told you those books were worth money," added Martin. "They're worth it because they're full of sensitive material the Kremlin won't want published. The Hungarians don't like the Soviets much, but they understand what they have to do to keep the KGB out of their affairs. So they'll want to make quite sure these don't reach the West through any fault of theirs."

Winckler kicked one of the books so it skimmed across wet leaves and fell open at Jenny's feet. "Then we hide them again. The Hungarian police don't know us. So long as they don't find your bodies until we're clear, we can wish them good evening and they'll let us through."

"You have a wounded man to pick up, remember?" said Martin softly. "And your man there has a wrist I just broke for him and the hell of a swollen nose on the way. I'd be surprised if I haven't marked your face as well. You are also foreign. I don't think any policeman worth his pay is going to let you past a checkpoint without wanting a lot of questions answered first."

Involuntarily, Winckler's hand went to his jaw, and Jenny saw a purpling bruise and blood around his ear. He would have abandoned a wounded man without a qualm, but as it dawned on Ginger that he, too, might be left behind, he exclaimed aloud and, holding his gun left-handed, swiveled to face Winckler.

For an instant Jenny held her breath, almost believing that in driving this wedge of dissension, Martin had at last made their chance. Then Winckler bawled Ginger into silence, at the same time reassuring him that they would certainly leave together.

"You see, you do need us to get you past the police," said Martin blandly.

Silence lengthened while they all stood staring at one another. Cold wind blowing through the trees, curved evening sky above. Each aware of the enormous distances separating them from safety; captors and captives both.

Winckler's gun still trained on Martin, Ginger's wavering between the two, Jenny straining against the chain on her wrist. And because they were silent, they heard an engine coming from a long way off, the changed gear as an automobile left the road to plunge up toward where they stood, the spin of tires on mud.

Hansi did not manage to drive right to the bluff. A door slammed, and moments later he came pelting up between the trees. Jenny respected Winckler in that moment. She loathed him, but he deserved respect; whatever it was that Hansi gulped out the moment he came in sight, and her German was not good enough to understand it, Winckler's gun never shifted even fractionally away from Martin.

"There are roadblocks," said Winckler curtly when Hansi finished. "He saw one on a bridge, and another where the marsh tracks join the road."

"If he went the other way, he would find one there as well," observed Martin helpfully. Just for an instant he was enjoying himself, Jenny realized with astonishment. In contradiction to what Winckler had said by the river, Martin was not a loser but a born winner who today had been forced repeatedly to lose; consequently, no matter what the pain or danger, winning, however slightly, brought its own enjoyment.

Winckler had no time for victories other than his own. "You said you could help us past those blocks."

"Yes, probably."

"Then tell me quickly, and I decide whether it is worth my while not to kill you yet."

Martin rubbed his face, and Jenny understood that what she saw was reluctance. She had guessed what he had in mind, the final twist of scheming he hated having to use. Yet once he gambled on telling Winckler about the diaries and lost, he had no choice. He was forced to use the only remaining way of keeping them, and possibly Benedek as well, alive a little longer.

He shrugged. "You never asked my name, and wouldn't

have recognized it if you had. But it's Rothbury, and I'm a minister in the British government."

"*Verdammt!*" This time Winckler's gun did waver for an instant, so great was his astonishment.

"Exactly. I'm leading the British delegation to the financial conference in Budapest. Or I hope to be again tomorrow. Which makes me a hostage the Hungarian police won't risk having shot in circumstances they can't easily explain. Their whole foreign debt depends on reaching agreement with the Western banks inside this coming week."

"Can you prove this?" Bruised and filthy as he was, Martin did not look like a minister in anyone's government, and yet . . . he did. Winckler spoke automatically, being a untrusting man, but Jenny sensed uncertainty.

Very slowly and carefully, watching Winckler's gun, Martin put his hand into an inside pocket, took out his passport and some official papers. "Accreditation and status in three languages."

"Shoot him, both of you, if he so much as moves his eyes," snapped Winckler to Hansi and Ginger. He snatched the papers and held them to the light, lips moving while he read. He looked up. "So what are you doing here?"

"What does it look as if I was doing?"

"It beats me," answered Winckler frankly. "But I can see that when I've finished with you, the British will have a lot of explaining to do to the Hungarian police." He grinned, good humor restored not only by the prospect of safe conduct through police roadblocks but by visions of immense deals to come on hush money. The British government might refuse on principle to pay ransom for a minister, but matters could be very different if that same minister had been doing something discreditable at the moment he was seized. Still, for Winckler, the first priority was to get away. Only if he succeeded would there be leisure later for interrogation over details.

"Right, boys," he said briskly. "Don't let's waste time; we're going to need all the dark we can get. So if you will be so good as to pick up those books again, *Herr Staats-minister*, we will try out our little game on the police, eh?"

The muscles of Martin's face tightened, but he picked the books up without a word, waited while Ginger unlocked Jenny, he and Winckler following them down to where Hansi had left a handsome cream-colored Mercedes.

But when they would have stopped there, Winckler beckoned them into the Lada, while Hansi turned the Mercedes and brought it down to wait for them on the road.

I wonder why, thought Jenny. The police might be forced to let them through their block because a gun was pressed into the back of a British minister's neck, but they would certainly follow on behind. If Winckler was to have any chance at all of shaking off pursuit, then a Mercedes would be the vehicle to choose.

"You drive," said Winckler to Martin when the books had been stacked into the Lada's trunk again. "Ganss will sit beside you, the woman in the back with me. Follow Hansi and pull in behind when he stops."

So Ginger's name was Ganss, Jenny thought. Not that it mattered. Winckler sat immediately behind Martin, and Jenny was again handcuffed, this time most uncomfortably to the strut of the front seat so she had to crouch to save her raw wrists from further chafing.

After traveling about a mile, the Mercedes pulled to the side of the road, and Martin stopped immediately behind. Ganss climbed out, swearing loudly about his wrist, and he and Hansi vanished into the forest. No vehicles passed, nothing happened during the time they were away. The land might have been deserted. It was, of course, sealed off. Jenny even dozed, too deathly tired to feel even terror anymore, the awkward drag on her arms deadened by exhaustion into a distant ache.

Winckler grunted, and she jerked instantly awake. Heavy, dragging feet were approaching from the trees; Ganss and Hansi bent over to support the man they had left behind, swaying on flabby legs. They heaved him into the

Mercedes, and Ganss came back to flop wearily into his seat.

"We go now," Winckler said, and jammed his elbow into Jenny's ribs. "When we reach the police block, Hansi will drive straight through if he can and not worry about bargainings which may go wrong. But if it is solid, he will stop and get out. Then you get out, too, and walk past him to talk to the Hungarian pigs. Tell them *Herr Englischminister* here will have his spine blown into splinters if they stop us. They will have to radio for instructions, but say I allow only twenty minutes for them to think before we roll. If they stop us then—" He shoved the gun so hard into Martin's neck that, because he was driving, by reflex the Lada swerved nearly into the ditch. "The Hungarians will have to borrow rubles instead of pounds and dollars, eh?"

Jenny's mind was clear, but sluggish. She wished she knew what Martin intended next. Probably he hadn't been able to think further than keeping them alive another hour, when that was as far as anyone could think. The Mercedes was pulling away from them in the dusk, belting around corners the Lada couldn't grip at speed. "It will serve him right if he has to stop in a hurry and gets shot," said Winckler viciously.

Possibly this might be one reason he had chosen to follow in the Lada: if anything went wrong, the larger car was likely to be the prime target.

The Mercedes's lights flashed, dimmed, came on danger-bright. Martin jammed on the Lada's brakes, and they slithered to a stop a few feet behind. Winckler bent over and unlocked Jenny's hands. "Out, now. Remember, it isn't worth my while to keep either of you alive unless I can get out of here." He shoved Martin's papers into her hand and slammed the door behind her, leaving Jenny in the road, unable to accustom herself to the sensation of being free and alone. A single day, and it seemed unthinkable to be standing quietly in a road without a gun at her back.

Hansi was waiting for her in the headlight glare of the

Mercedes, someone yelling in Hungarian out of sight in darkness just beyond. She half turned to look at Martin as she moved away, but all she could see was Winckler's gun, huge and steel-dark against white neck, as if his victim were already decapitated.

Panic swamping her now, the sheer physical effort of thrusting panic back in its kennel occupying all of her senses until she reached Hansi.

"*Antreiben*," he said. Hurry: his voice as dark and menacing as his stubbled face and thick thug's body.

Figures were coming toward them down the road, sharp shadows of guns and uniforms thrown against the trees by the Mercedes's lights.

Hansi jabbed his thumb at her and gestured. He looked flustered, and Jenny could hear breath whistle in his nostrils; he would kill police more easily than walk down the road to meet them.

"I'll go on alone," she said, alarmed that through sheer habit he might open fire.

"*Ja*," he agreed, and added a string of oaths that were probably meant to convey that he would shoot her if she did anything that made him feel like it.

So she walked the last few yards alone, to where two police cars drawn across the road formed a barrier the Mercedes hadn't been able to challenge. Three boys in blue-tabbed police uniforms were spread across the road waiting for her, squinting against the glare and holding automatic rifles. Out of the corner of her eye Jenny glimpsed another, lying behind a weapon in the ditch: possibly a machine gun there.

"Have you radio contact with your headquarters?" she asked at once; no point wasting time on a trio of eighteen-year-olds.

They goggled at her, astounded. "Who are you? No one may pass tonight. You are under arrest." Nervously they all spoke at once, then sniggered a little in embarrassment.

Communist police, thought Jenny, and somewhere a distant shred of amusement gleamed. As the daughter of an exile from the East, she, even more than most Westerners, had been brought up to dread and deride Soviet-style law enforcement; now these untried youngsters represented a security she craved. She tried again. "Do you know Inspector Nemeth?"

They shook their heads.

"But you do have radio?"

They did not answer, as if possession of a radio were a state secret, but she understood from sidelong looks that they did. "Then will one of you please call your superior at once and tell him that the people you are looking for are here, but held hostage. I'm Jenny Marshall, a U.S. citizen, and I need to speak to Inspector Nemeth of the Budapest police."

Twenty minutes, Winckler had said, and five must be past already.

"Please," said Jenny desperately. "Look, probably you can't see it because of the lights, but there's second car behind the Mercedes, and a man held prisoner in it with a gun against his neck. He'll be shot in a quarter of an hour unless I can speak to someone who understands a little of what is going on here."

"I can see the car you speak of," said the one lying in the ditch, a corporal perhaps. "Call up Kisvárda, Joszef."

Thank God, thought Jenny. He sounded older and sensible. "I was given twenty minutes to talk to you, then they said they would shoot."

"I will not stop you from going back to tell them what is happening, *asszany*," he answered courteously. "You came to us, and not we to you. I do not think you will go away."

She raced back, into headlights and out again, to where the Lada squatted, almost invisible to her dazzled eyes.

"Well?" said Winckler.

"They're radioing for instructions."

"Why come back, then, without an answer?"

"Twenty minutes," she stammered. "You said you would shoot if I hadn't fixed things in twenty minutes, but of course I see now that it's going to take a great deal

longer than that while everyone consults the man above."
She could see Martin's hands still clasped on the steering
wheel.

Winckler laughed, his nerve-tearing maniac's bray.
"Perhaps I wait easier than you, *mein frau*. It isn't every
day I shoot a British minister, after all. If they are radioing,
then we are halfway out unless you told me lies." He
wound up the window with a thump, cutting across something Martin said.

Jenny gripped her trembling fingers, absurdly upset she
had not heard what Martin said, although it could only
have been some trifling encouragement. Well, she would
just have to remember that single flashed glance by the
bluff, which said everything between them that needed to
be said. She walked past Hansi toward the police again,
very conscious of the need to keep her back straight and
her mind clear if she was to avoid drowning in that abyss
of panic.

"I spoke to our inspector at Kisvárda, and he told us to
wait but keep both cars covered," said the man Jenny
thought of as a corporal when she reached the block again.

"One of your policemen has gone," she said suspi-
ciously.

"I cannot keep two cars covered from here, *asszany*."

"But—" Jenny was immediately thrown into a fever of
anxiety. The corporal was intelligent but simple, his under-
lings the kind of country recruits who would spend their
service lives scooping up drunks and watching traffic. If
they tried anything against a man like Winckler, God knew
what would happen.

At that moment the radio crackled, and the corporal
went to listen: he stiffened while he did so, as if an invisible superior had stepped out from beneath the trees. "Inspector Nemeth of the Budapest police is coming himself,"
he said when the transmission finished.

"How long before he reaches here?"

"He was already at Kisvárda."

Which was fifteen or twenty miles away, Jenny supposed, trying to visualize the map. Nemeth at Kisvárda, though; it must be unusual for an inspector of Budapest police to stray so far from his beat.

The minutes dragged past. Hansi went to turn off his lights, afraid of running the Mercedes's battery down, and in the sudden darkness that followed, everything seemed to become more horrifyingly real. Jenny felt her lips begin to tremble and put her fingers to her mouth to stop them; the only result was that her hand began to tremble, too. It was cold, and she couldn't remember when she had last eaten, rested, or felt safe: a day and part of an evening, less than twenty-four hours. Eternity.

After what seemed an enormous length of time, headlights came slicing through the trees toward them, and they all stood up. The corporal scuttled to salute, Hansi vanished, and she was pushed to one side as unimportant compared to the ceremonies of greeting.

"Well, *Asszany* Marshall," said Inspector Nemeth. "You are giving everyone a great deal of trouble with your foolishness."

11

"**I** MUST GO BACK," JENNY SAID FOR THE THIRD TIME.

"When I am ready." Nemeth had listened intently while she attempted to explain a situation that became impossibly complicated as soon as she put it into words, adding, almost casually, "You bought some books from Andras Benedek."

"Benedek? I don't think—" She stopped, knowing she was too tired and overwrought to remember lies for long. "Please, we haven't time for anything except this man Winckler. I don't know what he might do when he gets tired of waiting for your answer."

"What answer can I give when you refuse to help with our inquiries into books which may upset our Soviet allies?"

Jenny stared at him, her mind shuttling, but surely she owed it to Benedek—and Berdeyev—not to confess anything if she could help it. "I don't know anything about that, only about the jewel robbery. Listen, do you believe me when I say there is a British minister being held hostage back there?"

Nemeth tapped Martin's papers, and shrugged. "It is possible."

"Then tell someone, for God's sake!"

"I have done so. I wait for an answer."

Jenny sighed, a long, deep breath of relief. "Then I must go back at once and say what is happening."

"No. I will go. I want to see this British minister for myself." He heaved out of the car and slammed the door in her face when she tried to follow. "Stay there. I do not part with wanted criminals once I have them."

He walked off down the road, after curtly ordering the corporal to guard her.

Lights flashed on almost at once, from the Lada, Jenny supposed, when Winckler saw someone coming. Nemeth stood a moment, his bulky figure thrown into relief, then she saw him hold his hands wide before walking forward again, stand a long time at the edge of her sight, presumably talking to Winckler. If Nemeth should guess that the diaries were in the Lada and knew what they contained, then he would order his police to shoot and not care if Martin died. A British minister saved or dead made little difference to him, and only the Hungarian minister of finance might take a different view.

The radio in the car where she waited bleeped its call signal, and the corporal clambered in to answer it, half slewed round to keep her in his sight. So far as he was concerned, she had already changed from a citizen in trouble to a dangerous enemy of the state, and courtesies were forgotten.

"Yes, sir," the corporal said into a microphone and sat rigidly at attention. "At once!" He climbed out and called to Nemeth.

Nemeth called back and the corporal answered; just for a moment he wasn't watching her at all. Very gently, Jenny pressed down the door handle farthest away from him and slipped out, took two steps to the side of the road, and dived into blackness under the trees.

She waited, hidden behind some thicker trunks, until Nemeth came hurrying back, then moved again while the noise he made bawling out the corporal covered the crackle of undergrowth. As soon as she felt soft moss underfoot, never far away in this land of marshes, she dropped to her knees and felt her way silently into cover. Behind her a great commotion had broken out: Nemeth yelling, the corporal yelling, one of the boys on guard by the barrier running up and down. Without warning, he brought his rifle to his shoulder and loosed a stream of shots into the trees behind her, hurtling pieces of branch everywhere.

A shocking silence followed. Then Nemeth said something very soft and deadly before flinging into the car to speak on the radio.

Using the most finicking care, Jenny came to her feet and began to work her way through scrub toward the Lada, while Nemeth was tied to answering someone too senior for an inspector of police to keep waiting. Not far away must be the policeman who had been ordered forward to keep the cars covered, but she would just have to chance him not firing at her when he had already seen her used as a go-between.

As soon as she came close to the Lada, she called out to Winckler before stepping into the road.

"Do you know, I did not think the police would let you go?" he said as she crawled into the seat beside him. "They ought to have known I would not make a fuss, so long as the *staatsminister* stayed where I want him." He poked Martin derisively with his gun.

Martin's collar black with blood from derisive poking with a sharp-snouted gun, his face turned toward her and his expression for once unguarded. He looked appalled.

"You didn't expect me back, either," Jenny said.

"I knew . . . I thought I knew that Nemeth would hold on to you once he had you."

"He tried to."

Winckler laughed. "You mean you escaped to come back here? I never heard of anyone coming back to be shot before."

"It's quick and depends on the company." Because Martin said nothing, she felt ridiculous. Felt bitterly hurt if truth was to be told, since apparently he thought she was capable of waiting in safety to hear whether he had been killed or not.

Then he said, "My dear, I am a fool." And touched her fingers before Winckler had time to snap out of laughter.

Which he did instantly, cramming his gun so hard into Martin's spine that his face hit the steering wheel with a crack and keeping him there while Ganss fumbled one-handed at fastening Jenny's handcuffs again.

Only when she was secure did Winckler sit back with a grunt. "Next time remember to stay holding the wheel, *mein herr*."

And as he spoke, Jenny felt his free hand squeezing her knee, grope leisurely up her thigh, and fumble with the fastening of her jeans. Winckler hadn't cared before that she was a woman, even now was strung so tightly while he waited for Nemeth's return that he didn't truly care, yet he was unable to resist the urge to pass the time in tormenting.

Hostages have no rights, least of all hostages of wealth or position. This Martin had known, while she only now began to grasp its full enormity. Winckler had held them all day, coldly and unemotionally except when Martin riled him, in case they came in useful. He would have shot them if it suited him, but only became interested in torment when he learned that Martin belonged within the hierarchy of power. Then, immediately, he was possessed by an implacable rancor that longed to watch privilege grovel.

Jenny bit her lip as Winckler's fingers slipped into her open jeans; in near darkness she could feel his eyes on hers, glimpse the malicious, unsexual smile on his lips. In the cramped Lada and with her hands chained to front-seat springs, there was nowhere for her to go. Above all, no movement or sound she dared to make while Martin sat within an arm's length, rigidly facing forward, blood on his face now as well as at his neck.

He had also understood the likely consequences of a single word of affection once his status changed from captive to valued hostage but still had broken his silence when she needed it. Now she must endure the consequences if she could, or watch him split apart by shame because he could not help her or crippled by Winckler's gun barrel if he tried.

Christ, how much longer would they remain stalled here, with nothing to do except share a car with evil?

Four people confined together, the only sound their roughened breathing, the enclosed air drawn tight by rage, cruelty, pain, and harsh restraint. Ganss still holding his wrist; Martin the steering wheel; Jenny's fingers thrust into front-seat springs as if the bite of metal could keep her mind away from—

Winckler's breath whining deeply in his throat while he waited for the moment when she couldn't, humanly, keep from shifting under his fingers; the gun in his other hand poised to slash at Martin, his mouth puckered into mockery.

Ganss stirred and wound down the window. "Someone's coming."

A moment later Inspector Nemeth came crunching down the road toward them.

"Tell him that's near enough, and keep his hands where I can see them." Winckler's fingers were gone from inside her pants instantly, his own life far more important than any woman.

Nemeth stopped a couple of paces from the car and held his hands wide. "I still have not received any orders."

"Ask him whether he spoke to this finance minister the Englander named."

Jenny translated, and Nemeth shrugged. "Yes, but he is thinking about it. Unlike Western nations, Hungary is not accustomed to dealing with hooligans and decadence."

"They don't think you are as valuable as you thought,

eh, *Herr Englischminister*," Winckler said, and this time wrung a grunt out of Martin with his gun.

"For the love of God!" cried Jenny, in anguish. "You want him to be able to drive, don't you?"

"*Ja, mein frau*, I do. Tell this policeman that I think he is trying to make a fool of me by wasting half the night. If he has spoken to this minister of his, then he has received orders, one way or the other. In two minutes I start up my engine and drive for the barrier. If he does not pull his cars aside, the Englander will have a bullet through his spine for the Hungarian government to explain to the British, whom I do not suppose they have told yet about anything happening here. Then his police will still have us to hunt through the trees in the dark." Winckler bawled at Hansi in the Mercedes, and its lights immediately came on.

Nemeth turned on his heel without a word and strode back toward the barrier.

"I have allowed the swine to delay too long already." Winckler slapped at Martin with the back of his hand. "Stay close to Hansi when he moves. This time I keep my gun in your wife's belly, so be careful, even over how hard you hit the potholes."

And as he laughed his idiot's laugh, Jenny felt steel where his fingers had been. Of the two she preferred the gun, quite simply thankful it was away from Martin's neck.

"If she is harmed, I will crash the car at the first blank wall I see," said Martin harshly.

"Then you and not I will be her killer," answered Winckler agreeably. "A bullet in the crotch can be recovered from, after all. Go now and keep very close."

The Mercedes pulled away ahead of them, exhaust fumes blowing in chill air, gathered speed, and flung itself up the short stretch of road. Jenny thought of those police cars across the narrow junction ahead and felt every muscle in her body tighten, then they were past, men leaping aside as the Mercedes sideswiped one of the cars that was still reversing out of their way, sending it into the ditch and giving the Lada a clear run up the open track ahead. Ganss pumped a couple of shots out of his window as they passed; Winckler never moved, as if he had all along been completely confident that the police would let them through.

The Mercedes quickly outpaced them down the narrow road, its expensive springs absorbing potholes while the Lada fell heavily into each one.

"I told you to keep up," spat Winckler.

"Take your gun out of my wife's stomach and rest it on your knees. Otherwise I refuse to take the risk of high speed over such a surface," answered Martin.

For an instant Winckler hesitated, then Jenny felt gouging steel withdrawn. Now they had started, he could not afford to exercise his mastery quite so capriciously as before.

"Jenny?"

"Yes," she said shakily. "It's on his knees."

"Tell me if he tries to hurt you again." Martin put his foot down as if acknowledging the limits of any bargain he could hope to strike, and the Lada leapt in the air as it hit the next rut at fifty miles an hour, slashed twigs from trees growing either side of the lane, and shot over the summit of a miniature rise to see the Mercedes just turning on to a wider road ahead.

Turning left or westward, before switching back into a maze of narrow tracks that seemed to last forever, then turning west again, this time onto the main autoroute for Budapest. Jenny never afterward retained any impression of that early part of their journey: scrub flicking past, ditches, an empty countryside flowing away on either side, occasionally punctuated by lone specks of light. Ganss screeched with pain on the rough surfaces, hammering with his good hand at Martin's arm and begging him to slow down. He took no notice, and eventually Winckler slammed the side of his gun against Ganss's head, so he fell back whimpering in his seat. Winckler did not speak and immediately returned to nursing his gun on his knees; if it had still been crammed in her stomach during such rough motoring, Jenny would have been in agony. Matters were bad enough as they were. At each leap of the car, her wrists snagged tight, and because she needed to lean forward if she was to ease the pressure on them, her face jolted against Ganss's seat. After he slumped back, she was able to turn her cheek against his shoulder instead of edged upholstery; he did not notice, and it helped reduce some of the shocks.

Once they reached the autoroute, relief was immediate. Their passage remained rough, since the Lada was not built for very high speeds and was beginning to protest under the fierce treatment it had received, but at least the curves were gradual and the surface good.

At first the Mercedes almost vanished, then Hansi must have realized that if he used his speed to pull too far ahead, he became completely vulnerable. Police would be stationed ahead of them as well as following on behind; if there was room to shoot him off the road without hurting the hostages in the Lada, then they would do so.

Jenny saw his rear lights flash on again, and soon afterward they caught up, in time to snake through a darkened town and see police and an armored car drawn up in its square.

"Much good the army will do now their government has decided it wants you kept alive, eh, Englander?" Winckler said, and slapped the seat in delight. "Keep very close, or they will shoot poor Hansi."

"We're close enough at this speed," answered Martin curtly.

"I said, closer. If they think they can pick him off without crashing us, they will do it." Quite calmly, he rolled down his window, took aim at an elderly Hungarian cycling in the dark, and fired. They heard a scream as bicycle and man snatched into the dark behind them. "I shoot to kill the next person we see unless you go closer."

The balance of terror swinging against them again. Jenny hid her eyes in Ganss's sweater, sickened by hideous, heedless violence; felt the Lada jerk as Martin instinctively lifted his foot from the accelerator as the cyclist swerved, then the engine bit again. When she looked up, the Mercedes's rear window was filling their windshield, red light thrown back in their faces as if to stain everything with the dye of fear. Ganss's slack body, Winckler's fingers curled tightly round his gun, all glowing crimson; sweat trickling like blood down Martin's jaw as he hunched forward, needing every scrap of concentration he possessed to keep two cars of unequal power from crashing as they raced in tandem headlong through the night.

Jenny put her head back on Ganss's shoulder, so exhausted by shock and pain that, incredibly, she must have dozed again.

She wasn't sure how much time flowed past while she swooped giddily between one nightmare and the next. Longer than she realized, because when she looked up again, she saw a sign flash past that said Budapest 55.

There seemed no traffic except themselves; probably the police had cleared the road, surely must have cleared it after what happened to the cyclist. The Mercedes still loomed as lethally as ever immediately in front; Winckler was saying something, Martin answering. Very gingerly, Jenny eased herself upright and began to concentrate again. She felt unbelievably dirty, stiff, and bedraggled, but something in the way Winckler sat, an undercurrent in his voice, told her they had come close to where he intended to make his bid to escape police surveillance.

By twisting awkwardly in her seat, she could see about a mile behind them a posse of lights keeping pace with their flight. Figures also guarded every crossing, sometimes beside a half-track or armored car, watching which way they went but without interfering. Yet Nemeth's superiors would never tamely let them cross Hungary's borders, must suppose that by heading for Budapest, Winckler hoped to shake off pursuit in the city's mesh of streets. Possibly Winckler calculated that the police might weaken their vigilance, even if only fractionally, as the capital came closer and they planned how to stop him from doing precisely that.

But the Hungarian authorities had not yet learned what a master of the unexpected a man like Winckler was; the kind of man who could cobble together a whole new strategy out of the ruins of the old. "Turn when Hansi does," he said now. "Pass him when he stops, and then pull up immediately."

Martin grunted; he must be utterly exhausted, Jenny thought. Anyone would be exhausted by driving two hundred miles in such murderous conditions even if they started fresh, and he had been so very far from fresh when they began that it didn't bear thinking about.

Next time Winckler cursed him for drifting back from the Mercedes, he took no notice, allowed twenty yards to grow between the two cars; the relief of even a fraction more space for error was immediate. A straggle of dark cottages coming up, but no one on the street. No time to think, either, because the Mercedes was already turning, its lamps glowing like bonfires as Hansi punched the brakes and wrenched thoroughbred engineering through ninety degrees on howling tires.

The inevitable police patrol that had been set to watch the junction was forced to leap for its life, a scream of anguish as the Mercedes hit and then jolted over a body that had moved too slowly. The Lada needed every fraction of the space Martin had given it to take such a turn at speed, swaying soddenly on the corner before unexpectedly and desperately swerving to avoid the injured policeman lying in the road. One wheel up on the path, Jenny ducking instinctively as fencing shattered Ganss's window, cottage walls flashing past her eyes before the Lada slammed back on the road with a jolt that made the engine screech.

"You crazy maniac!" yelled Winckler. "Do you want to kill us all?"

Martin did not answer, was probably beyond words, beyond anything except keeping the Lada scorching down a tree-lined residential track. Through instinct rather than thought he had indeed nearly killed them all rather than drive over a helpless man, and Jenny felt a long, slow curve of happiness at humanity rediscovered within this wilderness of brutality.

They hurtled over unguarded railroad tracks, and then down the length of a freight yard while bitter air tore in through Ganss's broken window. Left, right, and right again into a jungle growth of factories and unmade residential roads, before skidding across an intersection at a speed approaching eighty, to find fields unexpectedly opening up again on either side. Here Budapest's industrial suburbs sprawled without apparent pattern across the landscape, a labyrinth that Hansi apparently knew intimately.

The Mercedes stopped and, as soon as Martin passed, reversed to block the track behind them. Hansi leapt out in the same instant as a glow of light exploded on the passenger seat, flames spreading rapidly. No room for Hansi in the Lada surely, but he came running just the same. Hansi alone, who hadn't made any attempt to drag his injured comrade out of the blazing Mercedes.

Quite casually, Winckler leaned past Jenny, crushing her back in her seat so her hands snagged and she couldn't see what happened next. But she felt Ganss's door swing open, there was a coughing thud, and Winckler lurched back again beside her. Ganss was lying in the road with his feet still inside the car, Martin half turned, his mouth open as if he had croaked a warning when Ganss was already dead.

Then Winckler grasped a fistful of cloth and collar and heaved Martin bodily from behind the Lada's wheel, thrust him where Ganss had been sitting only seconds before, while Hansi opened the driver's door and helped kick him out of the way before sliding into his place behind the wheel. Martin half out of the car and hauled back anyhow, the door slammed as Ganss slumped clear and Hansi jerked in the gear.

Two more men killed, Loris because the Mercedes was needed to block the road and he mustn't be left behind to squeal information, Ganss because he was temporarily of no more use and Hansi needed his place if he was to escape. Two murders and a changeover lasting less than a minute, the Lada's wheels spinning on stones as they pulled away again. Headlights off this time, twisting and turning among shabby lines of cottages, through stacked building materials and out again into a tiny lane between some trees, down a greasy bank, and into a tunnel, the hum of traffic overhead.

Hansi certainly knew every fence and backyard hereabouts; Winckler might have come this time to buy Sandor Havasi's haul of jewels, but he must have traveled a great many goods secretly in and out of Hungary before.

They came out from the tunnel cautiously. Such a maze of yards, dumps, new buildings, and ragged vacant plots was bewildering, particularly when driving without lights, but Jenny thought it must be a farm track under a new autoroute. The reason Winckler had chosen the Lada was now completely clear. An automobile the size of the Mercedes would not have fitted into that tunnel, nor many of the side alleys they were using now.

Unlike dead Ganss, who had seemed human enough provided his humanity was not too sharply tested, Hansi was a solid brute of a man. Loris had even thanked her when she bandaged his arm, but Loris was now dead, too. Although only two enemies out of four were left, almost inevitably they were the two who seemed to lack a single chink of weakness or compassion.

"*Polizei*," Hansi grunted, and swung the car behind stacked timber.

Winckler answered and both men laughed, before Winckler returned to immediate problems and stabbed at Martin again with his gun. "Put your hands behind your head! Quickly, where I can see them."

Martin obeyed without answering, his laced fingers almost directly under Jenny's nose, and for an instant she rested her forehead on the cloth of his shoulder, felt the unseen twitch of muscle that was his greeting. Irrelevantly she thought how they had lived through most phases of a good marriage within a single day: from acceptance to love, love to exasperation, and on again to understanding; from half-reluctant gamble to irritation when he was made to look a fool; from what she had thought of as his smugness and he perhaps as her selfishness, to recognition of human complexities that only love made comprehensible. And faced by Winckler, each was as exhausted and bewildered as the other.

Now a flick of muscle under her cheek, and both knew what the other thought: some men and women lived whole lives together and never guessed the other's mind.

Very soon would come their best, perhaps their only remaining, chance, when they reached wherever they were going and before Winckler was able to tie or stun Martin out of the way. Perhaps there was another vehicle they must transfer into, a safe house, an aircraft even. For brief seconds they would be two against two, terrifyingly unequal though the balance was.

Hansi was slipping through the back lanes of some village, lights and a road away on their right allowing them a glimpse of traffic drawn up at a checkpoint while police stood by with leveled guns. Wet mud surfaces, huddled workshops, the unplowed edge of a field. Several miles passed while they skirted the edge of plowed-up strips, then Hansi swung the car sharply down again and through what smelled like a sewage farm, following some kind of service road that came to a dead end by some storage tanks; involuntarily, Jenny exclaimed aloud as Hansi simply drove straight on. There was a gut-twisting lift followed by a drop like an elevator as the Lada fell down an unseen slope and they all fell with it, to finish on four locked wheels at the bottom.

"Hansi is good, eh?" Winckler said, and giggled.

Very faintly rotating against the sky, as far as Jenny could see, were metal sewage arms dripping liquid into pools. Pipes snaked between them, valves, piled drums, a single rubble path dipping away into the dark. Many things that would be fenced in the West were not fenced here,

perhaps because vandalism was rare or because of slacker
safety laws. Lights showed all around a flat horizon, but
very few of them were moving, as if traffic everywhere
was stopped, complete and stinking darkness where they
were. They were jolting very cautiously forward now until
they reached a concrete ramp, so narrow they could hear
their tires slithering grit over the edge. At the bottom lay a
curved concrete channel, which, when Hansi drove along
it, canted the car steeply enough to throw Winckler on top
of Jenny. She bit back a cry. Her hands were numb, the
pain at her wrists not numbed at all.

Two against two; what kind of a joke was that?

Abruptly the channel became another tunnel. A culvert
taking them God knew where, in utter, disorienting blackness. A stench like plague pits, sheer panic terror of
drowning in such filth igniting like marsh gas as the engine
coughed, then they were out again and on a wide stone
spillway, the dark glimmer of apparently limitless water
ahead. This must be the Danube and the end of their journey, since the river with its few easily guarded bridges
would finally zip up the hunter's bag the police had already
spread behind them. There were some reeds at the water's
edge and a narrow beach along which Hansi drove to reach
a cul-de-sac of holiday homes, shuttered and deserted at
this time of year.

Here.

This, then, was the end of one nightmare and the beginning of the next. Unless they could escape within the following few minutes, there would be nothing to look
forward to except days, weeks perhaps, of arid bargainings
over ransom while Winckler enjoyed his pleasures with
them at his leisure. The only alternative, instant death. No
way out, no room for even a light aircraft to land, although
that was what Jenny had half wondered about. Surely
Winckler must be crazy to come to such a place as this
when the Hungarian police knew they must still be somewhere between their checkpoints and the river.

Hansi pulled up in front of a villa like a shoe box: the

great Hungarian ambition to own a second home spattered the Danube with structures not much larger than garden sheds.

He got out to open the gate, which just for a moment meant they were two against one, and Jenny felt Martin tense. She tensed, too, ready to fling sideways against Winckler's gun arm. But he was completely, dismayingly, ready. His foot slammed down on the chain holding her wrists so she lurched forward with a sob of pain, and Martin half turned, uncertain what was happening.

"A warning, *Herr Staatsminister*," said Winckler pleasantly. "I have brought you safely from the Tisza to the Danube and do not intend to lose you now. Get yourselves hurt if you like, it will not matter to me."

Hansi slammed back in the driving seat and drove round behind the villa, where a scrap of grass divided it from the water's edge. Then he came to Martin's side of the car and stood back, holding what looked horribly like a sawn-off shotgun. Not the shred of a chance for anything there, abject obedience the only possible reaction to Hansi holding an aimed shotgun.

Only when Martin was out and standing under Hansi's gun did Winckler lean down and fumble until Jenny felt the strain on her arms slacken at last. "Stay where you are."

She could not have done anything else, fighting nausea as she eased back for the first time in two hundred miles and blood poured into hands that felt like leather sacks.

"Get out now."

She looked up. "I can't open the door."

Winckler's lunatic laughter yelped between the trees as if there was nothing funnier in the world than a woman too numbed to open a car door. Hansi sniggering, too, both of them a little drunk on the adrenalin of their escape. Then Winckler jerked the door open and scooped her out, a loose grin of pleasure on his face.

Jenny found her legs were clumsy, too, and straightened cautiously, the snap of Danube wind welcome on her face.

Vinckler slammed the car door and turned to say something to Hansi, a numbed and still handcuffed woman no
cause for vigilance. She hit him as he turned, the steel on
her wrists driven at his head with the strength of desperation, and of terror, too. Because in the end she alone was
left to decide that this was the chance they simply had to
take, Martin's life thrown with hers into that single blow.
And because she was slow and clumsy Winckler had time
to hear Hansi's cry of warning and whip round to face her,
so her handcuffs caught him across the eyes instead of
above the ear. He gave a gulped moan and fired his gun as
he tripped. Where the shot went, Jenny didn't know, falling with him and frantic to stop him from firing again. She
was half his weight, and all she could do was hammer the
steel on her wrists again and again into his face until his
moans changed to a breathy wheeze and his body slack-
ened under hers. Trembling violently and half-stupefied by
horror, she nearly passed out, too. She couldn't see in the
darkness, through a darkness in her mind as well. Afraid of
leaving Winckler for an instant in case he recovered his
senses behind her back, panic-stricken by wasting fumbled
seconds while Martin and Hansi . . . Half-frenzied by impatience, she groped with chained and dulled fingers for
Winckler's gun, only truly believing he wasn't shamming
unconsciousness when she lifted it easily from his grasp.

"Martin," she said thickly, and stood. The darkness
hampered everything, clogged her reactions, blew off the
river, lay like soup over fighting she could hear. Vicious,
unskillful fighting like a quarrel between the insane.

But even while fighting Winckler, she couldn't have
missed Hansi's shotgun going off, which meant that Martin
must still be struggling for control of those sawn-off bar-
rels, forced to accept meanwhile whatever punishment the
much heavier and more practiced Hansi dealt him. Like
her, Martin was not in the same league as the man he
fought. He was explosively angry, though, possessed by
the rage of a proud man forced for hour after endless hour
to endure violence and derision without attempting to retal-

iate. He had kept this rage out of sight through a helpless day and night, an effort of self-control that, to Jenny at least, had shown in his stillness under insult, the hoarded words that were all he trusted himself to speak. She hovered, gun in hand, in an agony of indecision while the darkness denied her any target at all.

Then she heard two grunts, vomited on an outrush of air and saw the shadows change shape.

"Martin?" she repeated softly.

No answer except breath laboring in lungs; close, very close now.

At the last moment intuition warned her that Martin would have answered somehow—a croak, a whisper. If it had been he she would have known.

Very carefully she stepped away from where her voice had betrayed her position. One, two paces over wet grass, until she was just able to discern a blacker bulk against the blackness of the river, bent forward awkwardly and searching for the shotgun. At least the brute was hurt.

Yet for a fatal moment Jenny hesitated. She very much wanted Hansi dead but still instinctively recoiled from killing him. And as she hesitated she must have made some sound, because he straightened and came at her. She dodged frantically, the gun so unfamiliar, she forgot it, tripped over Martin lying on the grass and went sprawling. Before she could roll clear, Hansi caught her a glancing kick in the ribs, and by unthinking reflex she curled up tight, trying to protect her head, knowing it was all over after all. A heavy boot was coming directly at her face. She wrenched herself sideways, but Martin's body was in the way; then his hand moved, grabbed Hansi's ankle just above the boot, and thrust it aside, so he lost his balance and came crashing down beside them. This time Jenny did not hesitate. Hands chained together on the gun, as Hansi scrambled to his feet again, she shot him through the leg. The cough of the gun was followed instantly by his screech of agony; as he jerked up his injured leg, she fired again, at the other ankle.

With both legs shot from under him, Hansi collapsed with a whimper, and sobbing from reaction and lack of breath, Jenny groped where she had seen Martin move to deflect that face-splintering kick. Felt him grope, too, their shaking fingers blundering across Winckler's gun and steel handcuffs on her wrists until they clasped, unspeaking in the dark.

12

THERE WAS NO TIME TO LOSE.

When all they wanted was peace and rest, an enormous amount remained to be done, a pack of worries to decide.

First of all there was Winckler.

Martin turned on the Lada's sidelights, and since their eyes were accustomed to a starless night, at first everything seemed brilliantly lit. Winckler was still lying where Jenny had left him, breathing but inert. His face was bloody and his eyes glazed. "Will he live?" she asked nervously. Now he no longer threatened them, it seemed hateful that she might have killed a man.

Even Winckler, whom she loathed.

She felt Martin glance at her. "I expect so, if we get him inside out of the wet. Hansi, too." He went over to the shuttered villa, and Jenny heard the sound of tearing wood. Hungarian summer houses were not built to withstand determined assaults.

Nor, they discovered, was there much inside worth burgling, the two rooms chilly and scantily furnished.

"Let's get those handcuffs off you first." Martin searched through Winckler's pockets, transferring anything useful to his own. A switchblade knife, a credit card in the name of Willem van Koop, a flask of schnapps. "Drink some of this; it'll do you good."

Jenny shook her head. "I'd be sick."

"This looks like it." He stood, holding a bulky bunch of keys. "Now, I wonder which—"

He tried five before he found one that fitted her handcuffs, then snapped them on Winckler as soon as she was free.

Next came the difficult business of carrying him and Hansi into the villa. Hansi was so heavy, they had to drag him, squealing, part of the way.

Inside at last, they were able to turn on the lights, and it disemboweled their faces, revealing features sunk into bone by the past terrible hours. Martin held her then, until time knocked again, insistent, warning him they had to hurry.

"Time for what?" All Jenny wanted was to curl up somewhere and plunge into unconsciousness.

"I don't think Winckler would come to a place like this intending to wait around until the police found him. He certainly planned to ransom me but wouldn't have lasted a couple of days once they really began to search. So he knew how to get out, and from here that means a boat."

The Danube. To Jenny it had been the barrier that finally stopped their flight, but of course, much of the trade of the Balkans used its waters.

"Hansi," she said carefully. "There's nothing we ought to do for Winckler, but I suppose we can't leave Hansi to bleed to death."

"Can you manage to fix him up while I go to see what I can find?" He didn't sound as if he cared much about Hansi, which wasn't surprising; she didn't care about him herself, except for the purely selfish consideration that she didn't want his murder on her conscience.

"The police can't be far. Why not find a telephone and

simply ask them to come here?" As soon as she said it, Jenny knew the answer to that. The diaries. If they went to the police, they would have to destroy the diaries first. Yet by now she was so exhausted, she wasn't sure she cared about the diaries anymore.

"Even if we did ditch the diaries, I'm not sure they would let you go." Martin was watching her face. "At least two policemen have been killed and another injured, that wretched man on his bicycle as well. Nor do we know what your friend Benedek may have said under interrogation. I preferred to see you in Nemeth's hands rather than Winckler's when that seemed the only choice. Now, if it's possible, I want you out of Hungary by dawn."

Jenny swallowed, remembering again about hard labor in the marshes. She had seen enough Hungarian marsh to last a lifetime. "Breakfast in Austria would be nice."

His expression relaxed. "Very nice. It's quite a distance away, though. We need every moment of the time we've got."

Foolishly she hated being left alone.

She had thought of Hansi as pure brute; now he blubbered with fear and pain, clutched at her hands for comfort, and was impossible to hate. But Winckler—Winckler was different. Though he lay quite still with his face and hair sticky with blood and she knew he was securely handcuffed, he remained filled with menace, as if his curse would follow wherever they went, and he come again to trap them.

In her heart, Jenny knew they ought to kill him. Blow out his brains while he lay unconscious, because in his past there must be many other victims, who had prayed hopelessly for this chance that they now held.

Perhaps it was the temptation to shut her eyes and pull that trigger that made her hate being left alone with him so much.

She tightened bandages on Hansi's legs in angry jerks, tore towels with flabby fingers and wrapped strips round her own raw wrists.

"There is a boat." Martin came back on a blast of wet air. "Jenny?"

"Yes," she said, and turned.

"My dear, it won't be much longer now." He knew her as well as she now knew him.

"We ought to kill Winckler." She heard her own voice shake.

"Yes, we ought," he said, and laughed.

A bad grunting hiccup of a laugh that made her forget Winckler. He looked awful, as she must, too, worse than when he was shuddering on the banks of the Tisza; worse because he had driven for hours under Winckler's stabbing gun barrel, lasted for God knew how long without sleep, and at the end of it, tangled with Hansi's jackhammer of a body in the dark. "Let's throw the damned diaries in the Danube and chance what Nemeth might do to me. You simply have to rest," she said as he held her.

"If it was just the diaries . . . I'd say yes. But I want to spend the rest of my life with you, not in badgering the State Department and our foreign secretary to try once more to get you out of Hungary's jails." He bent stiffly to check that Winckler was still unconscious, flipped open cupboards looking for food and clothes. "Bring anything you can find to wear; it's cold out there."

It was cold. As soon as Jenny went outside, she began to shiver, and even the labor of carrying books from the Lada to a small launch tied up in a boat house failed to warm her.

The boat looked nondescript, and she wondered how far it was from here to the Austrian frontier. "Do you know how to start it up?"

"Well, the engine turned over with one of Winckler's keys when I tried. Otherwise I'm damned if I do." They had to slide from dock to boat, her wrists and his neck and spine so painful, both their bodies so stiff that any movement snagged bone instead of muscle. "It would have helped these past two days if I was a racing driver who spent his spare time in the SAS, but I'm not, I'm afraid."

"I'm not, either, and I landed you in this mess."

"Thank God for that, anyway."

"For the mess?" she said provocatively, and was rewarded by the touch of his hands as he guided her from the deck to a small cockpit in the stern.

The engine caught almost at once, the sound surprisingly powerful before Martin throttled back. "There are spare cans of fuel stacked; can you stow them somewhere if I hand them down?" Jenny felt the boat bounce as he climbed back on the tiny timber dock.

This was worse than carrying books, an enormous effort to wedge cans in spaces she could only feel. Sensation had returned to her hands, but the rest of her body seemed so distant, it was a surprise when sharp corners hurt.

"Do you think the police will be watching the river?" she asked when Martin slid back beside her.

"Probably, although it's easy to think of water only as a trap. There will certainly be frontier patrols closer to the border, customs along the Czech shore as well. Here." He wrapped her hands round a small, rough-feeling wheel. "Will you steer? I'll need all my wits to stop us going out of control."

Jenny soon saw what he meant. While she gripped the wheel and strained her eyes into the blackness on every side, he fumbled among levers, searching for a gear. When he found it, the boat surged out of the boathouse like a missile before he was able to set throttle and mixture to a safer speed, experiment with switches whose purpose was uncertain. Water flashed past as Jenny scrabbled at the wheel, unprepared for how long it took the bow to swing, for the smack and surge of the current.

The Danube was swift-flowing at this time of year. Clouds blew across a sky just light enough to show that somewhere the moon had risen, the most immediate hazard not knowing where the opposite bank and main channel were. Little to see except all-pervading blackness, nothing to feel except wind blasting out of the winter approaching from the eastern steppelands.

For a while after that first heart-stopping surge, they went more slowly. Then Martin began working the boat faster again, until Jenny needed to stand on tiptoe if she was to see anything above the lifted bow. As a consequence, her fingers scarcely reached the wheel, and her eyes streamed with tears from the wind. "Martin!" She had to shout above engine and wind. "I can't see! We're bound to hit something soon."

She felt him come to stand beside her but could scarcely see him, either. "I know, but I found a map down there. I'm not sure exactly where we are, but it's quite a way to the Austrian frontier. And for the last ten miles, both banks of the river are inside Czechoslovakia."

He didn't need to spell out what that meant. Although tonight was certainly an exception, normally Hungary was the most relaxed of the Communist states, with guards not too much in evidence, except at the frontier itself. Czechoslovakia was different, and if the last stretch was completely Czech, then those were miles they had to travel in darkness and with exacting care.

"It must be light by the time we reach so far," Jenny said, then thought she saw blacker blackness and swerved nervously, the boat slapping against the current.

"My watch gave up some time ago, but according to Winckler's it wasn't quite eleven when we left. Dawn comes late in November."

"I saw that, too. It must have stopped."

"It hadn't. Just after an early winter dusk when we left the Tisza, perhaps around half past four or five. About two hundred miles to the Danube; I watched the meter while I drove. Most of those driven very fast; say, four hours. Plus another hour at the house. Winckler's watch was right."

Jenny's watch had vanished, scraped off by handcuffs on the Lada floor. All the same, *only eleven o'clock*. It was unbelievable.

On the other hand, she was beginning to get an idea how to steer a boat, so long as the river ran wide and straight. Experimentally she touched the wheel this way and that, trying to feel how speed and current fought each other, a touch too much and their motion changed, the bows slanting against water coming down the river. Yet if they stayed in the main channel, where the current flowed fast against them, they would lose a lot of time.

"I'm going to take her over to the other side," she called. "It will be the Hungarian shore once we reach the Czech border, and at the moment it's further away from where they're looking for us. The current might be less as well."

He lifted a hand in acknowledgment. "I'll go forward and watch."

She liked his easy acceptance of her judgment at such a crisis point; perhaps he wasn't such a natural politician after all.

"All right." His words soft-spoken and snatched back by the wind, although the engine alone was loud enough to betray them if the river was being watched. "Keep her like that. A little left."

She could see the bank now, the sky beginning unexpectedly to lift in a silvered sweep overhead. The moon still hidden behind cloud, but its glow more brightly reflected, to the point that increasing visibility might soon become more of a hazard than objects in the water.

The river was opening up, too, wooded hills sloping steeply from the water, scattered with lights from a sleeping town. Soon the bank she was following curled sharply on itself until she could see the difference between black water and blacker trees. The Danube Bend, where the river swept in a great arc and several side channels rejoined the main stream. They were farther from Budapest than Martin had thought, and that much nearer to safety. Along the shore there was a road now, occasional headlights sweeping across the water as cars snaked through sharp bends. Tonight, roads meant police.

Jenny bit her lip, not knowing what to do.

Any policeman standing on that road might hear their engine and wonder what a boat was doing, not showing

lights. Nor was there much other traffic on the river at
night. Out in midstream a tug towed a string of barges, but
no other small craft at all.

Martin dropped back into the cockpit beside her, shivering violently. She was shivering, too, now she remembered
about it; but she remained too frightened to remember it in
more than snatches as long as danger was so close.

"I think we ought to go further out again," she said,
hating to hear herself say it. Out there was silvered water,
stronger currents, and visibility strengthening all the time.

"Not yet. I came to say the road looks as if it swings
inland just ahead. Pile on the speed once we're past this
next headland, and with luck there'll only be farmers
minding their business to hear us until—" he crouched,
holding the map to faint light from the compass "—Estergom. After that there's a main motorway along the bank,
and the country flattens out."

A truck was coming along the road on the bank, swinging—now. For an instant they were bathed in light and
ducked instinctively, every detail of the boat picked out by
glare. Then it was gone, jinking through corners up a val-
ley that took the road away from the river.

"We can't risk staying inshore near a motorway where
cars do that every few minutes," said Jenny shakily.

"No. We'll just have to shove her along as fast as we
can on this next stretch and make up time, because we'll
surely lose it later."

They would lose it when the hills ended and Czechoslovakia began, where frontier patrols were likely and customs launches checked river traffic all the time.

"How far to Estergom?"

"Ten miles perhaps, and worth staying in the shallows
until we reach it. Afterward the other bank is Czech."

"Here goes, then," Jenny said lightly, and recklessly
pushed the throttle over as far as it would go. The engine
note changed from rumble to roar; the stern settled into the
water.

"Winckler made sure he had plenty of power in re-serve," shouted Martin.

"It didn't look that sort of boat."

"Winckler didn't look the kind of swine he was. First time around, that is."

Jenny remembered his chilling laugh and gripped the wheel tighter. No good thinking about it. No good thinking of Winckler left alive behind them. Think instead how each mile brought Austria closer, in a boat most unexpectedly built for speed. She looked over her shoulder at Martin, smiling. "I never steered a boat before."

"I'll give you one for a wedding present if you like." His arm around her shoulders, hugging tight.

How enormously, unbelievably welcome a period of time in which tension at least appeared to slacken, and yet, almost immediately, instead of absence of tension, what they noticed was the cold; grinding, pitiless cold, as great an enemy as Winckler. It seemed a very long ten miles before more lights came into sight ahead, showing where Estergom lay shuttered and asleep. By then Martin was taking a turn at steering, and he throttled the engine back to the softest of rumbles while they crept past darkened houses.

No sound, no challenge, no police launch flinging itself at them without a second's warning. Their passage so far seemed too good to be true.

Once they were past Estergom, Jenny crouched in the shelter of the cockpit coaming to try and rest awhile, away from the wind. It felt warmer there at first but quite soon, with nothing to occupy her mind, even colder than it had been standing up.

They had found only a little powdered milk and ancient cookies in the villa. The milk stuck in her mouth since she didn't dare drink filthy Danube water, and the cookies appeared to make little difference to her ravenous hunger. "Have some cookies." She had difficulty in standing again, and her eyes felt gummy. In spite of the cold, perhaps because of it, she felt alarmingly drowsy.

She saw Martin straighten when she spoke, as if he drowsed, too; perhaps only by keeping together could they hope to stay awake. He wasn't steering well, either. Didn't seem to feel the current in the way she had learned to do, and kept wasting distance by letting the boat veer away from the shore.

"Martin?"

"Yes?" His voice was thick, and for a moment she wondered whether he had drunk too much of Winckler's schnapps on an empty stomach.

"Have some cookies while I steer."

"Where are we?"

"Just past Estergom," she answered gently. He had taken over only two or three miles back.

"Christ. Then . . . no. You stay out of the wind."

"My love. It isn't your fault if you're asleep on your feet." She kissed him, and there was no smell of spirits on his breath at all, only blood under her lips and crisping on his clothes. "Where are you hurt?"

"I'm not. Don't fuss, for God's sake."

"And don't you be a goddamn hero," she snapped.

He grinned unexpectedly. "I'm working at it. The only thing wrong with me is that Whitehall offices and chauffeur-driven cars don't prepare anyone for Winckler's brand of roughing up. But like most governments, I shall survive as long as I have to, just the same."

She laughed and stood beside him after that.

The river now flowed under a patchwork roof of clouds, the wind gusting strongly from behind, bitterly cold but helping to compensate for the current.

Jenny glanced astern as lights came into view again on the left-hand bank, showing where the Budapest motorway ran. "It's blowing up into quite a storm behind."

"Good. It feels more than cold enough for snow, which could be a help over that last stretch."

"Not yet, though."

"No." Ahead of them moonlight was increasing all the time, another tug and barges standing out clearly in the center of the river, red Soviet flag showing in the glow of navigation lights. "Will you steer now? I want to look at the map and top up our fuel. We can't afford to run dry at the wrong moment."

Jenny felt better with the wheel in her hands again. The thrash of their engine sounded good when no one seemed in the least interested in their passage, and her spirits began to rise; having reached so far, they simply had to find a way past guards and borders all the way to Austria before dawn.

As the motorway pulled slowly onto their beam, she began to edge away into the middle of the river. No point hugging the shore once it became a trap. But when they reached the main dredged channel, she felt horribly exposed and instinctively increased speed. Better to get this part over quickly. Caution merely left them as sitting ducks for longer.

Martin came out from under the coaming and stood with the map tilted toward a moon that had become quite bright enough for her to see river and roads crawling across the paper in his hands. "For the next fifteen miles or so, the river narrows until, by the time it reaches the twin towns of Komárno and Komárom, one on each bank, it's really not wide at all. I don't think we'll get past there without being challenged."

"Could we make a run for it if we were? How far to the border?"

"Twenty or thirty miles, so no, we couldn't. Once past that narrow stretch, though, we've got a better chance. The river becomes much wider again and fills up with islands. Then it's just that last stretch through Czechoslovakia, where, as luck would have it, the islands disappear."

Jenny stared ahead, blinking a little to keep her eyes focused. In her imagination the Danube was already becoming narrower. She soon realized this wasn't an illusion when a lighted buoy showed the dredged channel swinging ever closer to the shore; mercifully, another bank of clouds had blown across the moon, and she looked up, judging

.me. "Ten minutes perhaps," she said aloud.

Ten minutes more while clouds and darkness helped to
.ide them, then they would stand out like a beetle crawling
.cross silver paper, on a stretch of river where both Hun-
.arian and Czech guards were likely to be alert.

"We'll have to overhaul that tug," said Martin. "It's our
.nly chance. Risk the speed we need during these few
.ninutes of darkness and tuck into the shadow of the barges
.'s towing until we're past the narrows."

Jenny felt her hands tighten on the wheel as she thought
.bout the risks of tangling with strings of barges in the
.ark, but she knew he was right. Yet once she increased
.peed, it seemed wicked to tear along and leave a wake
.early as wide as the river itself. She couldn't see the
.zech shore but felt it on her right, very close and getting
.loser. She glanced up at the sky again, only to see a trans-
.ucent glow slipping toward the edge of that lifesaving
.ank of cloud. Not long to go before the river would be
.rilliantly lit again.

"Can you see the barges?" At this speed it was difficult
.o see anything; her eyes were watering more than ever
.rom the cold.

"White wake. Steer right a little."

Steering right would take them even closer to the Cze-
.hoslovakian shore. Jenny felt every muscle tighten as she
.ust touched the wheel right and almost immediately saw
.lecked water streaming back toward their bow from some-
.vhere not far ahead. She throttled back hastily, frightened
.f ramming barges in the dark. Throttled back too much,
.ecause the flecks disappeared again as tug and barges
.hurned steadily onward.

She set her teeth and cautiously advanced the throttle a
.iotch at a time. This was a blindman's buff that could
.lrown them both without a second's warning. A skilled
.ielmsman in daylight would be careful how he approached
.ive hundred feet of tow and tug bucking against Danube
.urrent. But she hadn't been wrong when she believed she
.iossessed a feel for this. With growing excitement she

sensed how the launch responded to her touch, her own
instinctive compensation for an unexpected kick of water.
If she had even a moment to think or listen to advice, she
could not have done it, would have been terrified by the
idea of attempting anything so insane, but here and now
with their lives as the stake, reality was banished. Exhaustion bred recklessness, foam-specked darkness unraveled
fantasy, until she steered a launch for the first time in her
life as a child might ride a dangerous stallion, without
comprehending the nature of the skills she used.

Jenny saw Martin scramble forward, an awkward journey as they struck the barges' wake. She glanced up again.
The moon already lit the edge of cloud that had been hiding it. When she looked back at the water, two barges were
poised like a slipping avalanche directly in their path; red
lights hung over each stern, white water coiling underneath. The barges were being towed in pairs, about fifteen
feet of broken water in between them. Now it was difficult
to think at all, once she overrode instinct and continued to
drive their frail hull onward instead of swerving away to
safety. Thirty feet. Twenty. Fifteen. This was like accelerating across cobbles on punctured tires, the boat shuddering, her bones shaking, face aching from concentration.

She wasn't strong enough to hold the wheel as steadily
as she ought once churned water from the barges' passage
skidded their shallow draft from one eddy to the next.
Jenny had thought they would be able to remain in what
looked like smoother water immediately between and just
behind the pair of barges, but it was impossible. Their
launch was swept forward in undertow, slewed at each
eddy, snapped backward in a sudden surge of current. It
could only be minutes before some misjudgment brought
them to disaster. They weren't close enough, either. Instinctively she had been dropping back again to allow some
margin of safety, and as the moon came out from behind its
cloud, they were nearly fifteen yards behind the barges.

She saw Martin gesture, his figure lit by the moon and
his meaning unmistakable. He meant to climb up on a

rge and secure their mooring rope so they became part of
e tow, and she must get close enough for him to do it.

Jenny swallowed, reality sweeping back on a wave of
rtigo. He must be crazy. She almost laughed, wondering
hat Westminster lobby correspondents would say if they
uld see one of Britain's rising politicians now: Martin
othbury had never enjoyed a particularly good press,
ing too aloof and formal in his dealings for journalists to
arm to him, but that would very quickly change if this
ght's lunacy ever become known. She must be crazy, too,
 think of laughing.

All the same, she understood why he thought he had to
y. If they could only tow along behind the barges, then
y watcher would think they were simply part of the same
ring, the Soviet flag become their safeguard, the rope
aintain the exact distance they needed.

And for a few miles they might be able to rest at last.

If they were to do it, it had to be now. This moment.
e light was so clear that only the fact they were directly
 the barge's wake could have prevented them from being
otted already. Without allowing herself to think any more
out it, Jenny put her hand on the throttle and increased
eed. A sheet of spray was flung against the windshield as
eir bow dug into the barges' wake, and she saw Martin
agger; it must be fiendishly difficult to balance on that
y, exposed bow. She was driving straight for the gap
tween the two barges, their hulls lifting like rock on ei-
er side as the launch crept closer. A spout of water shot
 the air as an eddy hit their bow, then dropped it into a
ack race of water between the two barge hulls. For a
nic-stricken instant Jenny thought everything was over.

 single blow from these wallowing monsters and they
ould be swept down and under, their bodies roll God
ew how far along the muddy Danube bottom.

They were caught in backwash she had not seen and,
bber that she was, had not known would be there. The
unch seemed to slide into a whirlpool, all her strength
rown on the wheel to stop them from ramming the left-

hand barge. Then they were running forward again and in
the darkness between the barges, too fast, as their massiv
hulls unexpectedly absorbed most of the current. She cou
not pick her moment to nudge a barge so Martin cou
jump aboard, but at least the barges' decks were almo
level with their own, since piled cargo left little freeboard
Two more barges ahead and then a length of tow to the tug
unless they were exceptionally vodka-free and alert, th
tug's crew ought not to spot Martin jumping aboard mayb
five hundred feet astern, a fugitive shadow against th
glow of the river and distant stern-lights.

"Hold tight," she said aloud. Oh God, take care, m
love. If he slipped, he would fall between launch an
barge.

The wave between the barges was still carrying ther
forward, curling, canceling out her tentative touches at th
wheel. Then the launch's bows swung suddenly, and sh
felt the deck lift as Martin jumped: at least Whitehal
taught you to calculate a chance precisely. She could edg
away slightly then, although not far enough to ease eithe
strain or danger, was forced to wait while Martin scrabble
to make fast their rope, hoping to God he knew how to ti
knots that held.

Had Her Majesty's fiscal secretary to the treasury eve
been a scout? This time Jenny did laugh aloud. One da
she must remember to ask him, but she doubted it. Martin
wasn't the scouting type, even though he had made a fai
job of jumping rusty barges in the dark. She saw him re
turn at a crouching run and gunned the engine gently, to
gently, because the launch was still sliding back. She ha
no choice except to come in faster, riding that inferna
wave and striking the barge a glancing blow; a screeching
metallic blow that made her stagger. She felt Martin jum
inboard and dropped back instantly, out of that hideous tra
of steel and water. Out of that millrace, danger. Bac
through spilling surf between the barges' wakes, back int
spray and the skid-pan of water beyond.

She cut the engine the moment the rope snapped tight

the launch's motion changing as they were drawn smoothly forward, bounding in the chop but no longer fighting it.

Only when she took her hands off the wheel did she feel trembling begin at the back of her knees, then spread to every aching muscle in her body.

13

AT FIRST THEY FELT TRIUMPHANT TO BE SWEEPING along in the wake of Soviet barges, but as soon as they became used to the motion, it seemed very slow. The night was passing, passing, and when dawn broke, they could not afford to be brazenly motoring through a Czechoslovakian waterway.

There was nothing to be done about it, however. Storm clouds continued to surge up from the east, behind them, but the moon still shone overhead, and the river became narrower all the time. On the Hungarian shore the motorway was brightly lit, and what looked like overnight vegetable trucks were pounding along it toward Budapest, close enough for Jenny to glimpse the drivers in their cabs. The Czech shore was even closer, the main dredged channel within fifty yards of an apparently empty land. No lights, no roads, no movement. Whatever there might be in this patch of the Communist world by day, at night its inhabitants stayed indoors.

The only exception was an occasional shaded glow almost down by the water's edge.

"Do you think those are police posts?" asked Jenny.

"Probably. Czechoslovakia has a bad reputation for fencing its people in, and someone will be watching along this stretch, I'm sure. Even Hungary has watchtowers, machine guns, and bare, plowed ground along its frontier with the West."

And as he spoke they felt the tow slacken speed, saw light and heard shouts ahead.

"Wait here," said Martin. "I'll go and shorten the rope."

Jenny knelt on the seat and watched him run forward, saw how he needed to lean all the remaining strength of his back and shoulders to haul them into the barges' shadow. He would never do it in time. Now that the tug was nearly stopped, the only place to be was right between those barges' sterns, where a casual search might miss them.

She climbed out and went to join him. Together, yard by yard, they drew the launch against the current until black shadow closed overhead, stood panting while voices shouted to each other somewhere ahead.

"A patrol?" asked Jenny softly when her breath returned. A police launch checking papers and bills of lading would be infinitely preferable to some kind of static checkpoint where barges might be searched.

"God knows. I hope they don't take long, whatever they mean to do."

"What time is it, do you think?" They ought to have brought Winckler's watch along.

"One, two in the morning, I suppose. More, perhaps." He held her again, so each could feel the beat of the other's heart.

From where they were standing in the launch's bows, their eyes were level with the barge's deck. They could see lights on a mast alongside the tug and peaked caps on its bridge, would have brief warning if searchers decided to board its tow as well. Not that a warning would do much good, since there was nowhere else for them to go.

Waiting was worse than anything, particularly when waiting was itself an enemy. Time now racing past like black Danube water, and taking with it the small margin of safety they had won, every second vital if they were to have any chance at all of reaching the Austrian frontier before dawn.

The jerk took them unaware as rope tightened like a spring, snatching the launch's bows almost out of the water before Martin had time to fumble loose more slack. The tug was under way again.

"Down!" Martin said suddenly, and pulled her flat on the deck beside him as a light swept by.

Jenny turned her head just in time to glimpse a motor cutter bouncing past, three uniformed men on board. They were talking and laughing together, submachine guns slung, the beam of a small searchlight wavering from water to blackness overhead as the tug's wake made their boat roll. For an instant the beam caught their launch and seemed to strike right through her eyes to the brain behind, then it flicked up and away, leaving purple cartwheels behind her lids.

The rest of the journey behind the barges was uneventful. The river became darker as the coming storm blew more clouds across the moon, and thankfully the tug picked up speed, which made their own launch swoop and slam even more painfully in its wake. They dropped back as far as their rope would allow and sat side by side on the narrow cockpit seat, dozing uneasily. Too tired to stay awake no matter what the cold and danger, the viciously seesawing motion, once there was nothing immediate they must do.

Jenny was roused eventually by lights so close on either side that she thought the police must be about to jump aboard. Felt her mouth open to shout a warning before she realized they must have reached the narrowest point on their journey, where the twin towns of Komárom and Komárno leaned across the Danube to greet each other. Her sight blurred as sleep reached for her again, this time a tilting slope of unconscious that might last for hours. Perhaps forever when it was so cold. It was enormously hard to stand on legs that felt like fencing posts and force herself back into full awareness. She turned and saw Martin with his head down on his knees, arms dangling, no need to wake him yet. In fact, every reason not to while the Danube remained narrow and the tug was making better speed than before. Even an hour of sleep would help to give him some shadow of strength again, as her doze in Winckler's car had given her.

He had said the Danube widened after Komárom and Komárno. Jenny searched her memory and decided she was sure he had said that islands began there, and then a wider channel. When could they expect dawn in a Balkan November? Seven-thirty? And just before dawn most guards would be counting minutes until their relief, and be wider awake in consequence.

Ever afterward, Jenny found it difficult to remember exactly how she felt at that moment, when her mind was such a jumble of impressions. Impressions of personalities more than of events. There was Winckler, laughing his jackass laugh as he shot a man, Inspector Nemeth, who would have let them die rather than pass them through his roadblock if his orders had allowed it; Sandy Havasi, with his buccaneer's outlook on the world, perhaps still lying trampled on a marshy path. And as a background to her thoughts, there was the steady throb of the tug's engine ahead, each thrash of her screw another moment hurrying past that brought them closer to a hostile frontier and the dawn.

She shook Martin awake soon after, needed to shake with all her strength and then throw Danube water in his face before he roused. The brutal business of rousing a completely exhausted man whose every bone and sinew had stiffened from the pounding he'd received. "My dear . . . my dear. I think we ought to cast off from the barges soon."

He straightened gingerly. "Where are we?"

"We passed Komárom and Komárno perhaps half an hour ago."

He muttered something, still half-dazed, but annoyed he'd slept while she remained awake. "The river looked wider than this on the map."

"It is; that's why I woke you. You aren't seeing bank, but the first island. Look, over there." She pointed.

The tug was negotiating a wide turn marked by buoys, and as it did so, they were able to see the Danube stretching ahead, broken into a maze of pewter-colored, gray, and gray-black shapes. The islands were indistinct, and so irregular that the dredged channel must need considerable care in navigation: already the tug was slowing down.

"Yes," Martin said after a pause, meaning he could see the islands.

"It doesn't look good, does it?" She agreed with his tone. "But I think we have to get going on our own or we'll lose too much time."

"Yes," he said again, and stretched as if deliberately using pain to force sense back into his brain. "We'd better choose a side channel, go fast and chance hitting something. You're better than I am on the wheel, so I'll go up in the bow. If I shout . . . it'll mean unless you're bloody quick, I'll hit the water a split second before you."

"Have you thought perhaps we might do better to lie up for a day? Among so many islands there has to be cover enough for us to stay undiscovered. Then tomorrow night—"

"Tomorrow I have to be back in Budapest."

She opened her mouth, shut it again. "You what?"

"The financial conference reopens tomorrow afternoon, and I have to be there if I can. I ought to be there now, scurrying around exploring possibilities."

"You can't. You can't be serious. What on earth would Nemeth say if his police reported you'd just strolled past the guard on Budapest's Conference Hall?"

"He'll know I'm on my way before that, since I've no intention of boating back up the Danube. I shall have to ask our Vienna embassy to fix emergency papers and an early flight into Budapest for me. It's no good, Jenny. If I wasn't about to resign anyway, I should be forced to after the way I've behaved these past two days, but at this moment I'm still a minister, and the moment we get out, if we do, I have to put British interests first. I've got briefing meetings to attend, feathers to smooth, the hell of a pile of work to master, before I walk back into that conference tomorrow afternoon. The only risk is that I shall fall asleep. Nemeth won't touch me if his masters hold him off, and they will. I'll clear things up with him as soon as I've got time. So let's get going, like you said, and hope it works out easier than it looks."

"Well," said Jenny critically. "Now I know how your opponents feel after you've used parliamentary language to tell them what damned fools they are."

He grinned and kissed her lightly. "I was the fool, not you. The damage was done yesterday morning when I let you rile me into hiding while the hunt went past, when I ought to have driven you straight back to Budapest. By force, if necessary. I'll cast off the rope; no point risking more than we have to by trying to jump that damned barge again. And, Jenny . . . we shall do better to try and reach Austria tonight. Another day without proper food or shelter would do us no good at all, and sometime tomorrow—no, today—I expect the police to find Winckler. Then they'll know a boat has gone."

She watched his dim shape in the launch's bows as they dropped back from the barge before sheering away into the shallows; she supposed she would get used to the way his mind worked, but at the moment he constantly surprised her. The odd thing was, it didn't matter. In fact, she liked it, since she hated drab predictability.

Meanwhile they had the Danube to navigate. Once the tug and its barges disappeared into the murk, Jenny opened the throttle wide. Whatever the risk of hitting sandbars in the dark, they needed to do this stretch fast and snatch some lost time back.

The river was sluggish in these shallows, and the slack water helped their speed. Banks, islets, and flotsam seemed to tear past. Martin stood braced to a scrap of rail at their bows, signaling which way to steer, and she simply had to trust him. Keep the throttle open and pray they would not drive on an unseen shoal at full speed. Because there were sandbanks everywhere. Some overgrown, others like beached seals gleaming in the dark; a great many more that were only breaking water seen out of the corner of her eye.

The sensation was exhilarating all the same, until she heard a shout from Martin and his whole body leaned as if willpower alone could take them clear of whatever he had seen. As urgency whirled back from him to her, something appeared in the darkness beside their hull—a tree nearly covered by water. It skidded past and behind them in an instant, but already Martin was shouting again and she was desperately spinning the wheel the other way, fingers clawing to close the throttle. The launch swerved, hesitated, then, under her urgent, unskilled handling, swerved so sharply that icy water poured over the cockpit edge and deluged across Jenny's feet. A sound like a cement mixer vibrated against the hull, and a twig whipped across her cheek. Christ, she hadn't even seen the islet where that bush grew.

"All right," called Martin. "It looks as if it opens up here for a stretch. Keep going, but take it slowly while I look to see if we've taken any damage."

Jenny decided they must be threading past long, narrow islands with varying depths of channel in between, the water beginning to roughen up again as the current reappeared. Suddenly she could also make out a shoreline against the darker bulk of land beyond, but even as she wondered whether they might not be more likely to strike driftwood as they came closer in, the launch grated on gravel, caught, freed itself, bumped, and stuck fast.

"We are taking in a little water, I hope not too much." Martin crawled out from the engine hatch.

"I expect some came in when we nearly turned over," said Jenny stupidly. "We're stuck."

"I know. Try reverse." They felt together for a notch that might be reverse, and after several mistakes felt the propeller bite. The launch stirred and slewed sideways, jarring heavily.

"Oh God, I suppose we'll have to get out and try to shove her off," said Jenny, shivering. Her feet and lips were frozen, the river filled with infinite menace.

"If we did, and succeeded, she'd probably float away before we could scramble back on board. Anyway, I've had enough swimming in ice water for one day. Give her full power and damn the Czechs. They can't keep permanent posts on mud flats, surely."

She tried again, advancing the throttle notch by notch, feeling the hull shudder and watching water boil over stones. If there were any guards among this maze of shoals, they would have to be blind drunk not to hear.

Without warning, they spun clear. Went roaring at the nearest island with only seconds left for her to grab at spinning spokes and slice the launch past bushes growing over water.

By the time she had recovered from the shock of that, they had reached a channel that seemed blessedly free from obstruction. Only mist and blackness everywhere, a little rain on her face. She supposed she ought to welcome rain, when they needed any cover they could get and she couldn't possibly be colder. Meanwhile, the only thing that mattered was to stay clear of further traps while they went helter-skelter down the Danube.

Quite soon she began to reduce speed again, though Martin wasn't signaling any warning from the bows. Such luck as they'd had simply couldn't last, and she suddenly became possessed by a superstitious conviction that it would be idiocy to test it for too long at a time. And the moment the engine note changed, she heard a booming sound ahead, as if the river ran through rapids. Martin turned at once and gestured—slower.

Soon afterward they hit a long slide of water over God knew what. No waterfalls on the Danube, Jenny thought disjointedly, but here unseen islands must end in a gravel shelf, and water was pouring unevenly off its roughness. But beyond it she glimpsed the main channel again, looking deeper and straighter than before, the most comforting sight since they cast off from the barge.

She could hardly believe how easy it became after that. Rain thickened steadily until she couldn't see either bank at all, although lit buoys away to her left marked where the dredged channel ran and made navigation simple. Minutes passed while nothing particular happened. Perhaps another half hour before she realized the river was again beginning a long, slow bend, the rain easing sufficiently to allow them to glimpse another tug thrashing up toward them.

Martin dropped into the cockpit beside her. "I think we must be very close to pulling out of Hungary and into Czechoslovakia on both sides. They've canalized the river here, by the look of it, which if I'm right, means Bratislava isn't far ahead. It's quite a big city, with road and rail bridges we have to pass." He pried her frozen fingers off the wheel. "I'll take her while steering doesn't need too much skill."

She tried to smile, since he had only steered badly because he had been nearly unconscious at the time, but her lips were stiff with frost, her only remaining sensation a distant feel of water slopping across her feet. "There ought to be a pump somewhere to help keep this water down, I suppose."

"There ought, but I can't decide which might be the right switch. Don't worry about it. Who cares if Winckler's launch sinks once we've finished with it?"

He was trying to cheer her up, and irrationally, she felt annoyed. However good a face he put on it, the launch was beginning to feel decidedly sluggish, and during these last dangerous few miles they might need all the speed they could find.

There was a large flashlight clamped to the side of the

cockpit, and after shading it in cloth, Jenny gingerly turned it on. Greasy water slopped across gratings in the engine well. She could see it trickling in each time their bows dipped. And the more water they shipped, the lower those sprung bows would dip. She remembered now the screeching metallic clang as they had struck one of those barges while Martin jumped across to make them fast; the hull might also have been further damaged when they stuck on the sandbank. Somewhere, surely, there ought to be a pump; certainly there seemed to be plenty of wires and switches with cryptic abbreviations etched on plates above them. Of course, Martin couldn't read Hungarian. In rising hope, Jenny discarded the ones whose purpose she guessed at from their labels. That left four. Two had no marking at all, so she decided, for no particular reason, that perhaps they were something more routine than pumps. Of the remaining two, one was painted red while the other was a plain brass casting, marked OZTH:Y. Which meant nothing at all to her. Either might cut out the engine, sound an alarm, anything.

She glanced over her shoulder again at water sloshing over engine mountings; the level was definitely rising.

"Can you see anything?" she called up.

"Lights which are probably another tug, but quite a long way ahead."

They were idling along now, making the minimum of noise and slipping across rain-swept water like a shadow. This was the dangerous stretch, the last obstacle before the frontier. Though speed might save them there, here the only possible way to evade detection was to rely on stealth.

Jenny touched the switches, torn by indecision. If she flipped the wrong one now, it could mean disaster.

Equally, if they took in much more water, the engine would stall and disaster certainly follow. "I've found what could be a switch for pumps. Shall I try it?"

"How much water is there now?"

"Quite a lot. It's over the grids and up to the engine."

"And you think the switch might really be the pump?"

"I don't know. There's two it might be, and others I haven't found, I expect."

"Of course, they might not fit pumps on a boat this size. I've only ever sailed a dinghy, and that was quite a while ago."

"Staten Island Ferry is about my limit. Yes or no?" She knew what his answer would be, reading his mind this time easily enough. For both of them, when faced by likely disaster whether they did something positive or refrained, the choice would be the same. And Jenny had a feeling that Winckler, that careful man, would fit pumps in his boat.

So the answer was yes, for both of them, and without hesitation she chose the brass switch, on the feeling that the red-painted one suggested fire rather than water.

The lights came on.

Lights at their stern and bow and mast, over the engine, blazing out across the river before she snapped them off again. In the intense blackness that followed, neither spoke, straining their ears for a challenge or the sudden roar of a pursuing engine.

Nothing, except the continuing beat of a tug ahead.

"Perhaps they don't guard this part of the Danube because both banks are inside Czechoslovakia," said Jenny shakily.

"Or they couldn't believe their eyes. You said there were two switches, so we might as well set the foghorn going as well."

This time it was hard to snap the red-painted switch. She stared at it, hating slipshod engineers who built boats without labeling every part. Then took a deep breath and flipped it down; there was an electrical whir and, almost instantly, splashing from over the side.

She hauled herself back to where Martin stood in rain blowing in bitter November gusts across the Danube, and suddenly, she didn't quite know why, they were both laughing. She put her arms around him where he stood at the wheel and kissed him. The first kiss which was entirely hers, full-hearted, owing nothing to him at all. He couldn't even take his eyes off the river. Settled, happy, themselves the only warmth in a sodden and hostile world.

Neither spoke, but she felt him smile under her lips.

The rain made steering enormously difficult as visibility shrank to a circle less than a hundred feet across, their bearings lost between one lighted buoy and the next. Their speed dropped to a crawl, and they could no longer hear the sound of that other tug ahead. After quite a long while Jenny felt something brush her cheek and put up her hand: rain was turning to sleet, sleet into snow. Winter had come to the Danube.

14

THEY STOOD IN THE LAUNCH'S COCKPIT AND WATCHED A glow ahead brighten through drifting snow.

"Bratislava," said Martin.

"How big is it?"

"I'm not sure. A solid manufacturing kind of place like Baltimore, I should think. According to the map, most of i is on the north bank."

A manufacturing city meant shift work, and shift work meant people awake at five o'clock in the morning, which it must be by now. Trams, early trains, police on duty.

The glow strengthened as the snow eddied between gusts of Siberian wind, became illuminated embankment and two bridges. Red lights on the bridge sponsons, spaced lights along its length. Crawling lights from a train that moved behind black shapes that might be overhead supports or could be manned checkpoints.

"Take over, will you?" Martin stood behind her for a moment while she settled on the wheel, then began groping in snow-shrouded lockers. Deck and bottom boards thick with slush, their clothes and hair plastered white. It was increasingly difficult to move or think as cold attacked their tiredness.

"The bridge isn't far now," said Jenny quietly. Light spilled down over the water, turning blackness into gold. "I can see what looks like a police launch tied up to a landing stage . . . another just coming under the bridge." What wicked luck to find a police launch coming back off duty, from the frontier probably, just as they must enter that spotlighted arena.

"Anything else?"

"It seems enough to me. The tug we saw is close to the first bridge, and a dredger is coming upstream."

Martin straightened, holding a jumble of color. "Flags. Not a Czech one, unfortunately." He began fumbling with the tiny flagstaff at their stern.

"What are you going to do?"

"Those lights you turned on gave me an idea." Jenny heard the sound of tearing. "There's red cloth here, and I'm pinning a piece of yellow in the corner. From a distance it ought to look Soviet, and since most barges on the Danube seem to be Russian, perhaps it won't seem too unexpected to see a Russian launch as well. Then we'll turn on our lights and hope for the best."

"At least we've got snow on our boots," observed Jenny. "Do you often get into trouble with your cabinet over your sheer damned effrontery?"

"I'm not in the cabinet," he answered imperturbably.

Rope squealed, and she snatched a quick glance over her shoulder at a square of red the size of a bedcover streaming in the wind. Some fuse wire skewered a scrap of yellow to one corner. "What on earth have you found?"

"Bunting left over from some communist anniversary, I suppose. Maybe most comrades have red banners tucked away somewhere, to prove their loyalty four or five times a year. Ready for the lights?"

"Wait while I steer closer to the bank, so it looks as if we've come from somewhere." They had nothing to lose by turning on their lights since the whole width of the river approaching and between the bridges was vividly illuminated, highlighting snowflakes that danced in every direction, fluttering and falling and fluttering up again. The police launch Jenny had seen was just swinging in toward its berth beside the nearer of the bridges; less than two hundred yards of black water remaining before they entered a floodlit arena where their every move could be studied at leisure.

Martin put his hand on the switch. "Say when you're ready."

"Yes . . . now." As the lights came on, Jenny increased speed. No point being illuminated any longer than necessary, and speed might look more innocently purposeful than furtive shadow dodging.

They both stood, anonymous white shapes in front of a red flag, while the boat broke into the light. It seemed unbelievable to be motoring calmly in such brightness, their eyes screwed up against it, cockpit, engine hatch, and navigation lights glowing. Black shapes hurrying on the first bridge above their heads, shoulders bowed against the snow and apathetic toward anything except the wretchedness of a dirty winter dawn.

"Quarter past five," said Martin. "I saw it on a clock tower over there."

"Ten miles from here to the frontier?"

"I should think so, but I'd like to do a further mile or so undetected on the Austrian side. I don't want to get hung up trying to explain the unexplainable to some immigration clerk if we can avoid it. It would be the best way out for everyone if this whole business could be shoveled quietly out of sight for good."

They were chattering like gossips in a street, willing the time to pass.

The road bridge looming overhead now, outlined in white by snow driven against metal girders.

"The police," said Jenny quietly. "There's a boat steering out toward us."

She had thought they were going to get away with it. No one on the bridge had given them more than a glance, Soviet traffic on the Danube too commonplace for comment; brazen lights flaunting their respectability. Now she could see a cutter veering away from the police landing stage, painted gray and with an ensign fluttering among a tangle of aerials on its stubby mast. A new shift coming on duty perhaps; it didn't matter, because if they were stopped, everything would be over, since Martin could not answer the simplest question in Czech or Russian, and Czechoslovakia is a far worse country in which to be caught as spies than Hungary.

"It's coming this way," she added. She and Martin still facing forward as if no anxiety existed in the world. "I think we have to go faster, don't you?"

"A notch at a time and see if we can run away without seeming to. Look out for that tug coming upstream."

The railroad bridge rushed past above them in a glitter of light, water spilling through its arches in a sleek black slope. More light beyond. "Oh God, I thought we'd be into the dark again the other side," said Jenny.

"Keep as you are. We're just holding them, which is about right when we don't want to look as if we're running away. They probably have plenty of spare power anyway, if they should decide they need to use it."

Jenny braced herself to shave as close as possible to a tug and barges coming down toward them, and so save yards on the bend.

"That tug's Russian," said Martin suddenly. "Haul out and half turn; take off most of our speed. Look as if we're passing some message. It'll cost us our distance, but the bluff ought to be worth it. A tug can't possibly stop to ask us what the hell we said while towing a string of barges with the current up its tail, and ordinary Czech cops may not want to interfere if we look like some special kind of Soviet business."

Since bluff was perhaps the only remaining chance they had, Jenny throttled back and began to pull out in a shallow half circle, that same trembling ache lodged behind her knees again. The police launch was already surging under the railroad bridge, overhauling them easily now.

Jenny had to drag at the wheel to make the turn in time and the launch wallowed heavily broadside-on to the flow. The oncoming tug and tow stretched away into darkness and was coming fast. Her hand on the throttle ready to go again, Martin standing directly under the light on their mast, his hands raised to hail the tug as it passed. They were going to cut their chances very close; hull bobbing, kicking against the swell, the police cutter frothing down toward them. At last the tug was close enough for Martin to shout, his voice loud and confident, a bellow carried on wet air. Jenny saw a figure on the tug's bridge as it swept past, staring at them, wondering what they could be up to. Probably the tug-master would radio, afraid when he saw their oversize red banner that he had missed something of importance. Ten miles to go until they reached the frontier. By the time a radio call from a tug filtered through sluggish bureaucracy, with luck it wouldn't matter.

The police cutter was aimed straight at their stern, less than fifty yards away.

Barges driving past them now; rusty sides, piled cargo, white water feathering their clumsy lines. As the last hull cleared the channel in front of her, Jenny opened up the throttle and shot across the bows of the police launch as if making back to the shore. "Are they following?"

"They're still coming . . . no . . . yes. They're arguing, I think. No, they're going on upstream. Perhaps they weren't after us at all."

"I think they were." Effrontery and nerve: the weapons of negotiation had shown their value this past night and day.

Jenny no longer felt afraid, nor even tired. Keyed up and exhilarated rather, but also strangely calm: as if she took it for granted now that they would get through. But lurking behind the calm she was very conscious of that ching tenseness, a kind of ever-widening daze as if she would soon faint.

She must not faint yet. Their lights were switched off again, and she needed every scrap of concentration she possessed to keep them out of trouble. They must also stay away from that police launch, going in the same direction as themselves. Even ordinary cops would think it suspicious if they reappeared, unlit, unknown, and unheralded, in Czechoslovakia's frontier zone.

She hung on to the wheel feeling very weak, forcing herself to stand upright until finally her dizziness washed away. But when Martin asked if she would like him to take the wheel again, she refused; she knew she would only last while something vital remained for her to do, and not a moment longer.

Not much longer now.

Not much longer for endurance, not much longer before they entered a restricted frontier zone where unauthorized intruders were shot on sight. Jenny had lost much of the feeling in her feet. Her wrists throbbed angrily. Her muscles quivered from the strain of staying alert through so many hours. And perhaps because utter exhaustion made her long for warmth and safety more than it was possible to imagine longing for anything in normal life, unexpectedly she found herself thinking about her mother. She supposed she had never really grasped before that cozy, ordinary Klari Keszthely had actually struggled through marshes, braved machine guns, lived for months in a squalid refugee camp when she, too, escaped from Hungary thirty years before. All she'd thought was: How dull to be happy always in Bridgeport, Connecticut.

Jenny chuckled to herself, the sound nearly frozen in her throat. After this past twenty-four hours, in future she herself would not so easily welcome avoidable risks, either. The pity of it was, when Klari fled west, she had saved the Keszthely necklace, guarded it through months of uncertainty and fear. Whereas she, Jenny, had lost it. Surely she had never appreciated before quite how much of

a wrench it must have been for Klari to give away anything
so precious, even to a daughter.

Jenny stirred uneasily as this new honesty made her realize other mistakes, with Sandy as well as her mother. A
further tally to add to her mistakes with Martin, when previously she had seen only his mistakes with her. But already her senses were sliding away from her again. This
was the most dangerous of all times for introspection; how
much better simply to decide that once mistakes were confronted and accepted, they also brought the hope of re-
splendent new beginnings.

They reached the frontier as a surly touch of gray
showed in the east. It had nearly stopped snowing, which
was a pity, since melting whiteness on both banks intensi-
fied such light as there was. The Danube itself was still
completely black but would not long remain so, and a
snowstorm now exactly what they needed.

With their engine throttled right back, Jenny tried to
take advantage of shadows on the water, a few scattered
sandbars, anything that might help them reach undetected
the lights they could now see about a mile ahead, illumi-
nating a wire fence stretching into the distance on either
bank. No roads or crossing points in sight, although the
river seemed rather different from a land frontier. As she
watched, a Romanian tug passed after stopping only to disembark what looked like an armed guard. Barbed wire
half-submerged in the shallows forced all traffic to use a
narrow channel confined by floating booms. Gray police
launches tied up to one bank were similar to those they had
seen at Bratislava. Of the two launches actually on patrol
one seemed more concerned with exchanging flashed sig-
nals with the tugs than stopping them, while the other col-
lected or put on board the armed men who presumably
searched cargoes en route. There was nothing in sight at all
on the Austrian side. Probably they were sensible enough
to use the nearest town as their frontier post.

"Most of the river traffic must be transit. Perhaps the
full fuss of clearance is reserved for vessels actually tying

p in Czechoslovakia, and then quite likely it's done in
ratislava. Plenty of searchers and watchers, though, to
ake sure the rest stay moving, and everything according
the manifest. Otherwise it looks as if they let Commu-
ist bloc boats through without too much trouble, once
ey've taken a guard on board," said Martin, staring up-
ream. They were just keeping pace against the current,
esitating before taking the plunge.

"There's a hydrofoil service from Vienna to Budapest,"
aid Jenny, remembering suddenly. "I thought I might take
as more interesting than flying, but in the end I hadn't
me. When I inquired, though, no one said anything about
zech visas, so that must go straight through, too."

"Then I think we have to wait until a tug and barges
omes upstream. When it does, we'll close up on the side
way from where they disembark their guard and hope we
et most of the way before we're spotted from the other
ank. We can't bluff here. They'd never let an unidentified
oat through without authorization, clearance, God knows
hat."

"We daren't wait long or it'll be daylight."

He shrugged. "We could do with some islands, too."

But here the Danube flowed unbroken by so much as a
andbank where they might have lurked out of sight. The
and stretched flat on either side, featureless under snow
xcept for that menacing line of brilliantly illuminated
atchtowers and barbed wire. Gray clouds scudding over-
ead, lighter grayness spreading from the east. A sheen on
e water already, imperceptible but growing all the time.

Jenny couldn't remember how many tugs and tows they
ad passed during the night, but now they needed cover
esperately, the only one in sight was coming down from
ustria. It was also maddeningly difficult to keep the
unch trimmed against the current without risking give-
way wash or more than an irreducible minimum of noise,
nd for some time she had been worrying about fuel. Mar-
n had kept their tank filled during the night, but it seemed

a long time since the last of the spare cans they'd broug
was empty.

"I can hear something," Martin exclaimed. Almost i
mediately she heard it, too. The wind was gusting harsh
out of the east, as it had all night, and cut like wire, but
last brought with it the thrash of propellers from aste
The sound grew agonizingly slowly, but at last blunt bov
and navigation lights hardened out of scudding graynes
Quite definitely grayness now. At this very last mome
when they only needed the dark to last a few more mi
utes, night had finally faded into a dull and bitter dawn.

The moment Jenny heard the tug's engine change be
as her skipper slowed to drop his Czech guard, saw t
fleck of white at its bow momentarily slacken and disa
pear, she began to edge their launch away from the ba
and into the main channel. There was simply no choi
left, and they had to risk everything on this single chanc
which wouldn't come again. As they hit the full force
Danube current, their launch plunged crazily, the engi
still throttled right back because a white wake might ale
shore sentries a fraction earlier to what was happenin
Already the tug was picking up way again. Long practi
no doubt made the guard transfer a slick operation. Su
denly very little time remained for them to squeeze past
great many trapping coils of barbed wire washing about
the shallows and reach the infinitely more hazardo
shelter of that tow. Eight barges this time, and the t
making a great fuss over pulling such a load against t
current. Even so, if she was to catch it in time, Jenny h
to open the throttle wide without worrying about wake, a
even so only just reached the rearmost barge as it enter
the narrow boom that squeezed the channel to an absolu
minimum width for the quarter mile or so leading to t
frontier itself.

Then it immediately became terrifyingly difficult
maintain the slow speed that was all the tug could mana
after its enforced stop, and at the same time avoid bei
crushed between barge and boom. Water, barnacled hul

ough, snagging boom, all were slopping wildly in wash,
he space between them not much wider than their launch.
After a few moments Martin came to stand behind her,
closed his hands over hers, and helped add the sheer brute
strength that might just be sufficient to keep them clear. An
awkward arrangement, but after a long night's steering,
Jenny possessed the sharpest instinct for what this boat
might do, and he the extra power they had to have.

An outrageously splendid arrangement, as she felt
warmth against her spine for the first time in hours, and
together they watched barbed wire, machine-gun-filled
towers, mined and plowed strips of infinitely alien earth,
slowly pull level with their beam. The floodlights on that
lethal barrier also mercifully paling with the dawn, while
still no one shouted or fired a shot. The anchored end of
the boom beginning to pull slowly into sight, coming
closer and closer still, the worst of the slipstream from the
barges smoothing out as the Danube reached in from
beyond its confines to absorb their passage.

"We're going to do it," Jenny said aloud. "We're going
to sail right past, and no one's even going to know."

The beam from a searchlight hit them as she spoke, then
almost immediately two more, a deluge of light reaching
out from the shore to grab them. They staggered from the
sheer impact of so much light, the launch yawing under
their hands. Jenny heard an indignant yell from the tug,
whose skipper was ignorant of the reason for such a harsh
inspection, had a blurred impression of him shaking his fist
at the land as they surged past.

Because suddenly this became the moment when speed
was everything. They had gone as far as stealth would take
them, and now only speed was left. Martin alone at the
wheel, because not getting in each other's way mattered
more than skill, the throttle wide and their improvised red
flag streaming out from the stern.

Perhaps even then it was that red flag that made the
Czech guards hesitate. With a mystery launch streaking for
the West under their very noses, they wasted precious sec-

onds before they decided to start shooting. Or it could ha~
been the tug, Soviet-registered and in the line of fire un~
they were clear and going fast, or the bitterly cold mor~
ing, the dismal hour. Who ever knows these things?

"Lie flat," Martin yelled, and ducked himself as a la~
thread of tracer reached deceptively slowly across th~
water and then slammed overhead with a noise like a tri~
hammer. Lying down wouldn't do much good, thoug~
Jenny, feeling very cowardly all the same. So she snatche~
down the red flag instead, more from instinctive Yank~
distrust of anything foreign in a crisis than animosity t~
ward the Russians, who had really been very helpful durir~
their journey down the Danube.

The deck tilted sharply as Martin nearly stood th~
launch on its ear, violently changing course; she lost h~
footing, was flung against a locker and rolled across w~
duckboards. One single shot hitting their frail hull wou~
tear it apart, and at this speed they would never know wh~
had happened. She struggled to her feet again, wincing ~
sharp pain in her ribs, and stared astern to where the Ru~
sian tug was slewed in confusion across the river. It ha~
zigzagged instinctively when the shooting started, tangle~
its tow in consequence, and probably helped to take th~
Czech gunners' eyes off their target. And even as sh~
looked, the banks of the Danube interlocked behind the~
so that tug, barges, and frontier lights vanished from sigh~
The firing died as quickly as it came, and as if to mark th~
everything was over, it began to snow again. More heavil~
than before, until all they saw was whiteness and a sma~
circle of water around their launch.

"We're through," said Jenny stupidly. "There's n~
much of it, but this must be Austria."

15

J ENNY WOKE IN AN UNFAMILIAR ROOM AND LAY STAR-
ing at the ceiling, a crack across it nightmarishly resem-
bling a river on a map. Yellow flowered wallpaper and pine
furniture. Beyond the window it was still snowing, filling
the room with soft light.

She pushed the bedclothes aside and stood up. She felt
light-headed and her body ached. Dully everywhere, and
sharply at wrists and a lower right rib; otherwise she
seemed neither injured nor ill. She looked down at the unfamiliar cotton nightdress she was wearing, fussily tucked
and embroidered, then across at a mirror hung above the
basin. The image staring back was startlingly unfamiliar:
her skin tight-drawn over bone, eyes darker and larger than
they should be, hair a ruffled crest. I look as if I'd been
slung into a New York precinct house to sleep off a jag, she
thought wryly. She remembered almost nothing since they
began groping their way beyond the Austrian frontier, up a
still hostile river in thickening snow, searching for sanctuary along its banks, a sanctuary they must have found, at

an inn or farm perhaps. No clothes in the room, but an
envelope propped against the bedside lamp. She crossed
the floor and opened it, everything strange and difficult to
do.

*Wait where you are and rest until someone comes from
the embassy. Love.*

No incriminating documents for Martin, she thought
vaguely. Not even his name left behind in Austria while he
returned to Budapest. She smiled. Well, after a hellish two
days caused by diaries, she couldn't blame him.

With a strange, not unpleasurable, sense of being under
orders, Jenny returned to bed. Martin. Theirs would surely
always be a relationship of risk. Where humor, intuition,
and delight must help to hold a delicate balance of emotion
between two ambitious, easily bored, demanding people.
But love. That overworked, glib old word. That fresh and
radiant word for those who felt its power like a physical
pain, experienced the upheaval its absolutes loosed into
their lives. For them there was never any possibility of
remaining uncommitted.

"I love you," Jenny said aloud to Martin's note on the
bedside table. As he had ultimately accepted the loss of his
political career because he loved her, so she must accept
that her own concerns no longer came first. But of course,
she thought, surprised. Argument, regrets, the slightest
doubt, all now equally absurd. But I'll still try to make
Marshall's Literary Agency successful, she reflected drows-
ily, while also laughing at herself. How lucky Simon
Druce lives in London. She slept again.

In Budapest Conference Hall, everything was bustling. The
reopening of proceedings had been delayed while the British sorted out some unspecified difficulty with the Russians; now the delegates were settling behind the miniature
flags of their respective nations.

The French, who possessed a notoriously sharp ear for

gossip, were heard to remark that all the British were doing was fouling things up for the sake of it. Why, anyone could see from the look on his face that Monsieur Rotbourg, the British delegation leader, must have passed *un* week-end *exceptionellement passionnel* with the beauties of Budapest and needed to work off his hangover on whoever crossed his path. Herr Schiller, however, the central banker advising the West Germans, merely sighed when this comment was repeated to him and replied that all Hungarians were thieves and Herr Rottburg had his sympathy. *Erwagt die Sacht!* The jewels of his wife, which she inherited from the Esterhazy, stolen right here in Budapest, and by the Hungarian police themselves, he wouldn't be surprised. His Hilde was prostrate with grief.

The Russians, on the other hand, appeared pensive after their discussion with the British. They were always the end of the line for gossip, because they couldn't be trusted to pass it on and generally laughed at things the other delegates didn't consider amusing. Comrade Berdeyev, their leader, sat inscrutably amongst his advisers, lids drooping over eyes that usually darted from face to face; restless doodling hands out of sight beneath the table. Only the prominent veins across his high, bald forehead revealed his thoughts as unpleasant. The array of aides, watchers, and rivals who made up the Soviet delegation stared morosely at papers they had spent the weekend preparing, no relaxation with the beauties of Budapest for them. They had also just learned that not a single page of their work would be needed.

As the Hungarian minister of finance began the business of welcoming delegates back to their labors, Martin Rothbury found his eyes straying across to Berdeyev. Poor devil. Life in the upper echelons of Soviet power was predatory at the best of times, and this was not one of them for Pyotr Ordonovitch Berdeyev. Martin had been as oblique in the polite phrasing of threat as ingenuity could suggest, but there wasn't any civilized way of telling a man that his son had tried to sell him to the KGB.

The deal Martin offered was clear, however.

Berdeyev might be old, but he had labored through fifty years of the most murderous politics the world had known since Byzantium and did not need bargains spelled out for him. A dozen snatched sentences in his ear while the rest of the British delegation quarreled noisily and on purpose with those Russians who normally strained to hear every word any of their number exchanged with the enemy, and Martin had seen the veiled lids drop, the pursed lips and sudden stillness that told him the old man understood what he proposed.

As he watched now, Martin saw Berdeyev stir, unclip old-fashioned glasses and wipe his face, refold his handkerchief in a precise square and replace it in his breast pocket. The Hungarian minister droned on about debts and crises of confidence and great new opportunities, while those delegates who made it their business to watch each Soviet move silently agreed with what they thought Berdeyev's gesture meant. The room, indeed, was insufferably hot.

Only Martin knew that the old man wept.

It was a few minutes past two o'clock in the morning by the marble clock on Inspector Nemeth's mantelpiece, and most of the other rooms in Budapest's Third District police headquarters were dark. Outside, a melancholy drizzle of sleet melted on the sidewalks, the city silent except for the occasional clang of an all-night tram.

"Sign these and then you can go to bed." Nemeth pushed the buff forms of Hungarian bureaucracy across his desk at the latest disgruntled bunch of subordinates to attempt to unravel the disastrous events of the previous three days.

They signed with sullen resignation and trooped out without speaking. A great many dirty cups littered the room, and an enamel coffeepot stood on an electric ring. The room was thick with fumes from cheap Hungarian cigarettes. Everyone knew that the record of what had happened since thieves snatched capitalist jewels from the Korona Hotel was sufficiently damaging to ruin the career of every officer mixed up in it, although a few imagined they might save themselves by lies and contradiction. For over eighteen hours Nemeth had been working inside these same four walls to make sure that everyone who had contributed to the catastrophe signed a truthful statement of his responsibility, so that as a new age of international crime approached Hungary, the state police might be better prepared to combat it.

Nemeth knew he came out of the whole affair worst of all: the jewels vanished without a trace and a kidnapped British minister strolling back as bold as a bull through Ferihegy Airport. Six men dead, although fortunately, four of them appeared to be criminals, and the state police made to look utterly incompetent. He stretched and swore; his throat was sore and his eyes dry from smoking and long wakefulness. The best he could expect was a return to a country beat, counting cattle ticks.

"There is a man downstairs asking for you." A sergeant put his head round the door.

"Who?"

"English, I think. Anyway, he can't speak Hungarian."

Nemeth was about to utter a single pithy sentence that expressed what he thought of all things English when he changed his mind. "Bring him up."

He was sitting at his desk when Martin Rothbury was brought in, the dirty cups hidden in a cupboard.

"Do you speak English?" Martin asked when the sergeant went.

"Enough, I think. Sit down."

Martin shook his head and gripped a chair back instead, leaning his weight on it. "I would pass out if I did."

They looked at each other, two gray-faced, exhausted men. One whose slept-in uniform showed a grimy shirt beneath, the other wearing a dark suit that only an expert would have pronounced an indifferent fit, hastily borrowed from the first secretary of the British embassy in Vienna early the previous morning.

"The man on a bicycle Winckler shot somewhere before we reached the Danube. Is he badly hurt?" asked Martin after a long silence.

"No. But six men have been killed, two of them police, and another policeman seriously injured at the roadblock in Szeleveny village."

"I will do my best to answer anything you want to ask."

Nemeth snapped his fingers and stabbed a bell. "For this, a translator and witnesses."

"Not if you want the truth rather than diplomatic lies."

"My two police are dead! I make you."

"I know they are, which is a reason why I came. But as you discovered when I flew into Ferihegy this morning, no matter what you'd like to do, you can't arrest me or force confessions I don't choose to make."

The sergeant reappeared at the door. *"Igen?"*

Nemeth swore at him, and after a moment the man shrugged and went away again. Inspectors were entitled to their tantrums after seventy-two hours on duty.

So Martin told him, as clearly and concisely as he could, most of the things he knew, one of several exceptions being very sketchy references to Russian diaries.

Nemeth scraped with his thumbs at the stubble of his jaw. "These Soviet books—" He stopped. Such matters were KGB, and doubly dangerous for him if the Soviets ever learned precisely what they had lost.

"Yes," said Martin, watching his expression. "The Russians know we have them, but not how or where they were obtained, nor who wrote them. When I described to the Soviet delegation today the kind of material we possess, they were more easily persuaded to cooperate over the matter of Eastern Europe's foreign debt. But part of our bargain is that nothing will be published, at least for several years."

"Oh," said Nemeth, uninterested in legitimate finance. "You found Winckler?"

"Yes. He say he is dazed, so we will question him until he remember. Now you tell me everything, it is not so important."

Martin looked down at his hands. "Keep hold of him, will you? I don't fancy being caught by Winckler somewhere lonely, twenty years from now."

"You think?" Nemeth considered; in captivity, Winckler had contrived to appear as a bewildered petty crook, scarcely worth bothering about. "Perhaps. But we keep him; do not worry." Then he added with sudden venom: "Our people are not like yours. Not yet. Yes, Hungarians rob and murder; a man hate his wife and he kill her. An official cheat the state. Pouf! I understand that, and I punish because I am police. No bad feelings afterward. Now I find drugs in Budapest. Jewel thieves come here, and kill police because they come. Perhaps they kill you, too, in twenty years, which is a sickness and not crime. Our children have what they need, much more than we ever had, but always they want more. So they start to break things and write on walls. Nothing is easy anymore."

"You have an officer called Ferenc Karolyi," said Martin carefully, after a pause. "He laid information against Andras Benedek."

"So?"

"Benedek must now be in prison, under interrogation."

"So?"

"I think perhaps I meant, some things are never easy. Thirty years ago, perhaps as little as ten years ago, Ferenc Karolyi would not have betrayed Benedek, hoping for preferment, because he would have known that in Hungary, as the state then was, the man who betrays a traitor is damned, too. A potential traitor by association, as it were. That's what Benedek forgot. An old-style Communist himself, he forgot that now the state is not quite so greatly to be feared in Hungary, things aren't simple anymore. Even family loyalties."

"Well?" said Nemeth with hostility. Martin had not said, but both of them understood that in the very recent past he,

too, would have been dead already, shot instead of dis-
graced for failure.

"I prefer the present," answered Martin, smiling. "It
may not be simple, but there are fewer bloodstained cellars
under Eastern Europe's buildings. You, too, I suspect, and
because of it, I also came tonight to ask for Benedek."

"No," said Nemeth, astonished. "He is criminal, now or
thirty years ago. You see his apartment and you know. Like
this . . . full with black market."

"I never met him, but I'm sure you're right. All the
same, it seems unjust if you are forced to leave me free
while he goes to prison for—"

"Fifteen years, I think."

Martin straightened tiredly, every bone like barbed wire
under his skin. Just for the moment his longing for sleep
was past, but when it returned, neither willpower nor Ben-
zedrine would prevent him from collapsing. "I've done one
deal today, as I've told you. Now I propose another. The
jewels Havasi stole. If I tell you where you may recover
them, will you release Benedek?"

Nemeth jerked back his chair, wood screeching. "They
are not lost in the river?"

"The deal first, Inspector."

"I cannot do deals to release criminals."

Martin did not answer, watching him.

Nemeth's brain raced over the catalog of disasters he
must report to his masters. Recovery of jewels that in-
cluded Esterhazy rubies would be something to set in the
balance. Especially when Benedek was only a minor crook
of a type he understood, who so far had denied any knowledge of Soviet books. Eventually, of course, he would be
broken, but wouldn't it be better for Hungary if nothing
ever was filed officially on documents important enough to
make a Soviet delegation change its mind? Better if Benedek never did confess, in case the KGB heard a whisper of
what had really happened? "If it was me, I would shoot
this Benedek. No one find him then," he snapped.

"But in exchange for the jewels, you will let him go."

Nemeth shrugged. "Say the deal you suggest, and then I tell you."

A week later, the British public was mildly titillated to learn that Martin Rothbury, sometimes tipped as a future chancellor of the exchequer, had resigned his post at the treasury, close on the heels of a considerable personal success at the Budapest financial conference. Lobby correspondents filed reports of quarrels with the prime minister or disagreements over policy; other rumors suggested that Rothbury had been too successful in Budapest, when the present chancellor had sent a subordinate because he expected the negotiations to end in disaster.

"What did the prime minister actually say?" asked Jenny, curled up on the sofa in Martin's Westminster flat. "Or put it another way, how many of your follies did you confess?"

"Well, I have spent happier fireside hours. I left Nemeth out of it, stolen jewelry not being a government affair, and the diaries sweetened things a little. Berdeyev had written pages of dirt about nearly everyone who is now opposing Gorbachev's reforms, together with chapter and verse on what they've got up to so far, most of it stuff we didn't know. You can hear the intelligence boys purring halfway down High Holborn."

She felt a pang of loss as he spoke, but Jenny never lingered over failure she couldn't help. "I meant me."

"The prime minister is not romantic. We agreed to differ on a matter which is entirely my affair."

"And mine. Martin—"

"Jenny. No, listen. I want to be rid of this. I enjoyed politics, and now I've enjoyed getting out, if only to watch everyone's face when I did. I would have stayed if I could, but I'm also glad my hand's been forced. I'll always like to be busy, I suppose, but politics are death on a marriage, and I don't want it to be that way with us."

"I don't, either," said Jenny, remembering her fuddled musings when she woke in an Austrian farmhouse. "It's just that, later, you might resent what you had lost. And me, because of it."

"As you might decide eventually that you wished to God you hadn't married me after all. It's the kind of thing we can't possibly know, so why waste time over it?" He felt her sharply caught breath as he held her and knew she was laughing. "Oh, my Jenny."

"Martin. Has anyone ever called you Mart?" Really, she laughed because she had saved instead of ruined him; he didn't realize it, but surely he would never have reached the highest positions in political life when he so signally lacked the egotism a successful politician needs.

"No, never," he said decidedly.

"Good. You know, you never did finish telling me what happened to Benedek."

"He's tucked away in Kennington and has filed for British citizenship."

"He'll be stealing Rolls-Royces, I expect," said Jenny pensively. "Can you suggest any simple way I could get Pushkin thrown out of the States? Preferably before I fly back next week."

"Ah, well, Pushkin—Grigor Berdeyev, by the way— has already been declared persona non grata by the U.S. government and left New York for Moscow two days ago. The Russians made so little fuss, I understand the CIA are afraid he must have been up to something worse than selling diaries on the quiet, so now they're quarreling with the State Department. They wish they'd had the chance to follow him for a while."

"There isn't anything worse than selling those particular diaries." Jenny had knotted an orange silk scarf around her neck, and the ends of it touched his face as she leaned back against his shoulder. "I wouldn't have been in your place when you had to tell Berdeyev what his son had done for a million bucks."

He was silent, thinking of the old man weeping in Budapest's conference hall. Their bargain stood, though. On the British side, no disclosure or publication of the diaries for ten years; on the Russian, agreement to help fund Eastern Europe's debts to the West. How had Berdeyev persuaded his masters to honor such a bargain? Martin did not know, except he would certainly not have said anything that might reveal himself as the diaries' author. But many things could be done in the labyrinth of Kremlin politics by an old man who knew the way to reach those who held real power, who understood how to hint and slant reports and which fears must be soothed and which exacerbated, before agreement could be reached. Because Berdeyev knew such things and had been forced to desire agreement— maybe he and his government had always secretly desired agreement and only haggled from habit over terms—this time the matter was concluded, much to the mystification of the other Western powers.

Jenny touched Martin's lips. "Perhaps we'd better spend our honeymoon looking for someone else's diaries to support Marshall's Literary Agency through an imminent move to London."

Winckler's, for instance, Martin thought but did not say. He put his hand in his pocket. "That reminds me. An engagement present for you."

She undid the paper like a child while he watched the soft curve of her mouth, the determined curve of her chin. She opened the box and stilled abruptly. "My pearl necklace. How did you . . . How could you . . . Where did you find it?"

"Here, let me." He fastened it around her throat, delicate gold tendrils quivering. "I never said exactly how I bargained with Nemeth for Benedek. Loans weren't his business, after all, so I offered the jewels instead. Bad luck for Frau Schiller with her Esterhazy rubies, but she'd lost them anyway. You remember when Winckler made me swim to reach that boat? The jewels were there although I said they weren't, and when I nearly upset it, I transferred them out of sight; but being naked at the time, I had nowhere to hide them once I came ashore. So I stuck the packet in some mud by the reed bed and hoped for the best, then traded information on where they were with Nemeth. Except for this." He flicked filigree with his finger. "Luckily, Nemeth is a man of his word. I might have held him to Benedek's freedom by being annoying over loans but hadn't a hope over one pearl necklet I wanted for you. He delivered it to me at Ferihegy Airport lounge, and I regret to say I smuggled it through Heathrow."

Jenny's fingers lingered lovingly on pearls and gold. "My dearest, what can I say? Grandpapa might have had the words to speak for generations of Keszthely, but I haven't. Do you know, I actually felt exasperated that you could allow men like Winckler and Hansi the chance to mock at you, by being clumsy with that boat?"

"Yes, but then, I wasn't faking. I'm not at my best floundering in freezing water. So if you could make sure you don't drop it in the Thames—"

They both laughed, clinging together and shaken with the laughter that comes from joyous passion, tiger-striped by the winter sun as it shone through the bare branches of London's trees outside.

ABOUT THE AUTHOR

Mary Napier is the pseudonym of an award-winning author who lives in England.